FOUR FATHERS

SAUNAK MITRA

BLUEROSE PUBLISHERS
India | U.K.

Copyright © Saunak Mitra 2024

All rights reserved by author. No part of this publication may be reproduced, stored in a retrieval system or transmitted in any form or by any means, electronic, mechanical, photocopying, recording or otherwise, without the prior permission of the author. Although every precaution has been taken to verify the accuracy of the information contained herein, the publisher assumes no responsibility for any errors or omissions. No liability is assumed for damages that may result from the use of information contained within.

BlueRose Publishers takes no responsibility for any damages, losses, or liabilities that may arise from the use or misuse of the information, products, or services provided in this publication.

For permissions requests or inquiries regarding this publication, please contact:

BLUEROSE PUBLISHERS
www.BlueRoseONE.com
info@bluerosepublishers.com
+91 8882 898 898
+4407342408967

ISBN: 978-93-5989-347-1

Cover design: Raghunath Sharma (Kedor N Santy)
Typesetting: Pooja Sharma

First Edition: March 2024

FOUR FATHERS

Contents

Jab Main Chota Baccha Tha 1

Kela 51

Abbu Ki Naaz 185

Papa Kahete The 251

Jab Main Chota Baccha Tha

– 01 –

On a nippy November morning, the football field echoed with the cheers of friends engaged in a spirited soccer match. Milind, 31 years old, usually a force on the field, found his team trailing by two goals. Uncharacteristically, he decided to call it quits for the day.

"Alright, guys, time to leave," Milind announced as he gathered his belongings to head home.

But Satvik wasn't ready to give up the advantage. For some inexplicable reason, he was outshining Milind today. "C'mon, man, hang around until I'm two goals ahead, will you?" Satvik pleaded. "You can leave after that."

Milind dismissed Satvik's request with a scoff, pushing his sweat-soaked hair back into place. "There's a week's worth of goals you'd have to score to get ahead of me," he retorted.

"That's what I plan to do, if you stop being a sore loser and continue the game," Satvik fired back.

"Let him go, Satvik," Rohan intervened, sarcasm evident in his tone. He knew Milind's circumstances all too well. "He has other, more important people in his life now."

Milind shot Rohan a disapproving glare, unimpressed by the underhanded comment.

"Is that so? Someone's getting some action," Satvik teased, a sly grin on his lips. He kicked the ball to Milind, hoping to entice him into another round of competition, but Milind caught it, signalling his reluctance to play.

"Why didn't you tell us?" Satvik asked, unable to contain his curiosity.

"Don't believe everything Rohan says," Milind countered, pointing an accusatory finger at his friend.

"The only thing left to do is getting married," Rohan remarked, signaling for Milind to pass him the ball. "For Milind," he clarified. "She's already married."

The revelation was uncomfortable, casting an awkward shadow over the group. Infuriated, Milind approached Rohan, his face displaying displeasure. "Stop it, Rohan," he warned, leaning in and grabbing Rohan with menacing intensity.

"Why don't you stop it?" Rohan reacted, shrugging off Milind's grip. "You're playing with fire."

The tension on the field was palpable as the friends grappled with unspoken emotions and the complexities of their relationships.

– 02 –

Milind purposefully rushed down the busy road, the engine of his scooter revving beneath him. His heart raced, not just from the anticipation of what lay ahead, but also from the incessant stream of words pouring into his ear. It was Rohan, his well-intentioned friend, whose anxious rambling seemed to be practically tugging along.

"Dude, think about this for a second," Rohan's voice was a persistent murmur. "She's like, what, six years older than you? And there's that kid of hers who's not exactly thrilled about meeting you."

Milind's fingers twitched on the accelerator as he fought the urge to roll his eyes. Rohan's overprotective instincts were well-meant, but Milind needed to see this through.

"That's not all," Rohan continued, his gestures punctuating every point he made. "Her dad's some high-flying lawyer in the High Court, and her husband? Yeah, he's swimming in money. And then there's you – the struggling writer". Rohan's hands spread wide as if to emphasize the gap between their worlds.

Milind's jaw tightened, his grip on the scooter growing firmer. He was well aware of the differences, the chasm that seemed to separate him from Shreya's life. But there was an invisible thread that bound them, something beyond reason that had drawn them together.

"Rohan, I get it," Milind interrupted, briefly tearing his gaze away from the path ahead. The flicker of headlights caught his eye, and he swerved the scooter just in time to narrowly avoid a collision. The rush of adrenaline surged through his veins, but he quickly righted himself, heart pounding.

Ignoring the close call, he pressed on. "You have to understand, this wasn't planned. None of it was. We just... connected, you know? It's like there's a force that pulled us together, and we want to see where it leads."

"Easy, man!" Rohan's voice cracked with urgency, and Milind could almost see his friend's hand extended towards him, ready to yank the brakes. "You're not invincible on that thing."

Milind's grip on the handlebars tightened again as he shook his head slightly. "I can't slow down, Rohan," he confessed, his voice tinged with desperation. "Time's not on our side. Her husband is leaving for the US soon, and Shreya's made it clear - she'll only consider us if her son approves."

With the force of his will, Milind brought the scooter to an abrupt halt, the tires screeching against the pavement. He glanced around, his surroundings suddenly coming into focus - they had reached their destination.

– 03 –

Milind rushed around his room, stuffing things into his backpack as if time was slipping through his fingers. Amidst the whirlwind of packing, a pair of boxers dangled from his hand, and he raised an eyebrow, shooting a questioning glance at Rohan. "Hey, these boxers - yours or mine?"

Rohan leaned against the doorway, a mischievous grin playing on his lips. "Think of it as a farewell gift," he quipped, pulling Milind into a warm, tight hug.

Milind chuckled, a touch of sentiment in his eyes. "Well, it's going to remind me of you," he replied, a hint of mock seriousness in his tone.

Rohan laughed heartily, giving Milind a playful nudge. "No chance of forgetting me, mate. I'll make sure to call you right on rent day."

Milind's phone buzzed, stealing his attention. He answered the call, a smile forming as he chatted with the person on the other end. "Yeah, not exactly bubbling with excitement," he said into the phone, his voice light and playful.

After a quick exchange, Milind hung up and turned to Rohan. "That was Shreya," he explained, a grin spreading across his face.

Rohan raised an eyebrow, a knowing look in his eyes. "Sounds like things are heating up."

Milind shrugged, a mixture of uncertainty and anticipation in his expression. "We'll see."

Rohan clapped him on the back, a reassuring gesture. "Don't worry, mate. You've got this. Now let's get your stuff downstairs."

Together, they made their way downstairs. Milind's backpack was loaded into the waiting cab, and Rohan pulled him into a final bear hug. "Take care of yourself out there," Rohan said, his voice tinged with genuine concern.

Milind nodded with a lump in his throat as he looked at his friend. "You too. And find a new flat mate, someone less... romantically complicated."

Rohan laughed, a twinkle in his eye. "Will do. Now go on, your adventure awaits."

With a final wave, Milind climbed into the cab. He watched as Rohan's figure grew smaller in the rearview mirror, a mix of emotions bubbling within him. As the cab pulled away, he knew he was embarking on a new chapter, uncertain but full of possibility.

– 04–

As the cab navigated the bustling streets of Mumbai, Milind's gaze was fixed on the cityscape that unfolded outside his window. The symphony of honking horns, weaving vehicles, and throngs of people mirrored the whirlwind of emotions churning within him. Eventually, the cab came to a halt in front of an imposing villa, its grandeur had a stark contrast to the chaotic streets.

Clutching his luggage tightly, Milind took a deep breath before pressing the doorbell. He waited with bated breath as the seconds ticked by, his anticipation growing with each passing moment. The door creaked open, revealing a young boy standing before him, a gaming remote in hand.

Milind shifted the carton in his grasp to get a clear view and smiled warmly. "Hey there, I'm Milind," he introduced himself, his voice friendly. "We met at your mom's office. I'm..."

Before he could finish, the boy turned and disappeared back into the house. Milind stood at the threshold, a mix of surprise and confusion on his face. Just as he was about to take a step forward, the boy's voice reached him again, prompting Milind to pause. "Do you like bees?"

Milind blinked, his confusion evident. "Uh, not really," he replied, somewhat taken aback.

"Then come inside and close the door behind you," the boy countered matter-of-factly.

A smile tugged at the corners of Milind's lips as he followed the boy's instructions, closing the door behind him. "So, I'm Milind..."

"Yeah, yeah! You're mom's friend and will be staying with us for a few days," the boy interrupted, his tone a mix of nonchalance and eagerness.

Milind chuckled softly, his amusement shining through. "A few days, huh?" he murmured under his breath.

The boy pointed towards a closed door. "Your room," he stated simply. "And the kitchen's on your right, in case you're hungry," he added before returning to his spot on the couch, resuming his gaming session.

Milind took a moment to observe the surroundings, his eyes wandering around the unfamiliar yet inviting space. He was lost in thought when the boy suddenly paused his game, turning his attention to Milind with a curious expression.

Breaking the silence, Milind couldn't help but ask, "What else did your mom tell you about me?"

The boy's response was swift and direct. "That's between her and me," he replied, a hint of seriousness in his tone.

Milind nodded in understanding, respecting the boundaries. He was about to retreat to his room when the boy spoke up again, his tone slightly more authoritative. "And one more thing," he began, "The television's available for use only when I'm in school, understood?"

Milind smirked, a playful glint in his eye. "Loud and clear," he confirmed, offering a mock salute before making his way to the room assigned to him.

As Milind settled into the new environment, he couldn't help but reflect on the intriguing encounter with Dev. It was clear that navigating this new dynamic would be an adventure in itself, a journey marked by surprises, challenges, and the unexpected wisdom of a 10-year-old.

– 05 –

Milind's room exuded a sense of careful arrangement, with a tasteful display of a bed, bookshelves, side tables, elegant lamps, and thoughtfully placed artifacts. After settling his belongings, Milind eased onto the bed, taking a moment to admire the neat surroundings. In the hushed ambiance as the murmur of voices reached his ears, he realised he could overhear Dev talking to Shreya over the phone.

Milind listened as Dev's voice resonated, carrying a mix of casual assurance and subtle exasperation. "Yeah, Mum, I told him," Dev remarked, his tone tinged with a touch of impatience. "Just give him a call, alright...Whatever."

In walked Dev, the bar phone in his hand, which he handed over to Milind with a knowing glance. Without a word, Dev made his exit, leaving Milind alone with the device.

"Hey," Milind greeted, his voice warm as he held the phone to his ear.

Shreya's voice flowed through the line, a familiar comfort that instantly put Milind at ease. "So, how's it going?" she inquired.

Milind leaned back against the pillows, a soft smile gracing his lips. "So far, so good," he replied, his tone quietly confident. "Trust me, we going to get along just fine."

Shreya's laughter danced through the phone, a melodic sound that echoed with affection. "High hopes, aren't we?" she teased. "Dev's no pushover, you know. He's got a mind of his own. By the way, how do you find the house? And your room?"

Milind's gaze wandered around the room, appreciating the meticulous details. "It's a bit cozier than what I'm used to, but it's nice," he acknowledged.

A playful banter unfolded between them, their voices weaving a comfortable tapestry of conversation. Milind's voice held a hint of mischief as he chimed in, "But you know, something's missing."

Shreya's curiosity was piqued, her voice curious. "Missing? What could that be?"

A mischievous glint sparkled in Milind's eyes as he replied, "You, of course."

Shreya's laughter bubbled forth, a sound that painted vivid images in Milind's mind. "Well, if that's all it takes," she quipped. "I'll make sure to hang a picture of myself there. Problem solved."

As their conversation neared its end, Shreya's voice softened. "Alright, I need to go now. We'll catch up later in the evening. Take care, bye."

Milind's heart was alight with a sense of anticipation as he responded, " See you soon."

With the call concluded, Milind found himself immersed in thoughts of the venture that had led him to this point. The room around him seemed to shimmer with the possibilities that lay ahead, and he closed his eyes for a moment, his imagination brimming with dreams of a shared future with Shreya.

– 06 –

As Milind sat in his room, his mind floated back to the day he first met Shreya. It was clear as yesterday. He was standing by the elevator door when it jolted to a halt, the soft hum of its mechanisms hushing into silence. With a subtle mechanical fizz, the doors had eased open, beckoning Milind inside. This was the first time he laid eyes on her.

"Hey Milind! Good to see you, man," Chirag greeted warmly, a bright smile accompanying his words. He stood alongside an attractive young woman, exuding an air of familiarity and camaraderie. "How are you still here?"

Milind's lips curled into a wry smile as he stepped into the elevator, his eyes meeting Chirag's. "The boss won't accept my resignation," he admitted, his voice carrying a hint of resignation. "I'll give it another shot soon."

Chirag chuckled, a touch of envy glinting in his eyes. "You lucky bastard! You know there's a massive majority that would give up a limb for your job. And then there's you. Anyway," he continued, his hand resting casually on the girl's shoulder, "This is Shreya. She's our financial advisor. Shreya, meet Milind.. He's a copywriter."

A short smile danced on Shreya's lips as she extended her hand in greeting, her eyes holding genuine interest. "A man of words," she mused, her tone gentle and inviting.

Milind's response was a modest shrug, his eyes glinting with a touch of self-consciousness. "Well... I try," he offered, a subtle playfulness underscoring his words.

Chirag's lips curled into a knowing grin, his eyes catching Milind's as he spoke. "A modest chap indeed. He's more than just a good writer; he was our college open mic champion."

A spontaneous spark of sarcasm ignited within Milind, his words flowing effortlessly. "Little did I know then that my destiny was to pen tales about soaps and shoes," he quipped, the trio erupting into genuine laughter, the sound echoing within the confines of the elevator.

Shreya's laughter resonated like a melody, her eyes fixed on Milind with a newfound admiration. "Well, you truly are lucky," she confessed, her gaze a mixture of warmth and curiosity. "I wish I could use words half as skillfully."

Milind's lips curved into a thoughtful smile, his gaze meeting Shreya's. "The grass always seems greener on the other side," he countered, his voice tinged with both contemplation and longing. "I wish I could earn in a fortune."

Shreya's laughter bubbled forth, a joyous sound that seemed to light up the small space. "Trust me, it's simpler than wrestling with words," she quipped, a playful glint in her eye.

Chirag, an amused observer of the exchange, interjected with a mischievous grin. "Perhaps you two could become mutual disciples," he suggested, his voice dancing with humor. "A win-win situation, no doubt."

Shreya's eyes sparkled with mirth as she glanced at Milind, her agreement swift and certain. "Deal!" she declared.

– 07 –

Exiting the bustling cafeteria, Milind navigated a beeline, his plate adorned with an assortment of delectable food items that had captivated his palate. His eyes roved the room, scanning for an available spot, and that's when he spotted Shreya seated at a table, engaged in animated conversation with her companions. There was a vacant seat, an unspoken invitation to join them, and Milind decided to accept it.

"May I...?" Milind's question hung in the air, his polite inquiry directed toward Shreya and her friends.

Caught in the midst of camaraderie, Shreya's attention shifted from her companions to Milind. Recognition sparked in her eyes, and a warm smile tugged at her lips. "Hey wordsmith," she greeted playfully, her invitation evident. "Sure, join us."

As if on cue, one of Shreya's friends swiftly signaled the other. "Chal, yaar, it's getting late," the friend's words carried a subtle urgency, and without delay, they excused themselves, leaving Shreya in Milind's company.

Seated now, Milind's presence created a moment of subtle intimacy amidst the cafeteria's bustling ambiance. He settled into his chair, a soft smile gracing his features.

"So, how's the shoe sale going?" Shreya inquired, her tone infused with light-hearted banter.

Milind's shrug held a nonchalant charm, his eyes glinting with a mixture of contentment and subtle humor. "Not bad," he responded, his words accompanied by a gentle nod.

Shreya's playfulness took a turn, her words catching on her realization. "Oh, I'm so sorry," she interjected, her genuine concern dousing the levity of their exchange.

Milind's response was easy, a casual wave of his hand dismissing any awkwardness. "No worries," he assured, his gesture a subtle gesture of comfort. "My resignation hasn't been accepted yet. So, I suppose things are chugging along. What about you? How's life treating you?"

The word "life" lingered on Shreya's lips as she contemplated his question, her eyes revealing thoughts that remained unspoken.

Milind's head gently bobbed back and forth, his mannerisms underscoring an unspoken understanding of the complexities beneath the surface. "Yeah, life," he echoed, his words a silent affirmation of similar experiences.

The ticking of a watch caught Shreya's attention, a subtle reminder of the fleeting nature of time. "But why are you quitting?" Shreya's curiosity bubbled forth, her genuine interest woven into her question. "I mean, can't you pursue your dreams alongside your job? Why resign?"

Milind's exhale held a touch of exasperation, his search for the right words evident as he closed his eyes momentarily. "It's a bit hard to explain," he admitted, his gaze returning to Shreya.

With her attention drawn back to him, Shreya glanced at her watch again, subtly acknowledging that time was on their side. "We've got time," she encouraged gently, her interest unwavering.

Milind's thoughts unfurled like a story being told. His fingers seemed to dance through the air, tracing the contours of an imaginary path. "Imagine being on a long drive," he began, his gestures painting a vivid picture. "You know your destination; it's locked in your GPS, alternate routes are planned. But despite it all, you find yourself going in circles. And sometimes, starting from scratch feels like the only way to break free."

Shreya's brow furrowed, her contemplation etched across her features. "Your point is valid," she acknowledged, her tone thoughtful. "But while you're looking back for the right path, your destination could be right in front of you. Sometimes life has its own course, leading you on a detour before you reach that crossroads you were seeking."

Milind sat with Shreya's words, weighing their significance. After a lingering pause, he met her gaze, a nod of agreement accompanied by a small smile. "Valid point," he declared, their exchange marked by a shared understanding, a bridge built between them through unspoken sentiments.

– 08 –

At the bustling tea stall just beyond the office confines, a medley of aromas mingled with the cacophony of street sounds. Milind stood there, a steaming cup of cutting chai held in his hand, while Shreya awaited her own cup, anticipation radiating from her stance.

"Do you believe in destiny?" Milind's voice carried curiosity as he extended the cup of tea to Shreya.

Shreya's fingers curled around the warm cup, her eyes lifting to meet Milind's gaze. The unspoken question hung in the air, a thread connecting their thoughts. "One could argue in favour," Shreya replied, her tone reflective. "And you, why the question?"

Milind's reply was candid, his expression earnest as he engaged in this exchange. "Because I don't," he admitted, his honesty woven into his words.

Leaning against the tea stall's counter, Shreya took a leisurely sip from her cup, the fragrant steam enveloping her. Her response carried a thoughtful tone. "In this vast world of countless people," she began, her voice carrying a contemplative edge, "only a select few weave themselves into the fabric of our existence. Like it's by design. Sounds like destiny, doesn't it? "

Milind's counterargument flowed effortlessly, his words infused with a touch of conviction. "Well, some of these connections can be mere chance encounters," he suggested. "Like serendipity unfolding before us."

As the breeze stirred the air, Shreya's thoughtful gaze met Milind's, a silent moment shared between them. "You have a valid point," she conceded, her words carrying the weight of agreement.

Under the bright sun, a cozy roadside ice cream parlor hummed with life. Colorful umbrellas provided patches of shade as customers indulged in frozen treats. Shreya stood before the ice cream counter, sampling various flavors with an air of playful exploration. Milind leaned against a nearby railing, his eyes fixed on her with an amused twinkle.

As Shreya savored a spoonful of ice cream, her lips curled into a delightfully satisfied smile. She glanced at Milind, her eyes catching his gaze. "These wisecracks of yours," she mused between licks, her voice carrying a light, teasing tone. "Are they born out of experience, or are they just lines you've collected?"

Milind's lips curved into a smile, his gaze dancing with amusement. "Madam, I assure you, every word is a page from the book of my life," he quipped, his tone infused with playful honesty. "My experiments with truth, part two."

Shreya chuckled, her eyes crinkling at the corners. "And did any of these experiments involve matters of the heart?" she inquired, her curiosity evident.

Milind's expression turned thoughtful, a mischievous glint in his eyes. "Ah, indeed they did!" he confessed, his voice carrying a hint of nostalgia. "First in standard one, then in class two, three in..."

Shreya's incredulity was impossible to hide. "Three?!" she exclaimed, her eyebrows shooting up in disbelief.

A chuckle escaped Milind's lips. "I was referring to my first kiss," he clarified, his words tinged with a touch of playfulness.

A mix of surprise and amusement played across Shreya's features. "What?! You pervert."

Milind raised a hand in mock surrender, his smile unrepentant. "We were the same age," he defended himself with a casual shrug.

Shreya's curiosity got the better of her, and she leaned in slightly, her eyes locking onto his. "How did you even know what to do?" she inquired, her voice soft and genuinely curious.

Milind's reply was nonchalant, his eyes sparkling with a hint of mischief. "Perhaps I saw it on television, or maybe it was just my instincts kicking in," he suggested, his words carrying a hint of playful ambiguity.

A roll of Shreya's eyes was accompanied by a teasing grin. "How convenient," she retorted, her tone marked by mock exasperation.

Milind's lips quirked into a playful smile. "Well, you did ask, though you seem to be the swift judge," he pointed out, his voice laced with gentle amusement.

Shreya's lips curved into a rueful smile, her playfulness genuine. "Can't argue with that," she admitted, her tone holding a hint of apology. "Sorry about that!"

Milind's curiosity remained unabated, and he leaned in slightly, his expression intrigued. "So, what about you?" he prodded gently, his eyes sparkling with genuine interest.

Shreya's gaze flickered away briefly, a thoughtful expression crossing her features before she met his gaze once more. "What about me?" she deflected, a touch of mystery lingering in her tone.

A playful glint danced in Milind's eyes as he pressed on, his voice carrying a teasing undertone. "I'm just curious about the number of hearts you've managed to break," he admitted, his smile a mixture of curiosity and humor.

A moment of hesitation passed over Shreya's features, her eyes briefly studying his before a decision was made. "Next time," she replied, her voice a mixture of intrigue and promise, leaving an air of mystery hanging between them.

– 09 –

The lobby of Milind's office was a blend of modern aesthetics and professional efficiency. Sleek furniture and polished marble surfaces exuded an air of sophistication. Milind emerged from his office, the door gliding shut behind him, his steps purposeful.

His eyes fell upon Shreya, who stood in the lobby, accompanied by a boy of about 9 or 10 years old. A genuine smile illuminated Shreya's face as she caught sight of Milind's approach, a subtle warmth touching her eyes.

"Hey! Good to see you," Milind greeted, his voice carrying a friendly resonance that echoed in the open space.

Shreya's smile deepened as she introduced the boy standing beside her. "Meet Dev, my son," she said, her tone both proud and affectionate. Her hand extended in a subtle gesture, directing Milind's attention towards the young boy.

As Milind's gaze shifted to Dev, his initial smile wavered. The boy's demeanor was markedly serious, his expression unyielding, revealing a depth of thought beyond his years.

With an effort to ease the atmosphere, Milind extended his hand towards Dev, his smile returning in a gentle attempt to bridge the gap. "Hi, Dev. Good to see you," he offered, his tone warm and welcoming.

Dev's response was measured, his handshake firm but without a hint of emotion. His eyes remained steady, as if assessing Milind with a matured glance.

Sensing the tension, Shreya intervened with a gracious gesture. "Coffee?" she proposed, her words laced with a deliberate intention to diffuse the palpable unease that hung in the air like a weight.

Milind's agreement was swift, his smile holding a sense of gratitude for the offered reprieve. "Sure," he affirmed, his readiness evident as he gestured them to follow him towards the exit.

As they began to move, the lobby's contemporary ambiance provided a neutral backdrop to the unfolding interaction. The marble floors seemed to absorb their footsteps, creating a gentle echo that mirrored the cautious steps they were taking in navigating this new encounter.

– 10 –

Awkwardness settled around the table like a veil as Milind took a seat opposite Dev.

"So, Dev! Are you a fan of story books?" Milind asked, hoping the topic would pique Dev's interest.

"Yes," Dev replied with a matter-of-fact tone.

"Oh, that's great. What kind of stories do you enjoy? Cartoons, perhaps?"

Dev nodded in a yes, almost killing the conversation.

"Ah, I like those too! Tom and Jerry, Mickey Mouse, Donald Duck..." Milind continued, trying to engage Dev.

Dev's gaze remained steady, a curious mixture of seriousness and detachment in his eyes.

"Dev, why don't you go get yourself a juice?" Shreya interjected, an attempt to diffuse the tension lingering in the ambience.

Dev nodded, his demeanor unchanged as he rose and made his way to the counter.

With Dev gone, Shreya took the opportunity to make her priorities clear. "Listen Milind, I'm a single mother," she said. "And Dev is my world. I'm looking for someone who can understand this, someone who will accept him as much as they accept me."

A weighted silence followed Shreya's admission, the gravity of her words filling the air. A reassuring smile found its way onto Milind's face.

"I'm willing to give this a chance," Milind said, his eyes locked with Shreya's. "Are you...?"

Shreya's response was a simple nod, underscored by a single teardrop that trickled down her cheek, silently acknowledging the proposal. Milind gently wiped the tear away.

Suddenly, their attention was drawn to Dev standing before them, holding a glass of juice. His gaze, still serious, rested on Milind with an almost assessing intensity, conveying that this young observer had something to say.

− 11 −

Present Day

Ever since the moment when Dev stumbled upon Milind holding his mother's hand, a shadow seemed to have fallen over him. Normally not much of a talker, his reticence had deepened since that day. The unease that had taken root within him was now etched onto his features, visible for all to see.

The sun lazily streamed in through the curtains of Milind's room, a quiet sanctuary where an intimate conversation between him and Shreya was unfolding. The room itself was a blend of their personalities - Milind's organized bookshelf coexisting with Shreya's scarf draped casually over a chair. It was in this space that their connection felt most at home.

At that very moment, the door creaked open, and Dev entered the scene. Milind, caught off guard, handed Dev his phone. However, their eyes met in that instant, a brief but intense exchange that conveyed more than words ever could. A sternness flashed across Dev's face, a warning that lingered like a storm cloud. Dev's departure was swift, but the weight of that moment hung in the air for Milind - a mix of relief and tension intermingling.

As the day wore on, Milind's culinary aspirations took center stage. The kitchen transformed into his realm, and the vegetables his muse. With a practiced hand, he orchestrated a symphony in the pan, flames leaping to his command. The tantalizing scent of the pan-flambéed vegetables wafted through the air, turning a simple act of cooking into a sensory experience.

In another corner of their shared space, Shreya engaged in a mundane yet personal ritual - drying her hair. Her presence in the room seemed to infuse it with warmth and familiarity.

Carrying his culinary masterpiece, Milind crossed the threshold into the dining area, each step imbued with purpose. His eyes met Shreya's, and he couldn't help but let out a playful jingle, a sound that seemed to break through the ordinary and elicit an unguarded laugh from Shreya. The walls absorbed the melody, becoming silent witnesses to a moment of pure joy.

With a seamless grace, Shreya transitioned from amused observer to an active participant. The dining table became her stage as she orchestrated the serving ritual, her movements a dance of nurturance and care. "You really shouldn't have," she said, her words a mixture of gratitude and tenderness.

Taking his seat opposite Shreya, Milind's response was genuine and heartfelt. "I wanted to, though."

With the scene set for a shared meal, Shreya's affectionate yet authoritative call brought Dev to the table. The television, a background hum, stood as a silent testament to Dev's reluctance to detach from his comfort zone. His arrival was accompanied by an exaggerated eye roll, a gesture that spoke volumes of his disdain for vegetables. He grabbed his share with an air of protest, and returned to his awaiting television.

The gentle clinking of cutlery against plates became the soundtrack as Dev and Shreya got engaged in their meal. The absence of words was filled with meaningful glances, shared smiles, and unspoken understanding, each movement a brushstroke on the canvas of their connection.

In the periphery, the television continued its monologue, a reminder of the world beyond their table, as Dev, a silent observer, embodied a whirlwind of emotions - the complexities of familial dynamics and the stirrings of something deeper.

- 12 -

Milind was busy reading when Shreya entered his room, coaxing him to abandon the book.

"I'm assuming, Dev's finally asleep," he asked.

Shreya replied with a nod.

"He's a good kid," Milind noted.

"I'm worried, Milind," Sherya replied after a long moment.

"Worried? Why?"

"This experiment," Shreya began, lines of worry etched deep on her face. "I don't know how it will effect Dev."

"I understand," Milind replied. "But this is a risk we have to take."

He gently removed Shreya's glasses off her face and opened her long hair. They cascaded down, giving Shreya a youthful appearance.

"I don't know if he'll accept me," Milind confessed, his fingers tenderly tracing patterns in Shreya's hair. His voice carried a mix of uncertainty and longing. "Or if you'll want to continue with this relationship two months from now. The only certainty we have is that, for the next two months, the three of us are in this together. And I want to cherish every single moment of it."

Shreya nodded in understanding, and they drew closer, embracing each other tenderly. With her eyes closed, Shreya simply savored the warmth and comfort of their hug. Meanwhile, Dev, sequestered within the confines of his room, abruptly fluttered his eyes open, his profound displeasure over the situation blatantly conveyed by the furrow of his brows.

In the cozy kitchen, the aroma of Milind's culinary creation filled the air. He was fully engrossed in his culinary endeavor, preparing his specialty for the day - a delectable chicken lababdaar.

In contrast, Dev occupied a corner of the room, lost in a book. However, his concentration was tenuous, his mind seemingly preoccupied with troubling thoughts. With a sigh of frustration, he slammed the book shut and reached for the remote control. The television flickered to life, its sound adding to the tension that hung in the air.

Milind, though acutely aware of the shift in the atmosphere, chose to keep his focus on the simmering chicken, offering a silent but supportive presence in the room.

The next morning, as Milind diligently went about his morning routine, a knock on the door from Shreya served as a subtle reminder of her impending departure for the day with Dev. Dropping his toothbrush, he rushed to the door, his eyes reflecting a hopeful anticipation.

"See you soon," Milind offered, yearning for a response from Dev.

But the response he yearned for never came.

Left alone in the silent house, Milind resumed his official duties with his laptop. The click of keys and the soft glow of the screen were the only sounds and sights that accompanied him, echoing the hollowness filling the house.

As night descended, Milind and Shreya found themselves in Milind's dimly lit room, the air heavy with tension.

Shreya, vexed by the persistent cloud of smoke surrounding Milind, furrowed her brows disapprovingly. "Weren't you supposed to quit?" she questioned, her tone laced with disappointment.

Milind, his eyes reflecting a hint of guilt, responded, "I will, Shreya, but it's a process."

With a hint of defiance, Shreya snatched the cigarette from Milind's hand and took a long, contemplative drag. She sighed, the exhaled smoke spiraling upwards like a fleeting thought. "I'm leaving for Bangalore tomorrow morning," she revealed. "That means you'll be taking care of Dev for the next three days. Also, Dev's results are out, and he's scored a D in two subjects. You'll have to meet with his teacher."

Milind's eyes widened in surprise, and he blurted out, "Me? But Dev hardly talks to me, Shreya. Are you sure he'll be okay with me meeting his teacher?"

Shreya's gaze remained steady as she responded, "He's fine with it. I've already spoken to him."

A sense of wonder crossed Milind's face. "That's surprising," he remarked.

Shreya leaned in closer, her voice tinged with a sense of resignation. "Fatherless sons grow up faster, Milind," she explained. "He knows he doesn't have much of a choice."

Around the expansive dining table, the members of Dhruv's family gathered for breakfast. The servants moved about efficiently, tending to their every need. Seated at the table were

Dhruv, Shreya, Dev, Dhruv's father, mother, and his younger brother, Gaurav.

As they indulged in their morning meal, Gaurav, a hint of desperation in his folded hands, cast a furtive glance toward Dhruv. In response, Dhruv offered a reassuring nod.

"Dad, how about considering Gaurav's MBA in Australia?"Dhruv proposed, trying to inject some humor. He playfully suggested, "Who knows, he might even bring home a goribahu for Mom." Amused by the idea of a "goribahu," Dhruv's mother let out a chuckle.

However, Dhruv's father appeared sceptical. "So, are you suggesting that those who don't invest a fortune in foreign education don't achieve success?" he questioned, his brows furrowed.

Ever the diplomat, Dhruv improvised, his tone measured and persuasive, "Not at all, Dad. That's not what I meant. But what's the value of all our wealth if we can't put it to good use? After all, it won't serve any purpose in the afterlife."

Offended, Dhruv's mother scolded him with a stern "Dhruv!" while he nodded, acknowledging her objection, deftly steering the conversation in another direction. "My business has been facing some challenges recently," he admitted, his gaze fixed on his father. "Would you consider lending me some money, say 20-25 lakhs..."

Shreya, evidently displeased by the request, placed her spoon down with an audible clink, her disapproval showing.

"Dhruv, you've already borrowed 75 lakhs from me," Dhruv's father responded, his frustration evident in the deep lines on his forehead. "And there's no sign of repayment anytime soon."

Dhruv defended himself, his voice calm but persuasive, "It's an export business, Dad. Building a client base takes time."

Dev, seizing the moment, chimed in with youthful eagerness, "I need new skates, Dad."

Dhruv, always quick to seize opportunities, added, his tone infused with paternal warmth, "Dad will get you those skates, champ, as long as you top your class this time. No settling for second or third place, alright?"

Shreya couldn't hide her irritation. "What kind of nonsense are you filling his head with?" she snapped, her voice laced with frustration.

Dhruv shrugged nonchalantly, his demeanor unapologetic. "It's just the typical carrot-and-stick approach, Shreya. That's how business operates."

Shreya, retorted, her patience waning. "Today it's skates, tomorrow it might be a motorcycle. Where does it end?"

Growing weary of the disagreement, Dhruv abruptly pushed his plate aside. "That's enough," he declared, his voice tinged with frustration. "Dev, let's go. We're leaving."

Shreya reminded him, her voice firm, "You promised you wouldn't ask Dad for more money."

"Shreya," Dhruv retorted sharply, his patience wearing thin, "perhaps you should refrain from meddling in business matters." With an air of finality, he turned his attention to Dev. "What are you waiting for? Let's go."

Dhruv's father, keenly aware of the palpable tension in the room, chose to intervene. "Leave him be," he said, wrapping Dev in a warm embrace. ""I'll drop him off later," he said.

With his pride wounded, Dhruv stormed out of the dining room. Shreya followed suit, leaving behind an atmosphere heavy with tension.

In the midst of a heated conversation, Dhruv's temper flared, and he slammed the ice tray down onto the dining table. His voice raised, he bellowed into the phone, "Don't blame me if you couldn't bother to call, you imbecile!" His outburst earned him a disapproving glare from Shreya, who was occupied with arranging dishes on the table.

"Come on, Dev, dinner is ready," Shreya announced, beckoning Dev to leave the television and join them.

Meanwhile, Dhruv was already engrossed in another conversation, and his choice of words remained crude and inappropriate.

Shreya, feeling the need to intervene, implored, "Dhruv, please watch your language."

Dhruv responded with irritation, taking a long, exasperated sip from his drink. "Why should I?" he snapped.

"For Dev," Shreya retorted, her face etched with anger. "Do you really want him to pick up this kind of language from you?"

Driven to fury by Shreya's interference, Dhruv's frustration escalated. He violently threw the cutlery aside and seized Shreya by the hair. "I think it's high time I teach you a lesson," he roared, forcibly dragging Shreya into the bedroom.

Shreya wakes up from what had felt like a horrifyingly real nightmare. Her heart pounded, and she took a deep breath, relieved to find herself safely in her own bed. The past had all been just a terrible dream.

The soft strains of a melody enveloped the car's interior as Milind navigated the morning traffic, driving Dev to school. Dev, his small frame nestled in the back seat, gazed out of the window, his expression a mosaic of subdued emotions, hidden behind the glass.

In the rearview mirror, Milind's eyes caught a glimpse of Dev's distant expression. He decided to break the silence. "Are you feeling worried?" he asked, his voice soft and comforting.

Dev continued to stare outside, his gaze fixed on the passing scenery, his thoughts locked behind a wall.

"Don't fret, buddy. Remember, we're a team," Milind reassured, his words infused with a gentle sincerity. "I'll have a friendly chat with your teacher, that's all."

Dev's response was swift and sharp, his tone unyielding. "Absolutely not. I don't need your help."

Milind nodded, understanding Dev's need for independence. "I get it, Dev. Just so you know, I'm not trying to help. Think of me as a friend."

A cold retort came from Dev's direction, his voice laced with defiance. "You're not my friend."

Milind accepted this with a resigned nod, raising his hand in a gesture of surrender as they continued their journey through the bustling morning streets.

The principal's office was adorned with merit lists and trophies, a testament to its grandeur. Milind and Dev occupied seats across an imposing, polished table. The principal, a poised figure with reading glasses perched on her nose, began the conversation, with the class teacher, Priyal, sitting nearby.

"There have been numerous complaints concerning Dev," the principal stated, adjusting her glasses, her gaze flicking between Milind and Dev. She then signaled for Priyal to elaborate.

Priyal sighed, her expression a mix of frustration and concern. "It's hard to know where to start, ma'am," she began. "Dev's performance in both Maths and English is, well, disappointing. Moreover, he appears disengaged in class, seldom participating or answering questions—often gazing out of the window." Her eyes darted disapprovingly towards Dev. "He's also displayed a lack of interest in sports activities. Just last week, he pushed another boy down the stairs, nearly breaking his leg. Isn't that right, Devansh?" she concluded, her cold stare locking onto Dev.

Dev, his face flushed with embarrassment, nodded sheepishly in agreement.

"Last time, your wife promised such incidents wouldn't recur," Priyal reminded Milind. "She must have informed you, didn't she?"

"Yes, she did," Milind replied, a soft smile tugging at his lips at the mention of the word wife.

"I understand your job requires extensive travel," Priyal continued. "But you need to make more effort. We can't do everything for you."

"Yes, ma'am," Milind responded.

"Sir," the principal interjected, "each class has an average of 50 students. We can't provide individual attention to each child. Parents only seem to wake up at the end of the year when results are poor."

"Of course," Milind nodded in understanding.

"I genuinely believe that Devansh should repeat the class," the principal declared.

Milind hesitated, expressing concern. "Repeat? He'd lose a whole year," he observed.

With a sigh of resignation, Priyal retrieved a paper from a stack beside her and proceeded to read from it. "Here's an excerpt from his English paper," she said before reading aloud, "When I grow up, I want to become rich. I want to earn a lot of money. Money is very important. Money can buy so many things. Money can make us happy. I will buy everything that I cannot afford now."

"Rich? Money? Who writes like this? Is this what we teach at school, Dev?" the principal asked, her tone exasperated.

Milind took a moment to intervene. "If I may, ma'am," he began. "While it's true that most children wouldn't write like this, you might consider that Dev is simply different."

"But the curriculum is the same for everyone," the principal argued.

"I understand that, ma'am," Milind acknowledged. "But life is often more complex than the syllabus."

"I see your point, but..."

"No, ma'am, I don't think you do," Milind interrupted. "I'm sorry to say this, but every child in your class is unique, not just a roll number; they're individuals. Granted, Dev may not excel by writing in the manner he does, but at least he's expressing himself. As an educator, you need to decide whether you want your students to be mere crammers or independent thinkers."

The principal pondered Milind's words for a moment. "I'd like to speak with Devansh's mother before making a decision," she finally stated, ending the discussion. "Thank you."

Milind took the cue to leave the room. However, before exiting, he paused at the doorway for one parting shot. "This child's future hinges on your decision," he said earnestly. "Please take that into consideration when making your call."

Dev slouched on a weathered bench, his head hung low in a cloak of shame. Nearby, Milind paced back and forth, engaged in a spirited discussion with Shreya over the phone.

"Why did you have to argue, Milind?" Shreya's voice reverberated from the phone's speaker. Her frustration was palpable. "You should've just listened and left."

"I would've," Milind countered, his tone edged with justification, "but then she started spewing nonsense."

"Can't you see," Shreya sighed, her patience waning, "now I'll have to personally rectify this mess."

Milind remained undeterred. "Well, Shreya, this mess is too colossal for you to tidy up alone," he retorted. "At least now we can step in and help our child."

"Our child?" Shreya echoed, a trace of amusement dancing in her voice.

Dev released a long, defeated sigh. "Whatever," he mumbled, disconnecting the call.

The drive back home was shrouded in an uncomfortable silence. The radio, once a source of soft melodies, now echoed the somber atmosphere that enveloped the car's occupants.

Breaking the oppressive quiet, Dev's voice suddenly pierced through. "I like pizza," he declared, his words catching Milind off guard. "Do you?"

Milind couldn't believe his ears. Dev, initiating small talk? He shot a quick glance at his son in the rearview mirror, searching for any sign that this was real.

"Can you see backward?" Dev inquired, his tone laced with impatience.

"Huh? What?" Milind stammered, momentarily distracted.

"Look forward, at the road," Dev directed him firmly.

Milind, realizing his lapse, quickly returned his attention to the road, his hands firm on the steering wheel.

– 13 –

The cozy Italian restaurant was bathed in warm, dimmed lighting, casting an intimate ambiance as the waiter deftly placed two steaming, large pizzas onto the table. The enticing aroma wafted through the air, and Dev couldn't contain his excitement. Without hesitation, he grabbed a slice and began devouring it, his enthusiasm palpable.

"Did you ever dislike school?" Dev asked between bites.

Milind, equally engrossed in his pizza, nodded in acknowledgment. "We had a different grading system in my time," he began. "Back when I was in fifth grade, I developed a fierce addiction to comics—Bhokal, Doga, Nagraj, and Super Commando Dhruv, to be specific. I was completely immersed in their fictional worlds. But as the exams drew near, I had no time for studies, and naturally, I failed in all my subjects. English was the worst; I scored a big fat zero. It left a deep scar. I even used to have nightmares about that teacher."

Dev's curiosity was piqued. "What happened next?"

Milind took another hearty bite of his pizza and continued, "Then, one day, a friend of my father's gifted me a book: 'Robinson Crusoe.' By the time I finished reading it, I not only learned how to read English but also write and speak it fluently.

That's when I realised that learning requires interest, not just books."

Dev, contemplating Milind's story, shared his own aspiration. "I want to learn cooking. Will you teach me?"

A warm, understanding smile graced Milind's face. "Of course," he agreed. "Consider yourself a student at the 'Milind Institute of Culinary Arts' starting today."

In the days that followed, Milind and Dev spent an abundance of quality time together. They delved into the art of cooking, experimented with recipes, flew kites, sketched, explored parks, and shared stories—activities befitting a father and son.

When Shreya returned from Bangalore, the sight that greeted her was beyond her expectations. Dev was peacefully asleep, cradled in Milind's protective embrace. Overwhelmed by the heartwarming scene, she couldn't help but approach Milind. She rested her head on his shoulder, and in that moment, their family portrait was beautifully complete.

Shreya stood in the principal's office, a sense of apprehension gnawing at her. She cleared her throat, ready to address the matter at hand.

"I apologize for the other day, ma'am," Shreya began, her tone sincere. "I was out of town, and as a single parent, I had to request my partner to attend the meeting in my place."

The principal, a seasoned educator with a warm demeanor, leaned forward in her chair, her curiosity piqued. She adjusted her glasses and offered a reassuring smile.

"You know, Shreya," the principal said thoughtfully, "there's no need to apologize. In fact, Priyal and I discussed our conversation with your partner, and his perspective made us reflect.

Sometimes, we tend to overlook the truth, even when it's staring right at us in the face. That day, your husband, or should I say, your partner, what's his name?"

"Milind."

"Yes, Milind. He certainly gave us a reality check. It's a good thing to be evaluated from time to time. And I've heard that Dev has been thriving in his classes."

A sense of relief washed over Shreya as she absorbed the principal's words. She couldn't help but smile, genuinely grateful for the understanding shown.

"Thank you, ma'am," Shreya said, her gratitude evident in her tone. With that, she bid the principal farewell, her heart considerably lighter than when she had entered the office.

– 14 –

Milind sat in his room, engrossed in a Zoom call with Rohan. The digital screen flickered with enthusiasm as Rohan delivered the news.

"The client loved the script," Rohan exclaimed. "They're thrilled with it. Just a bit of branding touch-up, and we're golden."

Milind responded with a grin, his creative juices flowing. "Let's sprinkle some stardust on this campaign, then."

Rohan couldn't help but roll his eyes playfully. "Please spare me your puns, Milind. Go revise the script. This project could be a game-changer for your career. By the way, the gang and I are planning a trip to Matheran next week. You should join us."

Milind hesitated for a moment. "I'll have to take a rain check."

Rohan shrugged, conceding, "Suit yourself."

As Milind closed his laptop, Shreya approached him, her expression thoughtful.

"I think you should go," she suggested.

Milind shook his head. "Nah, I'm good."

Sitting down beside Milind, Shreya continued, "You know, ever since my marriage with Dhruv, I've let go of many meaningful friendships and hobbies. I don't want you to make the same sacrifice."

Milind's conviction was evident in his voice as he replied, "I'm content right where I am, Shreya, with you and Dev."

Shreya let out a sigh of resignation. As she reached the threshold of the room, a sudden idea brightened her face.

"You know what," she said, a mischievous grin tugging at her lips. "What if we all went?"

Milind's curiosity was piqued. "What do you mean?"

"I mean, Dev would love to meet your friends, I'm sure," Shreya explained. "And I've never been to Matheran."

Milind's eyes sparkled with intrigue. "You'd want to?"

"Only if you want us to," Shreya replied, leaving the decision in Milind's hands.

– 15 –

Shreya meticulously packed her and Dev's clothes into a bag, her movements carrying a sense of urgency. As she opened a drawer, her eyes fell on her camera, a relic of memories she had once cherished. She hesitated, contemplating whether to take it.

Just then, Milind appeared, dressed casually in a T-shirt, shorts, sunglasses, and a golf cap. With a playful smirk, he struck a mock pose when he spotted the camera.

"Where there's a camera, there's a model," he quipped.

Shreya sighed, her reluctance apparent. "I don't think we need this," she said, reluctantly placing the camera back in the drawer.

Milind, ever the optimist, declared, "You know, you think too much," before heading out to buy snacks for their upcoming road trip.

Heeding Milind's advice, Shreya retrieved the camera once more and secured it in her backpack. She then focused her attention on helping Dev prepare for their journey.

Shortly thereafter, the doorbell rang, and Dev rushed to answer it, expecting Milind's return. However, as he swung open the door, an unexpected sight sent chills down his spine—Dhruv stood before him, his parent standing in the background.

"Hey, son, how are you?" Dhruv greeted, feigning warmth. "I thought I'd bring Granddad to meet you."

Shreya, alarmed by Dhruv's presence, rushed to the door. "Dev," she instructed, her voice trembling. "Go to your room and don't come out until I tell you to."

"He's going nowhere," Dhruv countered, pushing his way inside.

Dhruv proceeded to enter the dining area, his eyes falling upon a portrait of Shreya painted by Milind.

"Isn't it funny?" Dhruv sneered. "You're too ashamed to talk to me, but you have no qualms about displaying your escapades in front of Dev."

"Stop it, Dhruv!" Shreya snapped, her patience wearing thin.

"Don't raise your voice!" Dhruv retorted. "Or I'll have no qualms revealing your true colors to Dev."

"Enough!" Milind's voice echoed from the background. Undeterred by Dhruv's hostility, he interjected sternly, "I believe you've said enough. It's time for you to leave."

Enraged by Milind's audacity, Dhruv threw a punch that landed squarely on Milind's jaw, sending him stumbling backward.

"Stop it, Dhruv," Dhruv's father tried to intervene but was held back by Gaurav. "We came here to find a solution."

"The only solution will be getting this through the court," Dhruv declared. Turning to Milind, he issued a menacing warning, "I don't care if you sleep with my wife, but if you try to take my son away, I'll tear you to pieces."

Milind challenged him, "Did you even ask your son?"

"Dev?" Dhruv scoffed. "Who is he to decide?"

"It's his life," Milind argued. "He should be the one to decide."

Infuriated, Dhruv prepared to strike Milind again, but he halted when he noticed Dev standing between them, brandishing a tiny cricket bat.

"Don't you dare hit him," Dev warned Dhruv.

"My son," Dhruv sneered, "Who is he to you?"

"He's my mom's friend," Dev replied defiantly. "And mine too."

Milind corrected Dev, "Actually, he's more like Mom's new husband."

"In that case," Dev proclaimed, "he's my dad."

"Enough!" Milind exclaimed, seizing Dev by the arm. "You're coming with me."

"Stop!" Dhruv's father cried out. "Put the boy down right now!"

"Dad, I'm his father," Dhruv insisted.

"And I'm his grandfather," Dhruv's father declared firmly. "Unfortunately, you've done nothing to deserve Dev as your son. You never asked what he likes or tried to support him. Nothing at all."

Dhruv's father turned to Shreya. "What you did with my daughter was unforgivable, but I stayed silent. However, I won't make the same mistake again. Dev is my grandson, and if he's happy with Shreya, then he stays with her."

"Only the court can decide this," Dhruv protested.

"Very well," Dhruv's father announced, determination in his voice. "I'll fight on Shreya's behalf in court."

"But, Dad..."

"Yes, I will fight the case," Dhruv's father asserted. "This young man," he said, pointing to Milind, "has set an example worth following for Dev. That's what a father should do." He turned his attention to Dhruv. "Look at yourself. Your behavior is shameful, especially for a father."

Approaching Dev, Dhruv's father leaned down and asked gently, "Tell me one thing before I go, my child. Are you happy here?"

Dev, tears welling up in his eyes, replied with a heartfelt, "Yes, Daddu."

Satisfied with the answer, the old man embraced Dev, bidding him a subtle goodbye. Shreya and Milind watched as he left, a sense of hope and determination in their hearts.

– 16 –

After 48 hours had passed, Milind and Dev found themselves on a football field surrounded by Rohan and several other friends. They were deeply immersed in an exhilarating game of football, the air filled with the sounds of laughter and shouts. Milind, however, decided to take a well-deserved break. He strolled toward the edge of a nearby cliff, leaving the football game behind. There, he leaned on the sturdy railing, taking in the breathtaking vista of the valley below.

In his pocket, Milind carried a pack of cigarettes, tempting him with the familiar comfort of a smoke. Yet, he resisted the allure of nicotine. Instead, he made a resolute decision, pulling the packet from his pocket and with a flick of his wrist, sent it tumbling into the valley below. The wind carried it away, and as he inhaled the pristine mountain air, a sense of liberation washed over him.

Unbeknownst to him, Shreya observed the entire scene from a serene distance. A contented smile graced her lips, reflecting the inner peace she felt at that moment.

Just then, Dev, his chest heaving from the intense football game, approached Milind. Milind turned to him, curiosity in his eyes.

"Tired already?" Milind asked, his voice playful.

"Nah," Dev replied between breaths. "Just taking a breather." He paused for a moment, collecting his thoughts. "You know, the other day when I called you dad?"

"Yes, what about it?" Milind inquired, his interest piqued.

"Don't take it too seriously," Dev cautioned with a hint of a smile. "We're still friends, alright?"

"Absolutely," Milind agreed, feeling a sense of relief.

"But let me warn you," Dev continued, his eyes twinkling mischievously, "I'm likely to get bored very soon."

Milind chuckled warmly, playing along. "Oh dear. What do we do about that?"

"Perhaps," Dev suggested, his hands cupped together in a playful gesture mimicking a puppy, "if you could get me a small friend..."

"Is that so?" Milind teased, seizing Dev and starting to tickle him playfully.

Shreya, standing at her peaceful vantage point, overheard their heartwarming conversation. Her eyes sparkled with joy as she saw them through the view finder of her camera and clicked it, in order to freeze this favourite moment of her life.

Kela

– 01 –

Amidst the bustling streets of Howrah, Prashant and his family carved out their existence. Like any other common man Prashant has to work hard to make ends meet in a big city like Kolkata. He is a diligent middle-aged individual who has dedicated his every waking hour to provide for his loved ones. Though himself being the son of an ordinary vendor, he has big dreams for his only child.

The mornings in their household were a whirlwind of activity. The relentless hissing of the pressure cooker punctuated the air as steam billowed out through the open window, creating transient patterns in the morning light.

Prashant's wife Durga, was the orchestrator of this daily chaos. She swiftly turned off the gas stove, pouring fragrant tea into a cup for her aged and frail mother-in-law, Rampiyari, whose partial paralysis limited her mobility.

Meanwhile, Prashant found himself knocking impatiently on the bathroom door. He was running late for the office, and his frustration was evident in the sharp rap of his knuckles. Durga knew all too well the precarious water situation; it had run dry more times than they could count.

"Rahul, my boy, hurry up!" Durga helplessly implored her 16-year-old son. "Your father can't afford to be late again. The water will run out."

Rahul emerged from the bathroom, his indignation palpable. His eyes met his mother's, but he had little time for words. He stood before the mirror, meticulously taming his unruly hair. Next to the mirror stood an old wooden almirah adorned with trophies and medals, testament to Rahul's achievements. He swiftly grabbed his cricket kit and school bag, ready to embark on his day's adventures.

In her haste, Durga grabbed Rahul's tiffin box and handed it to him. He snatched it without a word and hurriedly made his way to catch the school bus. Durga sighed as she watched her son's retreating figure. "You always manage to delay my morning prayers," she muttered, the frustration of the chaotic morning evident in her voice.

Prashant stole a glance at his wife but chose to remain silent. At this juncture, all he yearned for was to reach his office on time.

– 02 –

Prashant began his day by splashing his face with the little water left in the bucket. He carefully applied talcum powder and dressed himself. Grabbing his tiffin box, he headed towards the door. But just as he took his first step outside, Durga's voice called him back.

"Please make sure to come back early today, and don't forget to bring a gift," she reminded him. "We're invited to Jay's birthday party at the Shrivastav's in the evening. You know how Pushpa Bhabhi can be if we show up without one."

Prashant nodded in agreement, his expression conveying a mixture of understanding and haste. "Close the door," he said, ready to face the challenges of the day.

As he checked his purse, disappointment washed over him. He had a meager 200 bucks, a stark reminder of their financial constraints. With a sigh, he went towards the bus stop, joining the long queue of commuters bracing themselves for another day of chaotic travel. Some mornings simply start on a jarring note, and it appeared that luck was not favoring Prashant that day. The overcrowded bus offered no respite, forcing him to stand for the entire journey.

Meanwhile, Rahul disembarked from the school bus and couldn't help but notice a luxurious car waiting at the entrance of City

International School. He recognized Krish, an attractive teenager who was widely admired. As Rahul and Krish entered the school premises, their peers greeted Krish enthusiastically.

Prashant, on the other hand, had reached the bustling Dalhousie area and was steadily making his way towards his workplace, Parekh Diary & Calendars.

– 03 –

Hasmukh Parekh, the proprietor of Parekh Diaries & Calendars, sat in his garden with his wife, Nirmala. The morning sun filtered through the leaves of the trees, casting dappled shadows on the lawn where they enjoyed their breakfast.

The servant who served them raised an eyebrow and asked, "What about young master's breakfast?"

Nirmala sighed and replied, "He's at Rohan's place again. He'll grab a bite there and head straight to the office."

Hasmukh Parekh was growing increasingly concerned about his son's behavior. Shaket seemed to be spending more time with his friend Rohan than at home. Perplexed, he turned to his wife and asked, "What's going on with him? Since he returned from the US, he's practically living at Rohan's. Why aren't you saying anything to him?"

Nirmala sighed once more, anticipating that the conversation would come back to her. She replied, "What can I do? Every time I ask, he tells me he's planning to start a new business. He never divulges any more details than that."

Hasmukh Parekh was clearly troubled. The current market conditions were already weighing heavily on his mind, and now his son's mysterious plans were adding to his worries. He replied,

"Tell him to sort out his affairs here first. The market is not favorable."

Before Nirmala could respond, the servant arrived with some medicines, interrupting their conversation. After they had finished breakfast, Hasmukh Parekh headed to his office, while Nirmala continued her household duties.

At the office, Prashant was having a particularly frustrating day. His computer mouse was acting up, adding to the chaos of his morning. He couldn't help but voice his irritation to his colleague, Ghosh Babu.

Annoyed, Prashant asked, "Ghosh Babu, why is this mouse acting up? It keeps lagging."

Ghosh Babu, ever the calm and collected one, replied, "Prashant Ji, be grateful it's working at all. I've been requesting a new UPS for three months now, but no one's listening to us." Prashant sighed and decided to focus on his work. But his day took a turn for the worse when Shaket, Hasmukh Parekh's son, stormed into the office holding a table calendar.

Shaket demanded, "Who designed this calendar?"

The office fell into an uneasy silence. Shaket's impatience got the better of him, and he barked, "Is everyone here mute?"

Prashant, trying to make sense of the situation, finally admitted that he had designed the calendar. Shaket glared at him and asked, "How far have you studied?"

Taken aback by the confrontation, Prashant hesitated for a moment and then replied, "I'm a graduate."

Shaket, not letting up, then asked him to spell "Global." Prashant, still feeling embarrassed, spelled it out, "G.L.O.B.A.L."

Shaket then pointed out the error on the calendar, where Prashant had inadvertently written "G.L.O.B.E.L."

Feeling humiliated, Prashant tried to explain that it was an honest mistake and that his glasses had caused the error. But Shaket wasn't interested in excuses. Frustrated by the commotion, Hasmukh Parekh emerged from his office and inquired about the situation. Shaket, still seething, demanded to know why his father employed such incompetent people and suggested firing them.

Hasmukh Parekh tried to defuse the situation and invited Shaket to lunch. He wanted to avoid a prolonged argument, so he instructed the servant to serve food. Once inside his office, Hasmukh Parekh tried to calm his son and lighten the mood. However, Shaket continued to express his dissatisfaction with the way his father was running the business. He believed it was time for a change.

Hasmukh Parekh, though proud of his son's ideas, was concerned about managing two businesses simultaneously. He questioned whether Shaket could handle both the existing business and his new venture.

Shaket, adamant about pursuing his own business, stated that he was only helping temporarily due to the licensing process taking longer than expected. He was eager to make his mark and wanted his father to step aside.

Hasmukh Parekh couldn't help but feel a sense of resignation. He understood that his son wanted to forge his own path, but he also cherished the legacy he had built. In the end, he encouraged Shaket but reminded him, "Once a businessman, always a businessman. A businessman never retires; he works until his last breath."

As they shared their meal and discussed their future, Prashant and Ghosh Babu took a break. They sat on a bench on the balcony, looking out at the world. Prashant seemed lost in thought, still bothered by the earlier incident.

Concerned, Ghosh Babu asked, "What's on your mind? Did you forget your lunch?"

Prashant, lost in contemplation, didn't respond immediately. Ghosh Babu gently patted his shoulder, urging him to share his thoughts. Finally, Prashant spoke, his voice heavy with emotion.

"I've dedicated so many years to this company. Shaket was just a child when I first started coming to the office with Mr. Parekh. I've seen him grow up, seen him play with the computer. And now, for all those memories, these kids should at least show some respect, shouldn't they?"

Ghosh Babu, understanding Prashant's sentiments, offered some words of wisdom. He acknowledged that the younger generation often lacked understanding of the struggles others had faced. Ghosh Babu reminded Prashant of his own humble beginnings and how those experiences had shaped his values.

Prashant began to share memories of his childhood and the hardships his family had endured. His father, who sold itching ointment outside Howrah station, had worked tirelessly to provide for their family. He had sacrificed his own meals to ensure his children didn't go hungry.

As they continued to talk, Ghosh Babu advised Prashant not to dwell on the humiliation he had faced. He urged him to let it go and focus on their work. Even Prashant realized that holding onto the incident wouldn't change anything. Spoiled brats like Shaket often failed to understand the value of hard work and struggle. With Ghosh Babu's support, he decided to move forward.

Together, they shared Ghosh Babu's lunch, knowing that life had its challenges, but they had the strength to face them.

– 04 –

After an intense practice session on the playground, the students rushed to the canteen, their stomachs protesting with hunger. Rahul and his group of friends gathered at a table, while Krish sat nearby, savoring a burger and sipping on a coke.

Rahul eagerly opened his tiffin box, anticipating a delightful meal. However, his enthusiasm deflated when he discovered Poha inside. Though his stomach rumbled with hunger, the prospect of consuming Poha failed to excite him. Just as he pondered his predicament, his friends chimed in, beckoning him to join them for lunch.

Despite the hearty invitations and the jovial atmosphere at his friends' table, Rahul shook his head, politely declined, and excused himself. He retreated quietly, his footsteps barely making a sound on the canteen's tiled floor. He reached the nearby dustbin, glanced around, hoping his actions would go unnoticed. With a sigh of relief, he disposed the unwanted Poha into the bin, all the while thinking he had successfully concealed his lunchtime rebellion. However, Krish, perceptive as ever, had keenly observed Rahul's every move.

− 05 −

After a grueling day at the office, Prashant found himself wandering the bustling street market, desperately searching for an appropriate gift for Jay's 17th birthday. Armed with a meager budget of 200 bucks, his quest for the perfect present was tinged with frustration.

As he meandered through the market, his eyes fell upon a humble shop nestled on the footpath. Here, a vendor peddled a variety of Chinese products. Amongst the array of trinkets, Prashant's gaze settled upon a small, yet enchanting wristwatch, priced at a mere 100 rupees. It not only fell comfortably within his budget but also exuded an undeniable charm. Without hesitation, he beckoned to the shopkeeper and requested the wristwatch as Jay's gift.

Meanwhile, when Prashant finally returned home, he discovered Durga impeccably dressed and ready for the evening's festivities. However, their son Rahul was conspicuously absent. Prashant handed over the carefully chosen gift to Durga and excused himself to freshen up. While he wasn't particularly eager to attend the event, social decorum demanded their presence, especially for the sake of their host, Srivastav.

In the interim, Durga stood before the mirror, scrutinizing her appearance for any imperfections. The anticipation of the evening's celebration weighed heavily on her, causing her to question her own appearance.

Upon their arrival at their destination, their eyes were greeted by the radiant spectacle of the second storey of the building, resplendent with a dazzling array of lights and vibrant balloons. The boisterous tunes of Bollywood hits reached their ears even before they stepped inside. The infectious rhythm of the music enticed people to dance to the beats of "Tara Ra Ra."

Navigating their way through the jubilant crowd, Prashant and Durga spotted Srivastav, deeply engaged in conversation with Mr. Monga, a jovial Punjabi gentleman. Srivastav cradled his glass of alcohol as he passionately extolled the virtues of Life Pharmacy shares to Monga, who, in his inebriated state, readily acquiesced. Their conversation was punctuated by excited exclamations about potential profits and investments.

Prashant and Durga approached Srivastav, who acknowledged them warmly before inquiring about Rahul's absence. Durga, with a congenial smile, explained that Rahul had a cricket practice session after school, owing to an upcoming tournament. She assured Srivastav that Rahul would catch up with Jay later to extend his birthday wishes.

Srivastav's praises for Rahul's cricketing talent filled Durga with pride. She listened with a warm heart as Srivastav expressed his admiration for their son.

With a discerning eye, Srivastav noticed the gift in Durga's hands, and he couldn't resist commenting on its size. Despite Durga's attempt to downplay it, he couldn't help but express his thoughts.

Prashant hesitated momentarily when Srivastav offered him a drink, acutely aware of Durga's presence. Srivastav, however, encouraged him, highlighting the special occasion. Reluctantly, Prashant accepted a glass of whiskey.

Observing the situation, Durga gracefully excused herself, citing the need to greet Pushpa Bhabhi. Srivastav directed her to the guest room, instructing her to present the gift herself. Durga accepted the gift and departed, leaving the men to their indulgence.

As soon as Durga made her exit, Srivastav's excitement soared, and he turned to Prashant, hinting at a relaxed atmosphere for their conversation. He welcomed Prashant into the fold and encouraged him to partake in the celebration.

Prashant's tentative sip of the whiskey betrayed his reluctance, but he tried his best to blend in with the party. Srivastav then introduced Prashant to Mr. Monga, the proprietor of Monga Timber Industry, applauding his business acumen and recent success. Despite his inebriation, Mr. Monga effusively praised the host for his financial recommendations, which had undoubtedly contributed to his company's soaring profits.

Prashant, standing silently beside them, held his glass, bewildered by the abrupt transition from business to social pleasantries. Srivastav, however, seamlessly pivoted to introduce Prashant as the father of the exceptionally talented Rahul. The comparison between Rahul and a well-known cricketer was not lost on Mr. Monga.

As the conversation flowed, Mr. Monga's delight was evident as he broke into a hearty Punjabi song, the sound of which prompted him to take to the stage in a spirited dance. Srivastav, wearing a sly smile, watched with amusement as Mr. Monga's uninhibited dance moves stole the limelight.

Meanwhile, Prashant stood in the midst of the festive crowd, his face reflecting a sense of displacement and detachment. Lost in his thoughts, he sipped his drink intermittently, struggling to immerse himself in the celebrations. Srivastav, noticing Prashant's disquiet, tapped his shoulder gently, inquiring about his apparent despondency. Prashant, caught off guard, attempted to deflect the conversation but failed to conceal his inner turmoil.

Srivastav, setting aside his glass, delved into a heartfelt conversation about life's uncertainties and the anxieties that accompany thoughts of the future. He emphasized the importance of investing in their children's talents and well-being. Prashant listened attentively, attempting to decipher Srivastav's cryptic message. The mention of investments and supplements left him puzzled and frustrated.

Finally, Srivastav revealed his budget-friendly solution: bananas. He urged Prashant to ensure that Rahul consumed four bananas daily to provide the necessary protein and vitamins. The simplicity of this advice left Prashant bewildered.

As their discussion continued, Prashant's bewilderment grew. He struggled to comprehend how a banana could be the answer to his son's future. In his state of confusion, he could only muster a hesitant, "What?" Srivastav reiterated his suggestion, extolling the virtues of bananas as a cost-effective source of essential nutrients. Prashant remained flummoxed, grappling with the unexpected advice.

Their conversation was interrupted by Srivastav's wife, Pushpa, who arrived with a touch of irritation in her demeanor. She chastised Srivastav for neglecting their duties at the party, reminding him of the impending cake-cutting ceremony.

Srivastav, choosing not to engage in an argument, agreed to join the celebration. He and Prashant decided to proceed, leaving their conversation temporarily unresolved.

As Prashant stepped onto the balcony, he sought solace under the night sky. The moon's reassuring presence seemed to encourage patience and contemplation. The fading music provided a backdrop to his introspection, and he found himself lost in thought.

After the sumptuous dinner, Durga and Prashant returned home, their minds swirling with the complexities of life and the unexpected advice they had received.

– 06 –

In the tranquil evening, Durga sat diligently at her sewing machine, the rhythmic hum of the needle punctuating the silence. Her thoughts were consumed by curiosity about the conversation between Prashant and Srivastav. As she meticulously worked on a sari, her fingers deftly stitching intricate patterns, she couldn't help but wonder about the nature of their discussion.

Meanwhile, Prashant lounged in a chair nearby, engrossed in the evening newspaper. The soft glow of the lamp beside him cast a warm ambience in the room.

Suddenly, the sharp ring of Durga's phone shattered the tranquility. She reached for the device, her nimble fingers quickly locating it amid her sewing tools. Sudha, one of her customers, was on the line, inquiring about her ordered sari. Durga efficiently provided the necessary information, instructing Sudha to send Munni with a payment of Rs 120, as both saris were ready.

With the call concluded, Durga resumed her sewing, her focus returning to the unfinished sari. A few moments later, she couldn't contain her curiosity any longer. Casting a sidelong glance at Prashant, she ventured to ask the question that had been nagging at her since their return from Srivastav's gathering.

"What was Srivastav Ji talking about with you for so long?" Durga inquired, her eyes filled with curiosity and a hint of suspicion. Prashant, still reading the newspaper, seemed somewhat preoccupied. He responded with a vague, "Just random stuff."

However, Durga wasn't about to be so easily brushed aside. She persisted; her tone tinged with skepticism. "Random stuff? Since when does that man say anything randomly? He must have been bragging about himself and his son," she surmised, her sewing momentarily halted.

Prashant folded the newspaper and laid it aside, his expression contemplative. After a brief pause, he responded, "He brags about himself because he is worth it. Anyways, why didn't Rahul come? What practice was he doing in the evening?"

Durga sensed that Prashant might hold Rahul accountable for not joining them at the event, potentially leading to a conflict. To defuse the situation, she tried to steer the conversation away from their son's absence. "Perhaps he doesn't enjoy going to their house anymore. He's growing up, and I don't want to force him into anything," she offered, attempting to change the topic.

Prashant nodded in agreement, accepting Durga's explanation. "Yes, he is growing," he murmured, acknowledging their son's transition from childhood to adolescence. With a sense of resignation, Prashant settled back on the bed, reflecting on the cyclical routine of his life—daily trips to the office and evenings spent at home, all in pursuit of securing their family's financial stability.

The following morning dawned with a sense of tranquility at the Parekh Printing Works. The muted hum of Prashant's keyboard was the only audible sound in the serene office space. After a while, Prashant was interrupted by a knock at the door. The servant informed him that Hasmukh Parekh wished to see him in his office.

Hasmukh Parekh, engrossed in a computer card game, welcomed Prashant to his office, though Prashant's eyes remained fixed on the television screen, where Roger Federer was seen munching on bananas during a game break.

Hasmukh Parekh, noticing Prashant's distraction, momentarily diverted his attention. "Prashant, please, have a seat," he encouraged, extending a hospitable hand toward a chair. Prashant, however, couldn't tear his gaze away from the television. His curiosity about the tennis player's banana consumption was palpable.

Hasmukh Parekh, recognizing Prashant's curiosity, chuckled before addressing the matter at hand. "Ah, the bananas! Well, they're a vital source of vitamins A, E, B6, and C—essential for athletes. They provide an immediate energy boost. Even I consume them while playing tennis," he explained with a warm smile.

Prashant nodded in comprehension, appreciating the impromptu lesson from his employer. Eventually, he excused himself and returned to his work, leaving Hasmukh Parekh to his card game. At lunchtime, Prashant's attention drifted away from his meal. He gazed out of the window, his thoughts wandering elsewhere. Ghosh Babu, noticed Prashant's preoccupation and called him to join for lunch. This time, however, Prashant wasn't lost in thought.

Prashant reassured Ghosh Babu that he would return shortly and then walked over to Jamal Ansari, a fruit vendor who had set up shop nearby. Jamal was selling bananas at three for ten bucks, a pricing detail that did not escape Prashant's scrutiny. Prashant questioned him about the reduced quantity, as he was accustomed to purchasing four bananas for the same price elsewhere.

Jamal, resolute in his pricing, asserted that he only sold three bananas for ten rupees. His unwavering stance left Prashant contemplating his options. As he made a move on to explore other vendors, Jamal, having packed up his remaining bananas, stowed his hamper and left the area.

Meanwhile, at Rahul's school, a different scene unfolded. Rahul and his friends were enjoying a lunch of noodles at the school's food plaza. The atmosphere changed when Krish, accompanied by a charming teenage girl named Riya, emerged from the crowd.

Rahul and his friends couldn't help but envy Krish's charisma, a topic they often discussed in hushed tones. Their admiration for him was palpable. One of Rahul's friends remarked, "Life should be like Krish's—top-notch quality in everything, be it a car or a girlfriend. Another friend chimed in, "Just enjoy the view from a distance. We won't stand a chance."

Rahul, however, was less amused by their admiration. He attributed Krish's advantages to luck and destiny, emphasizing that their circumstances were different.

One of the friends nervously cautioned the group not to stare too conspicuously at Krish and Riya, noting Krish's unpredictable nature. Rahul interjected, "Krish's mind isn't unpredictable; it's sharp. He used to be the best cricketer in school. I don't know why he gave up everything."

As Krish and Riya approached the group, the conversation fell silent. Krish greeted Rahul and his friends, teasingly compared the situation to a Bollywood film. However, Rahul's bashfulness in the face of Krish's praise was evident. He deflected the attention and modestly replied, "Don't say that, buddy."

Krish, undeterred, continued to extol Rahul's popularity in school, emphasizing the admiration he received from fellow students and the adoration of female admirers. Rahul, still somewhat uncomfortable, acknowledged Krish's compliments with a modest smile.

Riya, taken aback by the revelations, playfully suggested taking an autograph from the renowned Rahul. However, Krish insisted that a selfie would be more fitting for the occasion. Feeling self-conscious under the spotlight, Rahul downplayed the attention. "Don't mention it, guys," he said, acknowledging the compliment graciously.

Krish, eager to engage Rahul further, extended an invitation to a club. He urged Rahul to join them for some relaxation, citing the rule that a senior's invitation should not be refused. Although tempted, Rahul hesitated, mindful of his early practice the next day. He offered his apologies but was met with Krish's insistence that he accompany them. Krish even offered to provide transportation for Rahul and his friends.

One of Rahul's friends raised concerns about age restrictions at the club, but Krish assured them that a gate pass would suffice. To further alleviate their doubts, Krish displayed his wallet filled with cash and cards.

Krish's focus was on securing Rahul's attendance, and he made it clear that everyone was welcome. Overwhelmed by the invitation and Krish's persistence, Rahul decided to call his mother for permission.

Rahul borrowed a friend's phone and retreated to a corner, dialing a number anxiously. Durga, engrossed in her cooking, answered the call, her knife resting beside the cutting board.

Rampiyari sat in front of the television, engrossed in the latest news updates. Meanwhile, Durga diligently chopped vegetables on the kitchen counter, her knife slicing through the fresh produce with precision.

Suddenly, the phone rang, its shrill tone piercing the otherwise calm atmosphere. Durga glanced at the caller ID, her eyebrows furrowing as she noted the unknown phone number. She carefully set the knife aside and picked up the receiver, her voice cautious. "Hello, who is this?"

On the other end of the line, Rahul swiftly concocted his fabricated story. As soon as Durga answered, he adopted a composed tone. "Yes, Mother, it's me, Rahul. I'm calling from a friend's phone. I'll be at Sandeep's house tonight. It's his brother's birthday, and we're having dinner there. I'll be a bit late coming home." Rahul abruptly hung up, not giving Durga a chance to respond. However, she was still voicing her concerns, unaware that the call had ended. "But you're not dressed up! Hello... hello!! This boy!!"

Rampiyari, who had observed the entire conversation, sensed her daughter-in-law's irritation. She decided to intervene and seek clarity. "What happened, Bahu?". Durga, still perturbed by the phone call, replied with frustration in her voice. "Rahul is going to a party. It's his friend's brother's birthday, and he'll be home late."

Rampiyari, finding nothing amiss with Rahul attending a celebration, responded with understanding. "It's okay. Let him enjoy himself. Don't stop him. Whose anniversary is it anyway?".

Durga, exasperated by the continued misunderstanding, corrected her with irritation. "No, Maa, not an anniversary. It's Rahul's friend's brother's birthday."

Rampiyari remained puzzled, trying to make sense of Durga's words. She struggled to grasp the situation accurately. "Birthday? Yours? But your birthday was last month, wasn't it?"

Durga, feeling utterly frustrated, abandoned her task and grabbed a plate before heading back to the kitchen. Rampiyari continued to stare blankly, attempting to unravel the confusion that lingered in the air.

– 07 –

Jamal's weary footsteps echoed as he disembarked from the crowded bus at the Monipur Bus Stop, his thoughts burdened with the trials of the day. With a heavy heart, he took his way back home, each step a testament to the toil and struggles that had become his daily life.

As he made his way through the bustling streets, his eyes caught sight of a group of young men engrossed in an intense game of carom on the opposite side of the road. Laughter and banter filled the air, a stark contrast to the weight Jamal carried.

But the respite was short-lived, for his phone began to ring persistently. Fareed, who sat nearby, repeatedly tried to grab Jamal's attention. "Bhai jaan, oh, hello, did you get any information about Bhabhi ji?" Fareed's tone carried a mocking edge, and Jamal's irritation simmered.

Reluctantly, Jamal answered, his voice tinged with frustration, "Yes, I received a letter from Dubai just yesterday. She was asking about you. Do you wish to know about anything else?"

Fareed persisted, seemingly oblivious to Jamal's growing annoyance. "Brother! You seem to be quite angry. I was trying to find out what happened. How could a decent girl leave her husband, even though the husband is still around, and run away with someone else, leaving behind a little child? It's very unfair to you. Isn't it?"

Jamal's patience reached its limit, and he could no longer maintain a polite façade. With a fixed gaze at Fareed, he retorted, "Thank you very much. I wanted to ask you something. Do you genuinely care about me and my child, or do you itch to irritate us whenever you see us? If you're so concerned, why don't you keep the child at your house for a week? Raqib Bhai and Bhabhi will get some relief. I'll drop off the child at your place tomorrow when I leave for work. Is that okay?"

Fareed, realizing that Jamal would no longer tolerate his interference, tried to deflect blame. "Come on... I was only trying to help."

Jamal's temper flared, and he spoke earnestly, "Please, brother, keep your empathy to yourself. Stop taunting me whenever you see me, if you cannot do anything for us. Please leave me and my child alone. It's not right to rub salt on my wounds."

Fareed, sensing Jamal's resolve, attempted to walk away hastily, his words laced with disdain. "Abe, shut up. I don't need advice from a guy who sells bananas for a living. Get lost, you scoundrel."

Defeated and weary, Jamal could only watch Fareed's retreating figure. He knew that the world would not spare him or his family, not after his wife abandoned them. In silence, he headed towards Raqib Siddiki's house.

Jamal knocked on Raqib's door, hopeful to see his son, Shahrukh. However, it was Fatima who answered. He greeted her with a respectful nod. "Assalam o alikum Bhabhi Jaan. Where is bhai?" Fatima's warm smile welcomed him as she replied,

"Walekum Assalam. Your brother has gone to purchase jalebi. Come inside."

Jamal was puzzled by the idea of indulging in jalebi during the evening, and he couldn't help but inquire, "Jalebi? In the evening?"

Fatima responded with a grin, "Your shehzada wished to eat jalebi."

Jamal felt a pang of embarrassment, realizing that his son's desires had prompted Raqib's late-night errand. He sighed and remarked, "Ya Khuda, how much these children trouble. How is his health?"

Fatima reassured him with a warm smile. "Inshallah, he is absolutely fine. Why do you worry so much? We are here, no?" Just then, Raqib returned, holding a bag of jalebi. He joked, "At least, I got to eat some sweets because of Shahrukh's tantrum. Otherwise, your Bhabhi..." Upon spotting his father, Shahrukh's face lit up with joy. He rushed towards Jamal, eagerly exclaiming, "Abbu."

Jamal reciprocated the affectionate greeting, urging his son, "Beta, let's go home."

Yet, Shahrukh persisted, his eyes gleaming with anticipation. "Jalebi, jalebi..."

Jamal tried to reason with him. "Let's go home first, and then you can eat."

Shahrukh remained fixated on his desire. "Jalebi... Jalebi."

Jamal persisted in his attempt to lead Shahrukh home, assuring him, "Yes, let's go home and eat."

Shahrukh, however, was resolute. "Jalebi... Jalebi."

Raqib, growing weary of the impasse, intervened. "Arey, why are you saying home... home? Let him eat. What will he do after going home? What is there?"

Raqib's words hung in the air, an unintended barb that stung Jamal. Fatima, sensing the discomfort, looked at her husband with regret in her eyes. Raqib quickly regretted his choice of words and apologized, "Sorry yaar, I didn't mean that."

Jamal, understanding Raqib's intentions, dismissed the comment. He gestured with a resigned sweep of his hand, acknowledging the reality. "No, you are right. In reality, there is nothing there to call home."Fatima interjected, her voice filled with empathy. "Don't say like that, Jamal bhai. After all, even this is your brother's home."

Jamal nodded, appreciating the sentiment, as Raqib inquired, "Did you get any news of Shagufta? It's been more than 10 months now. She has not even called or texted."

With a heavy heart, Jamal stood, readying to leave.

Fatima offered a suggestion, born of concern. "Let me tell you something, Jamal bhai. If you want to wait for Shagufta bhabi, then do so. But also consider this innocent child. What will happen to him? You work all day long. Who will take care of this child? Today we are here, so it's not a problem, but you know that your brother has a transferable job. If he gets transferred, what then? Think about marriage again, not necessarily for yourself, but for your child's well-being."

Raqib echoed the sentiment. "Fatima is right. Think about it, or let us figure something out. Fatima, see what you can do. And, Bhai Jaan, try to leave that house and neighborhood as soon as possible. Neither that house nor that neighborhood is a place for decent people. Your landlady is also... Well, forget it."

Jamal nodded in agreement, resigned to the realities of his life. He chose not to argue, for what else could he do? His circumstances were harsh, and the world was unforgiving. With a final farewell, he took Shahrukh and left Raqib's house behind.

On their way home, Jamal realized that he would once again have to enter his room silently, avoiding any unwanted attention. As he approached the Watgunge red-light area, he glanced upstairs and carefully unlocked the door to a small, dimly lit room.

– 08 –

As Jamal entered his cramped accommodation, his eyes fell on the cracks of the walls, now more pronounced than ever. Shahrukh mumbled something in his drowsy state, and Jamal, understanding his son's need, handed him a glass of water. However, the steel glass slipped from Shahrukh's little hands, clattering loudly against the floor.

Jamal's stress mounted but he didn't want any unnecessary confrontations after a long and exhausting day. He looked heavenward and muttered, "Ya Khuda!"

A few minutes later, the sound of footsteps and tinkling anklets reached his ears. Jamal's gaze hardened as he could easily anticipate who the visitor was. He swiftly opened the door to find Razia, a woman in her late thirties. Their eyes locked for a moment, and it was Jamal who broke the silence with a resigned tone. "I will pay you the pending rent next month. I just need a little more time."

Razia wasted no time in launching into a tirade. "Did I say anything to you? You quietly entered the room like a thief thinking Razia is a woman of loose morals..... You'll quietly sneak out in the morning as well before I even wake up. How long do you think that this hide-and-seek will go on? You haven't paid the rent in three months. I also get hungry and thirsty, you know? I have no one to support me either. My home barely runs on the rent I earn. Should I start entertaining men again to solve your problems?"

Jamal, though frustrated, maintained his composure and replied, "When did I say anything like that?"

Razia retorted once more, her voice filled with exasperation, "What will you say, huh? Do you even have the right to speak? You can't handle your wife. You can't take care of your child. Tell me one thing, What is your actual plan? Are you going to raise a child by selling bananas? Or do you want to take over this house someday by murdering me?"

With defeat in his eyes, Jamal spoke softly, "I am toiling hard. I am not doing anything wrong. Rest, Khuda will see. "Razia, realizing that Jamal was going through a tough time, softened her stance. She looked at him and spoke with a bit more compassion, "Alright, I'm sorry. Maybe I said a little too much. Do whatever you want, but remember, it's my house, so do pay the rent on time. Remember that."

Jamal remained silent, his mind heavy with the weight of his responsibilities. Shahrukh mumbled again, drawing his father's attention. Jamal turned to Razia and mentioned, "He wants to go to the washroom."

A flicker of sympathy crossed Razia's face as she seemed to be touched by little Shahrukh's innocence. She spoke after a moment's pause, "I am giving you one month's time only for the sake of your child." With that, she turned and departed, leaving Jamal and Shahrukh in the dimly lit room, grappling with the challenges that life had thrust upon them.

– 09 –

Rahul and his friends found themselves in a pub for the first time, surrounded by the pulsating rhythm of loud music as the dance floor bathed in shining lights. While Rahul remained relatively unaffected by the sensory overload, his friends were thoroughly captivated by the vibrant atmosphere.

In the midst of this lively scene, Krish took it upon himself to light up a cigarette for both Riya and himself. He extended the offer to Rahul, who timidly declined, stating, "I don't smoke."

Krish couldn't hide his astonishment and queried, "Seriously?"

Rahul nodded in confirmation, prompting Krish to ask further, "You don't even drink?"

Once again, Rahul nodded, affirming his teetotaler status.

Krish waved his hand dismissively and suggested, "Come on, even I used to play cricket. Never mind, let's have a light beer."

Rahul hesitated momentarily but then, in a quiet voice, declined, "No dude, I have to go home."

However, Krish was determined not to let Rahul escape a drinking experience so easily. He looked directly at him and challenged, "No one will know anything. It's just one beer. You don't trust me or what?"

Rahul remained hesitant, but Sanjay interjected, attempting to sway his decision. "Yeah, buddy. Nothing happens with beer. We secretly had a beer each at my uncle's wedding. I swear, it was so much fun. We danced for 2 hours straight. No one found out anything."

Riya also joined in, coaxing Rahul with enthusiasm. "Come on, Rahul, be a sport!"

With these words of encouragement, Krish seized the opportunity and declared, "Now, you will have to listen to Riya. I will not take no for an answer."

Krish proceeded to pour a beer from the pitcher into a glass and handed it to Rahul. The group then raised their glasses, echoing Krish's sentiment, "To Rahul."

Feeling a bit more reassured and swayed by the camaraderie, Rahul couldn't refuse this time. He smiled and took a sip of the beer. In the midst of this moment, Riya took her phone, capturing a selfie with Krish and Rahul to commemorate the occasion.

In no time, the beers had their desired effect, and the group found themselves in a state of high spirits. Riya was enthusiastically dancing with Krish, while their friends unleashed their wild dance moves on the floor. However, Rahul remained a quiet observer, lingering at a distance.

Riya, noticing Rahul's detachment, decided to remedy the situation. She approached him and playfully dragged him onto the dance floor. In response, Rahul's gaze shifted to another girl, and he hesitated, muttering, "I cannot dance."

Riya, determined to change his mind, swayed her hands and encouraged, "Of course, you can. Just copy my steps."As Riya showcased her dance moves, Rahul found himself unable to follow her rhythm. Puzzled Rahul inquired, "What is this?"

Riya laughed heartily, her tipsy eyes gleaming with joy, and replied, "This is life. Dance for life."

Rahul looked at her enchanting face and muttered to himself, "Life, huh? My life is shit."

Sensing Rahul's hesitation, Riya pulled him closer and insisted, "Don't think about anything. Just dance with me!"

Rahul, won over by her insistence, smiled and began dancing. Some girls in the vicinity danced and laughed, thoroughly enjoying their friends' lively moves. For the first time, Rahul experienced the vibrancy of a party. Little did he know that his parents were anxiously waiting for him back at home. Rampiyari was asleep, but Prashant and Durga were lying in bed. Prashant glanced at the clock, which displayed the time, 11'o clock.

Meanwhile, Krish's car sped through the streets, blaring loud music. Krish brought the car to a halt near Prashant's house. Rahul and his friends disembarked, and Ansh, who was a bit tipsy, began to retch and express his gratitude to Krish, saying, "Thank you so much, you are the real boss. I love..."

Krish appeared concerned about Ansh's condition, but Sanjay intervened, assuring, "Don't worry. He lives near my place; I'll drop him off. Good night!" Krish nodded in agreement and bid farewell, saying, "Good night, bro. Take care."

Rahul looked at Krish and sincerely expressed his gratitude, saying, "Krish, thanks for everything."

Krish waved his hand casually and remarked, "Stupid, you are thanking your friend, huh? See you tomorrow."

Despite the heaviness in her eyes from the drinks, Riya managed to utter in a slurred voice, "Good night, Rahul. See you soon."

Rahul smiled at her and replied, "Sure."

Before driving away, Krish handed Rahul a piece of chewing gum, advising, "Listen, chew this gum. You won't smell. See you, buddy!"

As Krish's car faded into the distance, Rahul obediently popped the chewing gum into his mouth. Each of them then headed to their respective homes, their concerns momentarily forgotten. However, they were unaware of the storm that awaited Rahul upon his return.

Rahul knocked softly on his front door. Prashant, roused by the sound, woke Durga, who sleepily opened the door and allowed Rahul inside. As he entered the home, Durga inquired, "Where were you, beta? What took you so long?"

Rahul glanced at her, maintaining a certain distance, and responded, "I told you I was going to a birthday party; I knew I'd be late. It wasn't just any party, you know. But why did both of you stay up this late for me?"

Durga looked at her son, searching for words, while Prashant stepped in and asserted, "Because we care for you." Rahul's irritation became evident as he addressed his father, "I'm not talking to you."

Prashant, unflinching, stated, "But I'm talking to you."

Rahul vented his frustration, asking, "What do you want to talk to me about? Is there even a need for a conversation? And please, don't feign concern. It doesn't sound sincere coming from you."

Durga, observing the tension, interjected, "Rahul, what is wrong with you? How can you speak to your father like this?"

Rahul shrugged, his tone exasperated, and retorted, "That's why I don't say anything to anyone in this house. If I speak, everyone takes issue."

Prashant, maintaining his composure, addressed his son directly, saying, "Durga, don't stop him. Beta, say whatever is on your mind."

Rahul sighed and then, his frustration palpable, began to speak candidly, "Should I speak openly, then? Fine, listen carefully. But where should I start? What do you want to hear?" He paused momentarily, waiting for his father's response, before continuing, "You think that by enrolling me in a school like City International, you've done me a great favor, don't you? And even then, it was through the sports quota, thanks to my own talent. People should live within their means. It would have been better if you had admitted me to a government school. At least there, I wouldn't have to endure daily humiliation. Have you ever considered the financial status of students in that school? Do you know anything about their lifestyle? I don't belong among them at all. Last month, you paid the fees late. Everyone there arrives in cars, while here, even owning a scooter feels like a luxury. What were you thinking? That I would achieve all your unfulfilled dreams? And for heaven's sake, please don't expect your children to fulfill your unattained ambitions. Children aren't born to fulfill their parents' dreams. Do you remember your mantra, 'Live within your means'? What happened to that? Did you think that the child you brought into this world would play cricket, make a name for himself, and earn money? Do you even understand cricket? Leave alone the international stage; do you comprehend what it takes to compete at the national or EPL? Specialized fitness training, specific diets! Do you have any inkling of what that entails? And even if you do, what difference does it make? All of this is beyond your means. Why can't you accept this reality? Cricket is a lost cause! I want to secure a good job. I don't want to live in a fantasy world like you, nor do I wish for an ordinary existence."

Rahul waved his hand in exasperation, turned, and retreated to his room, slamming the door shut behind him. Durga and Prashant were left stunned by their son's outburst. Prashant remained silent, while Durga's eyes swelled up with tears. She whispered to Prashant, her voice quivering, "You should go to sleep. You have to go to the office in the morning."

Prashant nodded and headed towards the bedroom. Durga wiped her tears away and followed him. Prashant, gazing at the closed door to Rahul's room, muttered quietly to himself, "You are not ordinary, beta."

– 10 –

Razia diligently spread her freshly washed clothes across her terrace, the warm sun casting a gentle glow on the vibrant fabrics. Her focus was on her task until she suddenly sensed a presence below. Glancing downward, she spotted a man gazing up at her. It was Parevez, an unwanted figure from her past.

Parevez, undeterred by her initial indifference, ascended the stairs and joined her on the terrace. Attempting to break the ice, he greeted her, saying, "Assalam Waalekum, Raazi..."Razia continued with her chores, not deigning to respond to him.

Parevez, however, persisted, addressing her, "No greetings? Have you forgotten me? What's the matter, Rajjo?"

A surge of anger welled up within Razia as she shot him a furious glare. Parevez, sensing her ire, took a step back, eyed her cautiously, and quickly corrected himself, "Okay, not Rajjo. I will call you Razia. Sorry!"

Razia, in no mood for pleasantries, cut short his apology, demanding, "Why are you here?"

Parevez continued to scrutinize her with cunning eyes, a sly smile playing on his lips. He replied, "I have come because I am concerned about you. I heard that you are facing financial difficulties. You could have at least talked to me once."

Razia's patience ran thin, and she lashed out, "So, what would you have done? Build Taj Mahal for me?"

Parevez realized that small talk was futile in this situation. Cutting to the chase, he said, "Look, two businessmen have come from Delhi. I've completely changed the way we do business now. You don't have to do anything. Just get in the car. I'll handle the rest. You'll make enough much money to cover your expenses for the next six months."

Razia's fury intensified, and she yelled, "Get out right now. I do not want any drama here."

Parevez raised his voice slightly, emphasizing that Razia didn't belong in this 'world', as he said, "No matter how hard you try to become Razia, you will always remain Rajjo. Open your eyes and look around. No one respects you. I, however, still admire you. That's why I've come to you after five years."

Razia's voice grew even louder, drowning out Parevez's attempts at persuasion, as she retorted, "I don't even want respect from that world. As a matter of fact, not from you as well. And I'm done making compromises. Go and broker someone else's deals. Leave and don't come back here again."

At the adjacent part of the terrace, another woman stood silently, eavesdropping on Razia and Parevez's heated exchange. Her intent gaze was fixed on them as she strained to hear and comprehend their conversation. Parevez, feeling increasingly uncomfortable under her watchful eye, decided to make a hasty exit out of sheer embarrassment.

He concluded, "Alright, it's your wish. But my doors are still open. Remember that. If not today, then tomorrow, I will be the one to help you."

Parevez walked away, frustration evident on his face. Razia continued to glare at him for a moment before turning her attention to the woman who had been observing their confrontation. The woman quickly averted her gaze, pretending not to have been listening, and instantaneously shifted her focus to something else, choosing to ignore Razia.

– 11 –

Srivastav engaged in a conversation with his Bengali friend on his phone, sharing his concerns, "What's the matter, Komol Da? How will your business grow like this? I've been telling you for a long time to start investing slowly in mutual funds. Oh no, no. Shares have their place, but investment patterns change with time, right? What about risk? Isn't there risk in shares, Komol da? You Bengali people have this problem. You're afraid of anything new. That's why you can't progress. Well, my friend, risk is a part of life. If you don't take risks, how will you move forward in life? Alright, my friend, think about what I said with a calm mind. I'll call you again tomorrow, Namaste!"

After ending the call, Srivastav noticed his son Jay heading out. Although he wasn't one to pry too much, Jay's departure in the afternoon piqued his curiosity. He paused and then halted his son, asking, "Hey, where are you going?"

Jay turned to face his father and replied, "I am going to coaching, Papa. I have my test today."

Srivastav nodded in understanding and followed up, "Have you prepared?"

Jay met his father's gaze with a small smile and affirmed, "Yes, Papa."

Srivastav nodded his paternal pride evident. He encouraged Jay, saying, "Alright, go on then."

However, Jay lingered for a moment. Srivastav sensed that his son wanted to discuss something. He looked at Jay and asked, "What's on your mind?" Jay hesitated briefly and then opened up, "Papa, I wanted to talk to you about something." Srivastav gave his full attention to Jay, signaling his willingness to listen, "Yes, go on."

Jay paused for a moment, his gaze earnest, and continued, "Well, this coaching is good, but many of my friends are taking special classes with 'Dream Big.' Last year, their result was 100 percent." Srivastav took a moment to process their conversation. He hadn't heard of Dream Big before, so he inquired, "What is this, Dream Big?"

Jay stepped closer and explained, "It's the best coaching that prepares one to crack the IIT."

Srivastav got straight to the point, asking, "Do you want to join?"

Jay nodded eagerly and added, "Yes, Dad. I want to clear it in the first attempt so that I can save a year."

Srivastav considered the request, allowing a moment of silence to fill the room. Jay, with hopeful eyes, knew his father was likely to grant his wish. After a brief pause, Srivastav smiled and agreed, "No worries, I will see to it. You can go and fill out the form." Jay's eyes lit up with joy as he expressed his gratitude, "Thank you, Papa."

Seeing his son happy brought immense contentment to Srivastav. He returned the smile, and Jay left for his coaching with a heart full of hope and determination.

– 12 –

Following the memorable night at the pub, Rahul and Krish's friendship deepened. They found themselves sitting together in the school canteen, sipping on cold drinks, and engaging in conversations about life. Rahul had always harbored a burning question about why Krish had abandoned his promising cricket career. On this particular day, he finally gathered the courage to ask, "Alright, tell me one thing. You were such a talented cricketer. You could have effortlessly reached the state level, maybe even represented India one day. Yet, you left it all behind for alcohol, cigarettes, disco, and whatnot! Don't your parents scold you for it?"

Krish placed his bottle aside, turned towards Rahul, and met his gaze. After a moment's contemplation, he began to explain, "Whether anyone in my family knows about my habits, I'm not sure, and I honestly couldn't care less. I enjoy complete privacy at home. You see, I have my life all sorted out. After college, my dad is sending me abroad for management studies. When I return, I'll join his business. Eventually, I'll marry the only daughter of a wealthy businessman. This is the time to live life to the fullest! These moments won't come back. That's why I bid farewell to cricket. So now do you get it"

Listening to Krish's description of his life and family, Rahul couldn't help but feel a twinge of envy. He wished his life could follow a similar trajectory. However, his reality was different. Rahul nodded in agreement and confessed, "Yeah, you're absolutely right. We should live life on our terms. I just wish my family had the same outlook."

Krish smirked knowingly, having heard similar sentiments from others before. He swiftly changed the subject and enthusiastically declared, "Alright, listen up. Riya is throwing a surprise party this Sunday. She's booked a private resort, and her friends are also coming. Be ready right after school on Saturday, and come straight to my place. It's a two-hour drive. We'll return on Sunday."

Rahul hesitated for a moment, his family's reaction flickering in his mind. He wondered, "An overnight stay? But what do I tell my family?"

"Are you still a child?" Krish reacted. "Just make up any excuse!"

Rahul considered Krish's words and realized that he couldn't remain a "momma's boy" forever. He nodded in agreement and resolved, "Alright, I'll figure it out."

Krish grinned and then added, "And please, get yourself a mobile."

Rahul agreed, knowing it was high time he had one. He suddenly remembered he had cricket practice to attend. With a nod, he announced, "Okay, I need to go for practice now. Bye!"

Krish waved him off with a casual, "Goodbye! See you on Saturday." With a wave of his hand, Rahul left for his practice, looking forward to the exciting weekend plans ahead.

– 13 –

As the evening sun cast a warm glow over the CCR Club House, Shaket and his friend Rohan engaged in a spirited game of tennis. The court echoed with the rhythmic thud of the tennis balls, and the players displayed their athleticism with each powerful stroke.

After their intense tennis match, both players took a well-deserved break, settling down on a nearby bench to quench their thirst with refreshing glasses of juice. The tranquil surroundings enveloped them, and for a moment, they enjoyed the serene silence.

However, Rohan's thoughts soon drifted to business matters. He turned towards Shaket and broached the topic, "I had a conversation with a client from Florida yesterday. It seems there's significant potential for ready-made garment exports in that region."Shaket, ever the pragmatist, wasted no time in responding. He fixed his gaze on Rohan and advised, "Let's not dawdle, Rohan. I suggest you expedite the process of obtaining your import-export license. Have you already discussed this with your uncle? It's time to get the ball rolling, my friend."

Rohan shared Shaket's enthusiasm for launching their business venture, and he eagerly inquired, "I'm equally eager to start, Shaket. But remember, while you'll have your license by next month, we need to secure our own office space beforehand. Have you had a conversation with your uncle about this?"

Shaket casually brushed aside Rohan's concern, stating, "We already have my father's office space."

Rohan, however, couldn't shake off his apprehensions. He knew that Hasmukh Parekh, Shaket's father, had painstakingly built his own business from the ground up. He was uncertain whether Hasmukh Parekh would be amenable to their plans. With a hint of anxiety, he pressed further, "What about your father's business?"

Shaket appeared somewhat exasperated by Rohan's persistence, but he clarified his stance, "What about it? Let's face it, Rohan, his business is practically obsolete. Printing diaries and calendars! Can you imagine? I intend to propose shutting down that outdated venture and repurposing the space for our future enterprise."

Rohan's concerns lingered, and he probed further, "Do you think he'll agree to it?"

Shaket's frustration was palpable, but he remained resolute, "His business is on its last legs. He'll have no choice but to agree. Besides, I've known his clients since I was a child. They're like family to me. I'm confident I'll have their full support. We can even explore new opportunities through them. Establishing strong connections with local clients is crucial for our success."

With that, Shaket drained the last drops of his juice, got up decisively, and addressed Rohan, "I'll see you tomorrow. Have the proposal ready. The office space should be finalized by next month."

And with that parting statement, Shaket strode away, leaving Rohan deep in thought as he remained seated on the bench, pondering the challenges and opportunities that lay ahead.

– 14 –

Raj pulled up at the panwala's stall, and as he did, the panwala couldn't help but notice his sleek, silver Mercedes Benz that had come to a halt on the opposite side of the road. Instantly recognizing the car, he hastened towards it, offering a respectful salute to Raj, and greeting him with a warm "Namaste, Sahab!"

Raj, eager to get the information he sought, wasted no time. "Did Krish visit?" he inquired.

The panwala met Raj's gaze, acknowledging the query with a nod. He replied, "Yes, Sahab, he was here yesterday."

His mission accomplished, Raj promptly handed the panwala a fistful of money, and departed from the scene.

As the lunch hour approached, Prashant decided to venture out once more, his footsteps leading him towards the fruit vendor. He made a conscious effort to avoid Jamal, choosing a spot slightly farther down the road. The sun hung high in the sky, casting harsh shadows on the bustling street.

Unbeknownst to Prashant, Jamal had spotted him from afar. A warm smile crossed Jamal's face, and he called out, "Bhai jaan!"

Startled by the familiar voice, Prashant halted in his tracks, his curiosity piqued. Turning around, he faced Jamal, who returned his gaze with a friendly wave. With a nod, Prashant acknowledged Jamal's greeting and waited patiently as Jamal deftly packed ripe bananas into a plastic bag. However, as Prashant inspected his purchase, he couldn't help but voice his concern. "What are you handing me, my friend? I did ask for ten bananas, but these seem a bit overripe. Could you provide fresher ones?"

Jamal maintained his pleasant demeanor, offering an explanation. "Brother, even the most beautiful bananas suffer in this scorching sun. These poor fruits are no exception. That's why I sell four for ten rupees in the evening. Everything comes at a price, just like our politicians. Take them while you can."

Prashant found himself pleasantly surprised by Jamal's eloquence and responded with a smile. "You have a way with words. What's your name?"

Jamal replied, "I'm Jamal, Jamal Anshari."

Curiosity piqued; Prashant probed further. "You don't seem like you're from around here."

Jamal's expression shifted momentarily, a hint of nostalgia in his eyes. He sighed and said, "Times change, my friend. Our forefathers once owned ancestral mansions in Lucknow. But life takes unexpected turns, and here I am, a prince from a royal family selling bananas on the streets." His frustration was evident, but he quickly composed himself.

Prashant felt a pang of empathy for Jamal's predicament, for he, too, had started working at a young age and had witnessed life's hardships up close. Though he couldn't alter Jamal's circumstances, he could offer some kind words. He spoke earnestly, "No job is insignificant, my friend. Living with dignity is an accomplishment in itself. If you work hard, you'll find success. But, brother, I won't take these bananas."

Their shared understanding of life's struggles deepened the connection between Prashant and Jamal. Jamal, perhaps meeting a genuinely kind soul after a long time, exchanged the overripe bananas for fresher ones. "You're a good man. Here, take these fresh bananas," Jamal said, his appreciation evident.

A warm smile adorned Prashant's face as he accepted the kind gesture. Jamal, a man of humble means, exuded more warmth and compassion than many of the world's affluent. As he bid farewell, Prashant concluded, "Alright, we'll meet again tomorrow." Jamal met Prashant's gaze and nodded firmly. "You'll find me right here."

With their shared laughter lingering in the air, Jamal departed with his basket of bananas, and Prashant resumed his journey back to work, the bustling street a backdrop to the simple yet profound connection they had forged.

– 15 –

Srivastav lounged comfortably at home on a quiet afternoon when the shrill ring of his phone shattered the tranquility. His countenance transformed from one of calm to one of concern in an instant. The sudden plummeting of share prices had caught him completely off guard. He anxiously reiterated into his phone, "What? When did this happen? Please verify the information thoroughly."

Doubt and disbelief clouded Srivastav's voice as he continued his conversation, "How is this even possible, my friend? Double-check the facts. No... No, this can't be happening. Perhaps it's just that one particular share that has dipped. Or is there more to it? Very well, leave it to me. I'll head to the stock exchange and investigate personally."

Without a moment's hesitation, Srivastav terminated the call, leaving behind a sense of urgency in the air. He bolted towards the stock exchange, neglecting to inform anyone of his abrupt departure.

– 16 –

Durga sat at her sewing machine, diligently stitching clothes as the daylight streamed into the room. The soft hum of the machine filled the air, creating a soothing background melody. Her hands moved with practiced precision, guiding the fabric under the needle.

As Prashant entered the house, he carried a bunch of ripe bananas in his hand. He walked over to the kitchen where Durga was engrossed in her work. With a gentle smile, he presented the bananas to her.

Durga glanced at the bananas, her hands never faltering in their sewing. She inquired, her tone neutral, "For whom have you brought these bananas?"

Prashant met her gaze and replied, "Put them in Rahul's lunchbox for tomorrow."

Meanwhile, Rahul had observed Prashant's entrance and his interaction with Durga from a distance. He approached his mother, who continued to sew without acknowledging him. Attempting to initiate a conversation, he inquired, "What are you making?" She, however, remained unresponsive, her focus undisturbed by his presence.

Rahul, determined to engage her, shifted his attention to the bunch of bananas and asked, "Who brought these overripe bananas?". Durga's gaze turned steely as she finally responded, her voice laced with frustration, "They are for you. Your father has brought them for your lunchbox."

Rahul examined the bananas with disdain and voiced his irritation, "Rotten bananas? Even a stray cow would reject them after a sniff. Please, don't put this refuse in my lunchbox."

Durga had reached her limit with his attitude. She looked at him for a moment before firmly stating, "If they appear as refuse to you, then dispose of them yourself. And when you step outside, take a moment to consider the countless people on the streets who don't even have the privilege of such 'refuse.'"

Rolling his eyes, Rahul retorted, "If you're in the mood for lectures, you should become a teacher. Oh, by the way, there's a school friend named Krish. He's invited me to his house, and I plan to stay over on Saturday."

Durga continued her work without acknowledging his announcement. Frustrated by her lack of response, Rahul pressed, "Alright, I've informed you," before turning to leave. At this time Durga, however, replied coolly, "Whatever you need to discuss, speak to your father."

Rahul challenged her, saying, "You can go and inform him."

She firmly declined, stating, "I won't say anything."

Rahul, seemingly perplexed by her response, remarked, "Alright, no need to be formal."

He then left the kitchen, heading to Prashant, who had changed into comfortable pajamas after returning from work.

Prashant noticed his son's approach but chose to ignore him. Rahul stood in silence for a moment, waiting for a response.

Eventually, he spoke up, "My college friend Krish has invited me over on Saturday. I plan to stay at his place for the night."

Prashant, seemingly indifferent, continued his silence. After a brief pause, he relented, "Why are you asking? Go wherever you want to."

Rahul knew that the phrase "go wherever you want to" carried an underlying restriction. He wanted to protest and complain about his limited freedom but decided against it, for he truly desired to attend the Saturday party.

Prashant observed his son's internal struggle and broke the silence with a question, "He was your cricket team captain, right?"

Rahul nodded eagerly, confirming, "Yes."

Rahul stood there, still hesitant, and Prashant maintained his measured composure. After a few moments, Prashant finally relented, "Alright, you can go."

Rahul stood his ground, still not entirely satisfied with the conversation. Prashant cast another glance in his direction, silently urging him to speak his mind.

After a brief pause, Rahul gathered his courage and expressed, "I also need a smart phone."

Prashant responded promptly, his tone firm, "There are already two phones at home—one is mine, and the other belongs to your mother."

Aware that his father's response was less than encouraging, Rahul opted for a little white lie, "But I don't have one. It's causing a lot of trouble, Dad. Our team has a Whats app group, and I can't stay updated. Coach Sir mentioned it too. I'm constantly having to borrow someone else's phone."

Prashant, understanding the importance of communication for his son's cricket aspirations, nodded thoughtfully and conceded, "Alright, I'll look into it." Rahul's eyes sparkled with hope, and he reiterated, "I really need it urgently, especially before Saturday. Please try to arrange it as soon as possible."

With that, Rahul left the room without waiting for any further assurances, leaving Prashant to contemplate his request.

– 17 –

The news of the stock exchange's dramatic fall had hit Srivastav like a sledgehammer. He lay on the bed, staring vacantly at the ceiling, lost in the abyss of his thoughts. The absence of Srivastav from the dinner table was a rarity that didn't go unnoticed by his wife, Pushpa. Concern etched on her face, she decided to approach him.

Silently, Pushpa took a seat beside her husband, her expression reflecting her worry. She gently inquired, "What's wrong? Why didn't you have your dinner?" Srivastav, still in a daze, replied without making eye contact, "I'm just not hungry today." Pushpa paused, her hand landing softly on his shoulder. She persisted, her voice filled with care, "Why are you keeping things from me? Tell me, what's bothering you?"

Srivastav, upset and tensed, was hesitant to share his troubles, especially when it concerned his family. He offered a vague response, "It's nothing, just the usual ups and downs of the market. That's all."

Pushpa's concern deepened, and she asked, "How much have we lost?"

Srivastav sighed heavily, gathering his thoughts before confessing, "Around 15 lakhs... But don't worry, I'm exploring some options. You know me; I always find a way. The only issue is Jay's admission to that new coaching institute. I thought I could manage it by selling some shares."

Pushpa pondered the loss and then inquired about Jay's admission expenses, "How much does he need for the admission?"

Srivastav replied, his tone resolute, "Eight lakhs."

Pushpa, sympathizing with her husband's unwavering dedication for their son's future couldn't help herself and asked, "How do you plan to arrange such a substantial amount on this short notice?"

Srivastav weighed the risks and possibilities in his mind, a glint of determination in his eyes. He answered, "You know I don't shy away from risks, especially after all these years in the stock market. I'll need to liquidate our joint fixed deposit; it should be around 6.5 lakhs. The rest, whatever remains in your account, will cover the rest."

Though Pushpa had full faith in her husband's abilities and decisions, a trace of worry lingered in her voice. She expressed her concern, "But we only have one fixed deposit left. What if an unforeseen issue arises in the meantime?"

Srivastav, lying on his back with eyes closed, waved away her worries, assuring her, "Don't fret. Leave it to me; I'll find a way."

Seeing the unwavering determination in his eyes, Pushpa relented, resigned to the fact that when it came to their son's future, nothing could deter Srivastav's resolve. She stood up, determined to take care of her husband, and said, "Alright, if necessary, do it. But at least have something to eat."

Srivastav, still lost in his thoughts, barely acknowledged her as he murmured, "Let it be, I don't have an appetite."Pushpa knew her husband too well to accept that as his final answer. She left the room, determined to bring him a meal nonetheless.

– 18 –

Hasmukh Parekh sat at the dinner table with his family, enjoying their meal together. However, there was an air of tension, particularly from his son, Shaket, who remained unusually quiet throughout the meal. As Hasmukh took a bite of his food, he decided to address the issue.

"We have received fresh orders from Khanna, and Mehta," Hasmukh told Shaket between bites. "They need some new designs for diaries, calendars, and a few organizers. Please take a look; they are our old clients." Shaket, still deep in thought, didn't respond immediately. Hasmukh waited for a moment and then asked again, "What happened? Don't you like the food?"

After a brief pause, Shaket replied, "The food is good, Dad."

"Then what happened? Why are you so quiet?" Hasmukh inquired, concern etched on his face.

Shaket stopped eating and turned to face his father. He took a deep breath and finally broached the topic he'd been contemplating. "Dad, we need to talk."

Hasmukh nodded, indicating that he was ready to listen. "That's what we are doing. Tell me."

Taking another deep breath, Shaket continued, "Dad, I believe the future of the diary and calendar business doesn't seem very promising. Everything is becoming digitalized, and these traditional items may not have a strong market in the future. I have a plan. As you know, I'm planning to start an import-export business. The licensing process is almost complete, and I've made significant progress in discussions with foreign buyers. Now is the right time to move forward. I need an office for this new venture. Please, don't get caught up in the details of the diary and calendar business, and don't invest more of your time and resources in it. I will talk to Mr. Khanna and Mr. Mehta and explain our situation, or I'll consider outsourcing from elsewhere if necessary. Please don't worry."

Listening to his son's proposal, Hasmukh Parekh considered the weight of his decision. After a moment of contemplation, he responded, "Okay, you can take the office. However, remember, no business is small or big."

Shaket hesitated for a moment because asking his father to step away from a business he had built was a significant step. Nevertheless, he gathered his courage and continued, "Okay, Dad, can I open my company in the same office? Why waste money on rent? Moreover, I've seen your balance sheet, and your business is running at a loss. You should consider closing it down and let me take charge. I want to renovate that space for my new venture."

Hasmukh didn't take kindly to his son's suggestion, but he remained composed. He tried to make Shaket understand the importance of their family business with a sense of timidity. "Let me say one thing, Son, the respect and reputation of our family in this city today is because of this diary and calendar business. It's my identity. Profit and loss are part of business. You only looked at today's loss in the balance sheet. You didn't see yesterday's profit. The profit that has allowed us to reach this position today, your lifestyle, the expenses for your car's fuel, your

MBA degree from the US; it has all come from this business, my friend. Show some respect!"

Shaket quickly retorted, waving his hand dismissively. "That is the problem. When did I ever say that I don't respect your business? However, one has to adapt with time, or else they perish. It is the simple rule of nature. All I am trying to say is that we need to update ourselves. We need a new business idea. We cannot ignore the future in this way. I want to..."

Hasmukh looked at his son for a moment and then asked with a hint of frustration, "Do you want me to retire? You want me to sit back at home and watch Saas-Bahu serials?"

Shaket was not willing to let go of this moment easily, so he replied firmly, "Dad, you have done as much as you needed to do. Now, it's my turn."

Hasmukh Parekh stared at his son blankly, his emotions conflicting within him. He was about to say something, but his wife, sensing the escalating tension, intervened.

"Why are you two talking while eating? What's the enmity with food?" she asked, trying to diffuse the situation.

Hasmukh decided not to continue the discussion at that moment. He wasn't entirely happy with Shaket's decision, but he chose to let his son decide what was best for him. He washed his hands and then said, "I may belong to the older generation, but I understand the ways of the new era. I can comprehend what you're saying. You want to prove yourself, and that's a good thing. You should get your chance. Starting tomorrow, this company is yours along the office. Do whatever you want. All the best."

Hasmukh left the dining table, leaving a sense of uncertainty in the room. His wife glanced at him as he departed, while Shaket sat there, deep in thought.

– 19 –

The next morning, Prashant arrived at the Parekh Diary and Calendars like every other day. He placed his belongings on the desk when Ghosh Babu approached him with something to share.

"Do you know something?" Ghosh Babu asked, piquing Prashant's curiosity. Prashant looked puzzled and replied, "About what?"

Ghosh Babu leaned in and continued, "Deben told me that some people came here yesterday evening. They took measurements of the entire office."

Prashant, still puzzled, asked, "So?"

Ghosh Babu, in a weary voice, responded, "Chhote Babu doesn't seem to be in a good mood. I think this office is going to close down."

Prashant shrugged off the notion, not believing it could be true. "What? Nah, this must be some kind of joke."

Ghosh Babu nodded and remarked, "Seems like it's just a joke for us."

Prashant waved away the thoughts and said, "It can't be like that. You should check the design from Agrawal & Sons." He looked out of the window, contemplating his next moves.

During lunchtime, Prashant approached Jamal once again. Jamal greeted him with a smile and said, "Come, brother. Here are your four bananas." Prashant reached into his purse for a ten-rupee note while Jamal continued, "For the past few days, you've been buying bananas every day. Is someone sick at home?"

Prashant nonchalantly waved his hand and replied, "Oh, no, not at all. Why would anyone be sick? My son plays cricket. He's very talented. I buy them for him. Bananas are essential for athletes, you know." Jamal smiled and responded, "That's great. Next time when I go to the shrine, I'll definitely pray for your son. What's his name?"

Prashant felt blessed to have Jamal's friendship. He smiled and replied, "Rahul. Please do pray! Who's in your family?" Jamal took a deep breath before discussing his family. He then continued, "Just me and my 2 year-old son... My wife used to be here. But she's not anymore... She passed away."

Jamal's voice carried a sense of numbness, indicating that he was still grieving. So, Prashant shifted the conversation towards Jamal's son and asked, "What's your son's name?"

Jamal smiled and replied, "Shahrukh, Shahrukh Ansari."

Prashant wondered about Jamal's child and asked, "Wow! That's a great name. But who takes care of such a small child? You stay here from morning till evening!"

Jamal acknowledged the unspoken amicable bond between them and said, "I have a distant relative... like my brother and sister-in-law... I leave him with them when I come to work. Then, I bring him home in the evening. It's been going on like this for the past 7-8 months... but who knows what will happen in the future... They also have transferable jobs. Leave all that... do come visit our house one day when you have some free time... I don't say this to anyone... but you are a different kind of person... That's why I'm telling you."

Prashant nodded in agreement and said, "Certainly, I'll come to see Shahrukh but now I have to return to the office. I have some wok left."

They both smiled and bid each other farewell.

After buying bananas, Prashant made his way to a mobile phone store. He observed the lavish Smartphone's on display and wished he could afford one for his son. However, his budget didn't permit such extravagance. He turned to the shopkeeper and inquired, "How much does a Smartphone cost?"

The shopkeeper, sensing Prashant's budget constraints, went straight to the point. "What's your budget? A branded one will cost at least 6000."

Prashant didn't intend to spend 6000 rupees at the moment. He took out his phone and asked, "How much for a phone like this?" The shopkeeper glanced at Prashant's old model phone and promptly replied, "Uncle, we don't have this model anymore. Should I show you a Chinese one without a warranty?"

Prashant nodded and said, "Sure, go ahead."

The shopkeeper presented a box and explained, "This one is 1500 rupees. It's dual SIM, has 4GB RAM, cameras on both sides, and you can also expand the memory with an SD card."

Prashant remained unsatisfied with the price and asked, "Isn't there anything cheaper?"

The shopkeeper was determined not to let a potential customer walk away without a purchase, so he offered, "Alright, I'll give you a good deal, uncle. You can have it for 1200."

Prashant hesitated but played his last card, suggesting, "Eight hundred?"

The shopkeeper was taken aback by the low offer but quickly regained his composure. He agreed, "Alright, alright. I'll do it for 1000. Last offer."

With the deal sealed, the shopkeeper prepared the bill, and Prashant left the store with a sense of accomplishment. He felt a deep sense of satisfaction, believing that Rahul would appreciate his gesture. That evening, he secretly placed the mobile phone on Rahul's bed while he was asleep and went to rest.

– 20 –

It was Saturday morning. Rahul was still in bed, trying to get some extra sleep when Durga entered his room in order to wake him up for cricket practice. She called out, "Rahul...Rahul. Don't you have practice today?"

Rahul, groggy and still half-asleep, replied, "I won't go today. I have plans in the afternoon. I told you. Please go now, and let me sleep."

Although Durga remembered his request for permission, she was excited to see his reaction to the surprise gift. She continued, "Alright, if you don't want to go. Look what Dad brought."

Rahul turned to face her, curious, and asked, "What is it?"

A smile lit up Durga's face as she handed him the mobile phone box and said, "Take a look."

Rahul took the box, expecting to find a fancy Smartphone inside. However, to his dismay, he discovered a simple, non-branded Chinese phone. He felt a surge of anger and frustration, expressing his disappointment, "What is this?"

Durga's excitement quickly turned into frustration as she responded, "It's a new mobile phone. You were making such a fuss about getting one."

Rahul's frustration grew, and he replied irritably, "I asked for a normal Smartphone, not this cheap, non-branded Chinese phone. Seriously. I'd rather not have anything."Durga, feeling exasperated, retorted, "From where will we get 7 or 8 thousand rupees? We've already spent so much on your school admission. Plus, we have to pay the monthly fees."

Rahul, still frustrated, retorted, "You got me admitted to a lavish school, and now you're counting every penny? Just leave, Mom, please. Don't annoy me. Let me sleep."

Durga realized that talking to Raul at that moment would be futile, so she turned and left the room. Rahul, still irritated, added, "And take this box away with you. I don't want it," and with a careless gesture, he knocked the box off the bed, causing the mobile phone to fall to the floor.

In the evening, Rahul got dressed and headed to Krish's house. He wanted to get away from his home environment for a while. Upon arriving at Krish's house, he rang the bell, and a servant answered the door.

"Is Krish here?" Rahul inquired.

The servant recognized him and nodded, "You must be Rahul Baba, right? Please, go straight upstairs. He's waiting for you."

Rahul entered the grand house and was awe-struck by its opulence. He made his way to Krish's room, where Krish was applying perfume. Rahul stood at the door and commented, "Nice smell."

Krish turned around to face him, smiled, and said, "Well, you can use some too."

As Rahul entered the room, and Krish sprayed some perfume on him, both of them sharing a laugh. Krish placed the perfume on the table and announced, "Come on, I am ready."

Both of them headed downstairs to leave, but they were interrupted by Krish's father, Raj Bansal.

When Krish noticed his father, he introduced Rahul, "Hey, Dad. Meet my friend Rahul."

Raj Bansal greeted Rahul with a warm smile, "So, you're Rahul! I've heard a lot of good things about you. Krish talks about you quite a lot. You're very talented."

Rahul blushed and replied, "Uncle, you should let that pass. He often exaggerates."

Krish, checking his watch, interjected, "Dad, we're running late. See you tomorrow. Bye!"

Raj nodded in agreement and bid them farewell, "Okay, bye. Say hello to Riya's dad for me."

Rahul added, "Bye, uncle," as they made their way out of the house and into Krish's car. Krish drove them to their destination.

However, Rahul was unaware of their real destination. Krish had told his family they were going to Riya's house, but in truth, he didn't want anyone to know where they were going. He had even arranged for Riya's car to be brought to his house to maintain the illusion.

Krish explained to Rahul, "No, buddy. I don't want anyone to know where we're going. So, I told them we were heading to Riya's house. So, no one gets suspicious. That's why I had Riya's car brought here."

Rahul smiled and appreciated the strategy, "Smart move."

Eventually, their car stopped in front of a paanwala. The paanwala approached them and handed Krish a small pouch. Krish paid for it, and then he instructed the driver, "Drive." Rahul was puzzled by this unexpected stop. He asked Krish, "What is this?"

Krish smirked cunningly and replied, "Jaadu ki pudiya."

– 21 –

Rahul found himself at the Magnolia Outhouse for the first time, feeling like he had stepped into a dream. The space was lavish, the music was loud, and there was an air of excitement and peace in the atmosphere. Riya greeted them with a warm smile and hugged them. As the night progressed, they decided to play a game of truth or dare.

Riya spun the bottle, and it landed on Rahul, which caused everyone, especially Krish, to become excited. They cheered in joy, and Riya asked, "Truth or dare?"

Blushing slightly, Rahul impulsively chose "dare." However, before Riya could assign him a dare, Krish intervened, volunteering to give Rahul a dare.

Krish retrieved a packet he had purchased from a local vendor, containing a substance. He opened the packet and placed it on the table, locking eyes with Rahul. He then rolled a 100 rupee note, offering it to Rahul to sniff the powder. Confused, Rahul stared at Krish and asked, "What is this?"

Krish playfully responded, "Jadu ki pudiya," causing laughter to erupt from the group. They all began chanting, "Dare, dare, dare..."

Despite his confusion, Rahul took the note from Krish and sniffed the powder, which caused him to start coughing uncontrollably. Simultaneously, someone offered him a joint, which he also smoked.

Soon, Rahul began to lose his sobriety, and the world around him became a hazy blur. He observed people dancing, some taking pills, and others sniffing substances.

Riya approached him and asked, "Hey Mr. Cool! How are you feeling?"

Rahul, struggling to maintain his composure, mumbled, "It's okay. I mean, good."

Seeing through his lie, Riya smiled and said, "Really? Liar, come with me."

She led Rahul to the roof, where she hugged him. Rahul could barely register his surroundings, but her touch made him feel both comfortable and nervous at the same time.

Riya asked, "Feeling better?"

Rahul nodded and inquired, "Where is the washroom?"

Riya pointed to the left corner, and Rahul managed to make his way to the washroom. As he looked at himself in the mirror, he felt a disconnect with the person he saw. However, he was too intoxicated to dwell on those thoughts, so he shrugged them off and returned to Riya.

Riya observed him and remarked, "I know you're not a fan of parties. That's why I brought you to this place with a lively atmosphere. It's nice, isn't it?"

Rahul could only manage a faint, "Hmm..."

Moving a little closer to him, Riya innocently admitted, "I want to say something today."

Rahul nodded, and asked, "What?"

Looking into his eyes, Riya revealed her feelings, "From our very first meeting up until now, I've always felt a strong connection between us. The feelings I get when I see you cannot be compared with anything else. I've never connected with anyone as deeply in my life. What I want to know is, do you feel the same way about me?"

Rahul attempted to look for an answer, his senses muddled by the intoxication. He hesitated and eventually stammered, "Riya... you're Krish's girlfriend, and Krish is my friend. So..."

Riya clarified, dispelling any misconceptions, "Hey, what did you say? I'm Krish's girlfriend? Let me correct you; Krish and I are just good friends. Nothing more, nothing less. And this wasn't the answer to my question. I want to know your feelings about me, regardless of whether I'm anyone's girlfriend or not."

Deep down, Rahul grappled with his emotions, feelings conflicted about betraying his friend. He tried to explain, "Riya... please try to understand... You and I..."However, Riya was not ready to listen. She pulled him closer and stated, "I've got my answer, Rahul."

Unbeknownst to them, Krish watched their intimate moment unfold.

– 22 –

After a night of revelry, Rahul found himself missing his practice the following morning, sparking concerns amongst both his coach and fellow players. Amresh, their coach, stepped onto the field and quickly noted Rahul's absence. He queried his students, "Where's Rahul?"

Harsh promptly responded, "Sir, he's absent."

Growing increasingly concerned, Amresh probed further, "Again? Harsh, do you have any insight into Rahul's whereabouts? He had been missing practice for two days last week."

Harsh shook his head and replied, "No sir, I have no idea."

Amresh lets out a weary sigh and conceded, "Alright then, boys, let's continue."

With his concerns about Rahul mounting, Amresh decided to reach out to Prashant in search of answers. Prashant was en route to the office when his phone rang, displaying Amresh's name. He promptly picked up on the second ring. As the teacher introduced himself as Rahul's cricket coach and expressed his growing worries regarding Rahul's erratic attendance at practice. He sought Prashant's perspective on Rahul's overall well-being.

Prashant assured Amresh that he would have a conversation with Rahul and address the issue at hand. Amresh, emphasizing the critical role practice played in Rahul's cricket career and academic progress, reminded Prashant of the primary reason Rahul attended the school – his cricket talents.

As Prashant ended the call, a cloud of unease hung over him. He had been oblivious to his son's frequent absence from the practice and couldn't help but feel anxious as he made his way to the office.

On his way, Jamal noticed Prashant's visibly distressed countenance. Out of concern he inquired about Prashant's well-being, wondering if something was amiss. Preferring not to burden Jamal with his worries early in the morning, Prashant offered a reassuring but strained smile, replying, "No, nothing's wrong. Everything is good." He then proceeded to the office.

Upon his arrival at the office, Prashant was greeted by a bewildering sight – the entire office staff had gathered outside, and the office door was securely shut. A feeling of unease settled in the pit of his stomach. He approached Ghosh Babu, in search of answers. With a heavy heart, the latter somberly informed Prashant, "My fears have come true. I had a sinking feeling that something was awry."

Prashant was momentarily dumbfounded, he stammered, "Are you suggesting... our office?"

Ghosh Babu confirmed the grim news, "It's shutting down."

As they conversed, a servant approached them, relaying a message that the management had summoned all the employees for a meeting. They joined their fellow colleagues who had congregated outside. Hasmukh Parekh stood before them, anguish etched across his face, alongside Shaket.

Shaket addressed the staff, acknowledging their years of dedicated service to the company. He proceeded to explain that the company had been running at a loss for three consecutive years, making it impossible to sustain the operations. He reluctantly revealed that they had no choice but to cease business operations and, as a gesture of goodwill, offered to provide one month's salary in advance.

The staff listened in stunned silence, their expressions reflecting their deep disappointment. Ghosh Babu couldn't contain his emotions and implored Shaket, "ChoteBabu, where will we go at this stage in life? How can you shut the office like this?"

Unyielding in his decision, Shaket avoided making eye contact and departed, leaving their pleas unanswered. He promptly called the company's lawyer to oversee the necessary procedures.

As the staff began to disperse, Prashant felt an overwhelming sense of despair and apprehension. Thoughts of financial responsibilities and an uncertain future weighed heavily on his mind. He found a chair, sat down, and buried his face in his hands.

Seeking solace, Prashant turned to Jamal, whose concern had been evident since the morning. Jamal had sensed that something was gravely wrong and finally asked what had transpired. Prashant, defeated and disheartened, confided in Jamal, recounting the shutdown of the office followed by the uncertainty regarding his future.

Jamal tried his best to console his friend, but the weight of the situation was undeniable. Nevertheless, he made an attempt, saying, "Hold on to your courage, brother. Something will surely work out, Inshallah. For now, take these bananas and head home to clear your mind." Prashant nodded, reaching for his wallet to pay Jamal for the bananas. However, Jamal halted him and said, "You can settle this later; right now, go home."

As Prashant prepared to leave, a customer arrived at Jamal's stall, requesting a dozen bananas. Jamal asked for a moment's pause before turning back to Prashant, reassuring him once more, "Brother, don't dwell on this too much. Something positive will come your way. We'll meet tomorrow."

Seeing Jamal's hopeful smile and feeling his attempt to instill optimism filled Prashant with a sense of comfort. He returned the smile before heading home.

Meanwhile, Jamal turned his attention back to the waiting customer. The customer had been standing under the scorching sun, waiting for his bananas, but Jamal had been preoccupied with Prashant. The customer, growing impatient, made his request once more, "Brother, please give me a dozen bananas!"

Jamal felt awful about what happened to Prashant and on top of that, the customer kept asking for bananas. He irritably replied, "No, it's finished. Take it from someone else." The customer looked at him with frustration and asked, "What do you mean by 'it's finished'? It's right here."

Jamal stood in a serious position and irritably said, "I am not selling them, the shop is closed. I told you, take it from someone else."

The customer started moving ahead, cursing, "Insane human..."

Jamal said, "Okay." Then he remembered something. He figured out a way to help Prashant. So, he immediately turned and saw him walking slowly in defeat. He called out to him again from behind and yelled, "Brother... brother?"

Prashant heard his name being called and retraced his steps back to Jamal. He walked toward him and asked, "What happened?"

"Do you have a typewriter?" Jamal asked, his enthusiasm showing.

Prashant nodded in agreement and said, "Yes, I have an obsolete typewriter. Why?"

"That's it. Come meet me tomorrow morning, okay?"

Prashant's face displayed confusion. "What? But why?"

"Just come!"

Prashant nodded in agreement and said, "Alright... see you tomorrow."

Jamal kept his smiling face and said, "Bye." He then went toward his dala and packed up. Both headed toward their respective homes.

– 23 –

As Prashant made his way home, his mind raced with thoughts about how to break the news to his family. He walked alone, his head filled with anxiety and uncertainty. By the time he reached his front door, he had concocted a white lie to ease the situation.

As Durga opened the door and laid eyes on Prashant, concern immediately crossed her face. She inquired, "You're back so early? Is everything alright with your health?". Her husband stepped inside, as she closed the door behind them, turning to face him expectantly, awaiting his response.

Taking a moment to gather his thoughts, Prashant finally spoke, "The boss's son has returned from America, so we were given the day off." Durga let out a sigh of relief. She smiled warmly and remarked, "Well then, you've finally got a day off." Returning her smile, Prashant glanced towards the storage room, his mind still burdened by the events of the day.

– 24 –

Prashant perched on a stool in front of his modest storage room, rummaging for his old typewriter. After a minute of searching, his hands finally met the familiar keys. He gingerly carried the typewriter to his bed, where he took a seat. It had been ages since he last laid eyes on this relic, and the sight of it stirred memories of his early days. A faint smile crept onto his face as he began to type, relieved to find that it still worked flawlessly.

The rest of the day passed in solitude as Prashant sought to avoid Durga, fearing that she might see the concern in his eyes. Prashant had little appetite during dinner and found sleep elusive that night. His thoughts were consumed by the uncertainty of the morning ahead. He had no clear idea of how Jamal would assist him, but he clung to hope.

The following morning, he woke early and left the house with the lunch Durga had prepared. Clutching the typewriter on his lap, he boarded a bus headed for his former workplace. For a fleeting moment, he forgot the purpose of his visit, but upon seeing his former colleagues, the grim reality returned, etching a somber expression on his face. He entered the office to collect his final salary, sparing one last glance at the place he had spent the past twenty four years. Memories flooded his mind, and though a tear welled up, he held back his emotions.

Prashant exited the office without looking back and made his way to meet Jamal. Scanning the area, he spotted the vendor approaching from behind; Jamal had taken the day off. He led Prashant to the collectorate, where he introduced the former to Wasim. Wasim greeted Prashant with a warm smile and informed him that he would be paid for typing legal documents for customers.

Prashant nodded appreciatively and thanked Jamal, who then went off on his way. Placing the typewriter on a small desk, Prashant got to work. Instead of a conventional salary, he now earned money directly from his customers. During lunchtime, he found solace beneath a tree near his workstation and quickly devoured his meal. Typing legal documents all morning had left him drained.

Prashant toiled tirelessly for the sake of his family, while Rahul, despite his own hardships, embarked on a different path. Following that fateful night out, Rahul began frequenting parties with Riya and Krish, neglecting his classes. He even stashed his cricket gear in Riya's car and changed into casual attire there.

While Rahul's teammates diligently practiced on the cricket ground, he reveled in the teenage nightlife. Amresh repeatedly inquired about Rahul's absence but never received any satisfactory explanation. Worried about his star player, Amresh remained oblivious to Rahul's newfound activities.

Krish's father, too, was living a life of deceit, unaware of his son's escapades. However, the day came when he discovered the truth about Krish's wild parties and wayward life. Once he witnessed Rahul and Krish entering a bar from his car and, though shocked, chose not to react. He simply instructed the driver to head home, disappointment weighing heavily on his heart.

The stock market losses continued to plague Srivastav, who now began training a group of new boys at Bharosha Capital Insurance.

Meanwhile, Hasmukh was in his car, passing by the Parekh Diary and Calendar Office. He couldn't help but reminisce about the past, prompting him to instruct the driver to stop momentarily. As he gazed fondly at the office, his office board lay on the roadside due to renovation, and an inauguration card rested on the car seat. Hasmukh glanced at the card, then told the driver, "Drive on."

On the other hand, Jamal began to envision Razia instead of Salma as he fed Shahrukh at home. Everyone's lives had suddenly taken unexpected turns.

Srivastav meticulously filled out the last entry in his checkbook, which now read: "Balance: Rs. 8,000 only." A heavy sigh escaped his lips as he placed it back in the drawer.

Prashant wrapped up his final typing session and headed home.

The next day, Prashant met Jamal in front of the Parekh Diary and Calendars. Jamal offered a warm smile and remarked, "Brother, you've been attracting excellent customers from day one."

Grateful for Jamal's support during his trying times, Prashant nodded and replied with a smile, "Thank you, Jamal." Jamal quickly interjected, "If you truly want to express your gratitude, come to my humble home someday. I'd be delighted."

Prashant smiled back without uttering a word. After a brief pause, Jamal continued, "Come on, today is Shahrukh's birthday." Prashant's face lit up in surprise. "Is it?". Jamal nodded and shared, "My son is turning 2 years old today."

Without another thought, Prashant headed to a nearby small cake shop and purchased a cake along with some chocolates. As he reached for his wallet to pay, Jamal intervened, "Let me take care of it." Prashant halted him with a warm response, "You've called me your brother, right? So, he is my nephew."

With gratitude, Jamal accepted Prashant's gesture. Together, they proceeded to Jamal's home. Jamal made a brief stop at Raqib's place, returning a few minutes later with Shahrukh in his arms. The kid's joyful giggles filled the air as he gazed at Prashant, who couldn't help but smile back, feeling an instant connection with the child.

Once inside Jamal's modest abode, Jamal looked at Prashant and announced, "Brother, this is our little palace, and that chair over there is our throne. Feel free to sit wherever you like."

Prashant glanced around and settled onto the bed. Jamal turned his attention to Shahrukh, who was eagerly awaiting his birthday cake. Jamal lowered Shahrukh to the floor and presented the cake, asking, "Today, uncle brought a cake for the little prince. Who's going to enjoy it?"

Shahrukh's excitement was palpable as he eagerly reached for the cake. Prashant watched the young boy with affection, gently patting his cheek. Jamal offered a slice of cake to Prashant, who gratefully accepted it. Throughout their meal, Prashant grappled with a pressing question. He finally mustered the courage to ask Jamal, "Can I ask you something?"

Jamal nodded, encouraging Prashant to proceed. After a brief pause, Prashant inquired, "His mother..."

Recognizing that he could confide in Prashant, Jamal chose not to lie this time. He looked into Prashant's eyes and revealed,

"That day, I told you a little lie. His mother didn't leave us. She ran away with someone else."

Prashant sat in stunned silence, struggling to find words. Both men remained silent for a moment before Prashant finally responded, "I don't know what to say. When I see you and Shahrukh, it's clear that there's a strong bond between father and son."

Jamal nodded, his smile tinged with melancholy, and he shared, "What's done is done. We can't fight destiny, my friend. We've grown accustomed to it." Prashant pressed further, "Why haven't you remarried?"

Jamal pondered for a moment before answering, "Brother, didn't I tell you, we can't fight destiny. If it's meant to be, it will happen someday. Back in Lucknow, my father owned a large furniture store. One night, it all went up in flames. My father survived the shock, but my mother could not. I ended up on the streets, begging for alms. Look at destiny's game: I came to Kolkata, found work in a bakery, fell in love with Salmaa and we got married."

Prashant listened, processing Jamal's story with empathy.

Jamal continued, "Just a year after Shahrukh was born, Salmaa left us. I don't know why. Perhaps, she wanted something which is beyond our reach."

Prashant fell into a contemplative silence, deeply affected by Jamal's words.

Jamal eventually broke the silence, saying, "Now, whatever I have is right in front of you. I had no reason to live except for him. What else can I do? I'm his father. But let's put all this aside. Make sure to arrive at Wasim Bhai's place on time tomorrow. You remember, right?"

Prashant nodded, still processing the revelation. They finished their cake in silence, and after a few minutes, a knock sounded at Jamal's door. It was Razia.

"Oh, it's you," Jamal said. "Come in, come in. Meet Prashant; he's like a brother to me. And brother, this is Razia Ji, our landlady."

Prashant nodded, acknowledging her.

Jamal went on to share, "You see, I've fallen behind on rent for the past three months, but she hasn't said anything. That's why..."

Razia cast Jamal a serious look and clarified, "I didn't come here for rent today. It's the child's birthday, so I made some kheer. Please give it to Shahrukh."

She handed a bowl of kheer to Jamal, blessed Shahrukh with a prayer, and then departed.

– 25 –

The meeting room was adorned with sleek, modern furnishings, where Shaket and Rohan sat in earnest conversation. The door creaked open, heralding the entrance of a distinguished figure, Khanna, a man in his late sixties, radiating an air of wisdom and experience. Instantly, Shaket rose from his chair, a mark of respect for the venerable elder.

Khanna, with an air of unassuming authority, gestured for Shaket to retake his seat before settling comfortably into his own. He smiled warmly, his eyes crinkling at the corners, and asked, "How are you, beta?"

Shaket reciprocated the smile, showing genuine affection for the older man. "Good, uncle. What about you?"

Khanna's nod conveyed contentment as he replied, "I'm well, beta."

Shaket leaned slightly forward, his enthusiasm palpable. "Uncle, you must have heard about my new start-up. I'm sure Papa must have mentioned it to you."

Khanna acknowledged this with a knowing smile. "Yes, Parekh bhai did mention it. Good, beta, very good. What kind of business have you ventured into?"

Shaket, shifting in his seat as if to better prepare for the conversation, answered, "Import-Export, uncle, with a specific focus on the textile industry. We're starting with the Indo-US route. Given your extensive connections and impressive list of US buyers, I wanted to discuss potential collaborations."

Khanna's head bobbed in understanding, and he inquired further, "And where have you established your office?"

Shaket paused for a moment before delivering unexpected news. "Actually, Khanna uncle, we've decided to discontinue Dad's diary and calendar business. So, our new office will be set up there."

The shock on Khanna's face was unmistakable; he had been oblivious to this significant development. His eyes fixed on Shaket with disbelief. "Parekh Bhai's diary and calendar business is closing down? But why? He never mentioned anything about this on the phone. We were about to place a substantial order this month."

Shaket, feeling the weight of Khanna's scrutiny, leaned in to clarify. "Uncle, you know as well as I do that there's hardly any profit in printing and stationery. It's more like charity work. Dad, bless his heart, doesn't quite grasp the dynamics of the modern business world. I've returned after completing my MBA in the US, and I want to explore new horizons. What's wrong with wanting something different? I can assure you, uncle, our new venture promises substantial profits!"

Khanna regarded him sternly, and his voice carried a note of wisdom. "Son, one should never forget their roots."

Shaket, somewhat puzzled by Khanna's cryptic remark, inquired, "I'm sorry, uncle, but I don't quite understand."

Khanna sighed, as if lamenting a generation gap. "Son, this company you see today was on the brink of collapse twenty years ago. It was saved by a person whose guidance was invaluable, reviving it to become the city's premier engineering firm. Do you know who that person was?"

Shaket's curiosity piqued. "Who?"

Khanna fixed Shaket with an intense gaze. "Parekh ji."

Shaket blinked, a sense of realization slowly dawning upon him. Khanna continued, his voice heavy with meaning. "He never held an MBA, yet he possesses knowledge that could still enlighten even the most educated of MBAs. Prominent Kolkata businessmen still seek his counsel. And you call him old-fashioned! Anyway, best of luck to you. We are old-school people; we value the relationships with those who've stood by us."

With that, Khanna rose from his chair, signaling the end of their discussion. However, he couldn't resist offering Shaket a piece of advice. He turned to face the younger man and said, "One thing to remember, son: To know the road ahead, ask those who had been there since the bygone times."

Khanna wasted no time and left the room, leaving Shaket and Rohan in a state of subdued embarrassment and reflection.

– 26 –

Srivastav sat at a polished wooden table in his dimly lit office, engrossed in calculating his expenses. The room bore the signs of a life deeply affected by financial turmoil, with stacks of paperwork scattered haphazardly.

Amid his calculations, his phone buzzed with an incoming call from Pushpa. He answered it swiftly, his eyes never leaving the sea of numbers on the table. Her first words were filled with concern, "Did you have your lunch?"

Srivastav's mind was preoccupied with the impending visit of Dutta Saab, and he replied, "I'll do it. Mr. Dutta is coming to the office. Remember Dutta Sahab? Back when I used to work at Bharosa Life Insurance, he was my boss. Now, he's the director of the company. We'll be having lunch together. It's been so long since I visited his office. Oh, by the way, I forgot to mention it in the morning rush, I've closed that fixed deposit. Jay's draft is in the drawer. Tell him to go and get his admission tomorrow. Alright?"

Pushpa's concern grew palpable as she pondered their precarious situation. Her worry deepened as she asked, "How can you handle everything? The business losses, Jay's expenses... I'm getting worried now." Despite his own concerns, Srivastav was resolute. He knew he had to bear these burdens for child's sake.

He replied firmly, "I'll have to handle it now. What other options do we have? Don't worry. Everything will be fine."

Just then, as if summoned by fate, Avinash Dutta entered the room, interrupting the call. Srivastav hung up the phone, a warm smile lighting up his face. "Oh, come in, Dutta Saab. It's been so long!"

Dutta reciprocated the smile, his presence filling the room with a sense of nostalgia. "How are you, my 'Life Boy'?"

The affectionate moniker stirred a hearty laugh from Srivastav, the memories of their shared past rushing back. "Life Boy... You haven't forgotten that yet?". The former boss waved his hand dismissively. "How could I forget? In this particular industry of ours, there has never been a salesman like you, and there never will be. That's why everyone in the entire life insurance industry knows you as the 'Life Boy.' Even now, when a new guy joins as a salesperson, we still refer to you. The way you bonded with customers is exemplary and needless to say your sales techniques were brilliant."

The flood of affection and camaraderie warmed Srivastav's heart. "When both hunger and necessity exceed their limits, 'technique' comes naturally. What do you guys call it in English? 'Necessity is the father of invention,' or something like that. Anyway, let's forget all this. Let's have some home-cooked food first."

Dutta settled into a chair, his gaze fixed on Srivastav, and then he revealed the true purpose of his visit. "You know, I didn't just come here for lunch, leaving my work behind. Monga informed me about your situation. And the inside scoop is that the market is going to decline even further. I thought I should warn you." Srivastav's keen business instincts detected the unspoken proposal in Dutta's words. He didn't beat around the bush and inquired directly, "And in these circumstances, what is your proposal for me?"

Dutta smiled, acknowledging Srivastav's shrewdness. "Your mind is still sharp when it comes to business. A nod is enough. So, I propose that you continue with your share trading, but as a part-timer, and at the same time rejoin my company. I want you to handle the entire Eastern region's sales. You'll have a workforce of around 30-40 employees under you. You won't have to be directly involved; you'll supervise them. But it's not the same as before. In the last few years, so many multinational insurance companies have flooded the market that sustaining oneself has become a challenge. I am also facing pressure from management. So, I need my old people back, especially my 'Life Boy.' The difference now is that you don't have to be just one 'Life Boy'; you have to create two or three more. Our company used to be number one in the Eastern Region back in the day; let's reclaim that title, and in return, you can decide your commission."

Srivastav, deeply touched by Dutta's proposition, took a moment to reflect. Then, he said with a sense of gratitude, "This is something I can learn from you. When you help someone in their troubled times, do it with so much respect and sincerity that the other person doesn't even realize it. Just because I left the insurance industry doesn't mean I'm not keeping tabs. There's competition in the market, but your company isn't in such a dire state that 'Bharose' would have an urgent need for me to join!"

Dutta, not wanting Srivastav to feel pressured, emphasized their bond of respect. He replied, "Since when did you learn to argue with your seniors? You've become a bigger share broker than an insurance agent, but in age and designation, you're still junior to me. Understand! So, just follow my order. Okay?"

Srivastav nodded in agreement and said, "Right, sir."

Dutta beamed at him, his eyes revealing the depth of their friendship. "Come to the office next week to complete the paperwork and collect your advance. You know, Srivastav, I understand that after running your own business for so long, it's not easy to work under someone again. But sometimes, to move one step forward, you have to take two steps back. That's also a principle of your own business. And tell me, how are Pushpa and Jai? The food is amazing as always, and now I know why your weight is increasing day by day! One day, I'll have to visit your place and eat to my heart's content."

– 27 –

Prashant sat under the unforgiving sun, fingers rhythmically tapping away at the keys of his typewriter, as if trying to harness the sweltering heat into words on paper. Beads of perspiration glistened on his forehead, testimony to the arduous task at hand. He typed with a determination that transcended the discomfort of the weather, each keystroke etching his dedication.

As the sun's relentless rays bore down, a familiar figure approached. Jamal, with his humble cart, observed Prashant's unwavering dedication. A pang of sorrow tugged at his heartstrings, for he knew that this was the same man who once occupied a cushy chair, tapping away on a computer. Yet, time had a peculiar way of altering one's circumstances, and now, Prashant toiled under the scorching sun.

Stepping closer, Jamal brushed aside his somber thoughts and addressed Prashant, "Brother, can you type an affidavit for me?". Prashant's eyes lifted from the typewriter; his fingers momentarily suspended above the keys. Amusement danced in his gaze as he saw the customer before him - none other than Jamal. A genuine smile bloomed on his face, and he exclaimed, "Jamal, how come you're here today?"

Jamal returned the warm smile, his eyes reflecting the deep bond between them. "You could say life felt incomplete without you. So, from today onwards, our shops will stand side by side."

Prashant's happiness swelled at the prospect of having a beloved companion by his side. "Wow, that's great."

With a nod of determination, Jamal continued, "I'll ask Wasim bhai to arrange something like a small shed. The sun is very harsh." Prashant acknowledged the twist of fate that had brought them together once more, his heart filled with gratitude, though he didn't utter a word in response.

– 28 –

Prashant stood at the grand entrance of Krish's opulent mansion, a sense of awe washing over him as he gazed at the imposing structure. The sheer luxury and scale of the house were overwhelming, a stark contrast to his own humble abode. After a few contemplative moments, a gardener approached him, his curiosity evident.

"What's the matter?" the gardener inquired. Prashant, feeling slightly out of place, met the gardener's gaze and replied wearily, "I wanted to meet Krish's dad. He invited me."

The gardener considered this for a moment, then asked for his name. "Your name?"

"Prashant. I'm Rahul's dad."

A nod of understanding from the gardener was followed by an offer of assistance. "Wait here; I will call him."

As Prashant waited on the manicured grounds, he couldn't help but take in the lavish surroundings, his eyes drawn to the impressive array of cars parked nearby. The sprawling mansion loomed large before him, evoking both curiosity and apprehension about the reason for his invitation. Unbeknownst to him, the complexities of the situation were largely a result of Rahul's own actions.

Finally, Raj emerged from the magnificent house. Prashant's heart raced with anticipation as he regarded the man who had extended the invitation. Raj, however, greeted him with a warm smile and a welcoming gesture.

"Please come in," Raj invited, breaking the momentary silence that had enveloped them.

Prashant followed him inside the grand residence, taking in the lavish furnishings and ornate decor, all of which stood in stark contrast to his own modest surroundings. The meeting ahead held a sense of mystery, and Prashant couldn't help but grew more anxious thinking about the purpose behind his summon.

– 29 –

Raj did his best to create a welcoming atmosphere, offering Prashant a beverage. "Tea, coffee, anything to drink?" he inquired politely.

Prashant, though appreciative of the gesture, declined, opting for a glass of cold water instead. "No, thanks. Just a glass of cold water." Raj turned to a servant, issuing an order with a calm authority. "Bring orange juice."

As they engaged in light conversation, Prashant couldn't help but be captivated by the elegance and sublimity of Raj's character. Their discussion touched on various topics, although a sense of anticipation lingered in the air. Prashant savored the orange juice, finding relief from the oppressive heat as he wiped his perspiring brow with a handkerchief.

Raj, mindful of the weighty matter at hand, decided to broach the subject directly. He wasted no time in addressing the issue that had brought Prashant to his home. "Look, let's get to the point," Raj began. He reminisced about his own youthful indiscretions, sharing a personal anecdote. "When I was in school, I used to secretly smoke cigarettes. One day, my dad caught me, and I got a good scolding. I remember it well. But times have changed, and our generation is different. Nowadays, kids are way ahead when it comes to cigarettes and stuff. Do you know what heroin is?"

Prashant was taken aback by the sudden shift in conversation. He responded with genuine confusion, "Heroin?"

Raj took it upon himself to explain the gravity of the situation. "Drugs. It's like white powder. My son, Krish, takes it. It might shock you, but I know that Rahul has also acquired this ill-habit from his friend. He's started drinking, smoking, and doing drugs."

Prashant struggled to absorb this shocking revelation. He shook his head in disbelief and insisted, "Rahul? Rahul can't do that!"

Raj sympathized with Prashant's disbelief but knew he had to share the difficult truth. "I'm Krish's father, and I know him well. He is always in need of new company. Today, it's Rahul; tomorrow, it could be someone else. You might find it strange, but at the shop where he buys these drugs, I pay the shopkeeper every month, so he gives Rahul fake drugs. Placebos! I mean, he thinks he's taking real drugs, but he's not. But I don't know how long I can keep doing this."

Prashant sat there, reeling from the revelations, and voiced his bewilderment. "I don't understand what's happening. He's just a kid. He has a long way to go. How did all of this happen?"

Raj offered comfort and advice, approaching Prashant with empathy. He reached out, placing a reassuring hand on his shoulder. "I can understand. My intention isn't to distress or scare you. But you need to know the truth. I know I can handle Krish, but I'm worried about your son, Rahul. I know he's extremely talented; I've known him since his childhood. I've seen him play. But now it seems that he's lost interest in cricket. And I also know that you're doing more for him than anyone else. As a father, I understand your emotions. But there's still hope. Talk to him as a friend. He will find his way back. You have to bring him back."

Prashant sat in silence, contemplating his own actions and choices as a parent. He was overwhelmed by self-doubt, lamenting, "Where did I go wrong? I can't figure it out!"

Raj, displaying a blend of empathy and wisdom, consoled Prashant with a shared sense of responsibility. "It's not anyone's fault. Or maybe it's everyone's fault to some extent."

Prashant looked up at Raj, gratitude and determination in his eyes. He stood up to take his leave, saying, "Thank you very much. It was a good thing you told me all this. I will talk to him." Raj nodded and accompanied Prashant to the main gate. Before parting ways, he offered his support. "If you need anything, please don't hesitate to ask. I've also seen tough times."

Prashant acknowledged the sentiment with a somber expression. "Sure. I'll take a leave now."

– 30 –

Prashant trudged aimlessly along the rain-soaked road, his thoughts weighed down by an overwhelming sense of despair, his heart heavy with concern for Rahul. His steps lacked direction as he wandered, oblivious to his surroundings. As the rain intensified, drenching him to the bone, a passing car slowed and then reversed – it was Srivastav.

Srivastav peered at Prashant through the car window, concern etched across his face. "Prashant, why are you walking alone in the rain? Come inside." Prashant remained unresponsive, his gaze vacant, and Srivastav repeated his offer. "What are you looking at? Get in the car, bhai."

With a numb nod, Prashant entered the vehicle, his vacant expression far removed from his usual demeanor. Srivastav couldn't ignore the stark change in his friend's disposition. Concern etched lines into Srivastav's face as he probed further, his voice laced with genuine worry, "What happened? Is there anything serious?"

Raindrops danced on the car's windowpane as Prashant turned his gaze away from Srivastav. His voice, barely above a whisper, held an air of finality as he muttered, "Everything is over." Srivastav couldn't fathom the depth of Prashant's despair, and he was determined to lift his spirits. He spoke urgently, trying to dispel the despondency, "Bhai, why are you blabbering nonsense?"

The rhythmic pitter-patter of raindrops seemed to intensify Prashant's melancholy, but Srivastav was unyielding in his efforts. He reached for a glimmer of optimism, urging his friend with unwavering enthusiasm, "Brother, it's raining outside. The atmosphere is beautiful. The night hasn't even properly begun yet, and you're talking about it ending. Come on, I'll take you to a great place."

Defeated, Prashant simply nodded, his compliance signaling a willingness to be led out of his emotional quagmire. He uttered softly, "Take me wherever you want."

Srivastav, sensing a spark of opportunity to pull Prashant from his despair, instructed his driver to steer them toward the Green Palace Bar, a place where a change of scenery might offer some respite from his friend's inner turmoil.

- 31 -

Srivastav strode into the dimly lit bar with an air of confident anticipation. In stark contrast, Prashant's presence seemed to be weighed down by an overwhelming sense of grief. The bar exuded an atmosphere of shadowy contemplation, populated by a diverse assembly of patrons. Some of them reveled in the triumphs of life, their laughter mingling with the haunting strains of melancholic music, while others sought solace in their sorrows.

The bar was filled with an assembly of men, each harboring their own joys and burdens. The music, a soulful serenade, played at a subdued volume, adding to the ambiance's reflective quality. In the midst of this emotional spectrum, Prashant and Srivastav claimed their corner seat, seeking refuge from the storm of emotions that raged within them.

The waiter, courteous and attentive, approached them with a warm greeting, "Namaste, sir!"

Srivastav responded promptly, "Bring whiskey for me and my friend."

The waiter, well-versed in the art of serving, offered a culinary suggestion, "And would you like some fried fish?"

Srivastav agreed to the suggestion with a nod, and the waiter departed to fulfill their order. Meanwhile, Prashant's gaze remained transfixed on the worn walls of the bar, his thoughts wandering through the labyrinth of his emotions.

Srivastav, sensing the need to break the melancholic silence, attempted to infuse some cheerfulness, turning toward Prashant and offering, "The fish fry here is world-famous." Prashant acknowledged the comment with a vacant nod.

After a brief wait, the waiter returned bearing their drinks and the delectable fried fish. Srivastav's eyes widened with delight as he beheld the tempting spread before them. With an air of celebration, he declared, "Today's a toast to the rain! Cheers."
Raising his glass, Srivastav awaited a reciprocal gesture from Prashant, but instead, he found Prashant's glass untouched, his expression remote. Srivastav, growing increasingly puzzled, urged him, "Oh, brother! You haven't come for moderation. Raise your glass. Why are you sulking?"

Prashant kept staring at the glass and asked, "Is being an ordinary person a crime?" Srivastav looked at him with confusion and asked, "What do you mean?"

However, Prashant didn't reply. He stared at the glass for some seconds, lifted it, and then drank in one go. Srivastav was staring at him blankly hoping for some response, but Prashant didn't say anything. Instead, he wiped his mouth with his hand.

Srivastav waited till Prashant said, "As my father was dying, he held my hand and said, 'I couldn't give you a good life, but try to make your children happy.' Well, forget it! But I made a promise to him. And I'm trying to educate them, make them successful..."

Prashant wanted to say more but he looked at the waiter and asked for more. The waiter nodded and refilled the glass. Prashant again drank it one go, while Srivastav sat startled.

Srivastav put his hand over his shoulder and asked, "Is everything alright? You seem quite disturbed today. If something is bothering you, you can share it with me."

Prashant did not look at Srivastav. He stared blankly at something in the air and said, "Do you remember Rahul playing in the neighborhood cricket tournament? Despite being the youngest in the team, he scored 77 runs all by himself. He was just ten years old back then." Srivastav nodded while looking at him and said, "Yes, I remember."

Prashant continued, "The chairman had awarded him the Man of the Match trophy. That day, I realised that my son is talented. He's not ordinary! I'm promised to make him a great cricketer, and he will become one." Srivastav nodded and said, "He will definitely become one. I know you won't give up until he does."

Prashant nodded as if he were listening to what Srivastav was saying. However, he was not able to hear or feel anything. He continued, "When a child is born, parents are born alongside. It takes time to become a good parent. But I left no stone unturned in fulfilling my responsibilities as a father. What did I get in return? Rahul was only twelve when he got hit by a ball. It hit his forehead. Blood was pouring out. There was a taxi strike that day. I carried him on my shoulders and ran 2 kilometers to the hospital. His head was on fire; the blood was burning. Why didn't I send him to a government school? Huh!"

Srivastav still had no idea about the actual matter, but this time he figured out that Rahul had messed up. "Look, I don't know what happened between you and Rahul, but give it some time. They won't understand right now what we parents do for them. That's the kind of age they're in."

Prashant nodded and said, "Leave it... Let it go." He looked at the waiter and said, "Bring me one more glass, buddy."

The waiter nodded and poured another drink for Prashant. In no time, Prashant got drunk. Meanwhile, Durga opened the window and looked for any sign of Prashant as it was getting late. She was worried for him because of the heavy rain.

Prashant got another drink but the glass slipped from his hand and fell. He immediately said, "Sorry...sorry, it slipped."

Srivastav held his hand and said, "Forget it, the waiter will clean it. Let's go home. Bhabhi ji must be waiting for you."

However, Prashant didn't listen to him. Instead, he said, "Just one more!"

Srivastav got a little irritated and said, "Come on, Prashant. Today's quota is done. Get up. What kind of childish behavior is this?"

Prashant looked at him and asked, "Tell me one thing. Am I your neighbor or your friend?"

Srivastav glared at him and said, "You are my friend. Why?"

Prashant scoffed in frustration and said, "You're lying, aren't you? I know... I'm not your friend, I'm just your neighbor. I can never be your friend. And you'll never want that. Nobody here wants an ordinary friend, an ordinary father, an ordinary husband, a son, or an employee. There's no place for ordinary people! No respect! But how can everyone... I mean, how can anyone become the best? Is there room for everyone to reach the top like you or Mr. Raj Bansal? Everyone has their limits!"

Srivastav understood something was wrong, so he just replied, "That's not true." Prashant: "It is true! You say, right... the more you invest in your child, the better the return. I invested my entire life in my child. What return did I get? He feels ashamed to acknowledge his father in front of his friends. But he has no shame in smoking, drinking, or doing drugs with those same friends. This is my return!" Srivastav looked at Prashant blankly. There was silence between the two until the thunderstorm roared outside.

Srivastav eventually sighed and confessed his feelings. "Yes, I indeed discussed investment with you. I admit it. But today, I want to share my heart with you as well. You know, my friend, a father's life is like a one-way street. The returns are almost non-existent. We only say such things to solve our dilemmas. But if you think about the returns, my friend, you'll find nothing but sorrow. Our job is to nurture the tree and watch it grow. Whether it bears fruit or not is not up to us. What do you think? Jay... my son... does he have any idea where the money for his education is coming from? He doesn't care. He's good at studies... as soon as he gets a chance, he'll leave everything behind and run away, to the US, Canada, anywhere. Then a job, marriage, US citizenship, children... a settled life. Once every 4-5 years, he'll come home during winters and show his parents what life in America is like. That's it, duty fulfilled. And in a way, this is fine... because how can a broker like me, who can't even speak proper English, fit in with his IIT engineer friends? Making a career with the hard-earned money of a father is possible, but accepting it openly in front of everyone becomes difficult for them. I've seen so many like this. So, what should I do in this situation? I only have two choices. Either spend my life waiting for him... or live my life the way I want to. You should be happy that at least your son is with you. What's mine? Just waiting for a flight. When we grow old, we won't have our children around us. It'll be just us, watching out for each other. So, let's raise this last peg to our second innings. Cheers!"

Prashant was drunk, yet he heard him patiently. Srivastav's words made sense to him. He didn't say anything after that. Srivastav waited for a response but when it didn't come, he turned to the waiter and said, "Get the bill, bhai."

He helped Prashant to the car and then drove off. On the other hand, Durga was feeding Rampiyari but her heart kept worrying for Prashant. After a few minutes, she heard a knock and rushed to the door hoping to find her husband standing before the door. However, she did not think expect to see him staggering. Srivastav was holding Prashant because he was barely able to stand by himself.

A look of disbelief crossed Durga's face and she asked, "What happened to him?" Srivastav looked at her, his face contorted with shame. "Nothing Bhabhi ji, we just drank a little too much today," he chuckled.

Durga looked at them with distress and continued, "I tried calling so many times. He just wasn't reachable. We were getting so worried." Srivastav nodded and escorted Prashant to the sofa. Almost in a hurry he said "I'll take my leave, Bhabhi ji,". Please feed him something and let him rest. He'll be fine by morning. Namaste!"

"What were you celebrating that you drank so much?" Durga asked, the moment Srivastav left the house.

Prashant spoke irritably, "These days, even little kids are drinking, and smoking cigarettes... who knows what else they're addicted to? Can't I have a bit of alcohol? I don't need anyone's permission. Everyone in this house is doing as they please. And Babuji worked hard for every brick of this house. This house is not running on charity."

Durga knew there was no point in arguing with Prashant at this time. "Alright," she said. "Have your meal." Prashant looked at something on the ground, swayed his hand, and said, "You eat, give it to Mom. I've already eaten."

"Come on, go to your room and rest," Durga replied.

"I know. I'm not a child."

Prashant somehow stood up and staggered towards Rahul's room. Meanwhile, Rahul was listening to everything. The moment he heard the approaching footsteps, he closed his eyes, pretending to sleep. His father opened the door, careful not to wake the boy up. "Don't do this, my son," he said, his voice hushed. "Don't indulge in all this. You have a bright future ahead of you."

As Prashant walked away, his words hung in the air, laden with a sense parental concern.

– 32 –

In the heart of their modest home, Pushpa toiled away in the bustling kitchen. The aroma of spices filled the air as she prepared a meal with practiced precision. The rhythmic clatter of utensils provided the soundtrack to her labor. It was in this domestic sanctuary that her son, Jay, made his entrance, his voice carrying a sense of purpose.

"Mom, I'm leaving for tuition," Jay announced, his youthful face a canvas of earnest determination. "I'll be back in the evening. There are extra classes today."

Pushpa paused her culinary dance, acknowledging her son's plans with a nod of understanding. Her eyes held a mother's pride in her child's pursuit of knowledge as she responded, "Of course, Jay. But listen, your dad has kept the draft for the new coaching in the drawer. I forgot to tell you yesterday. When you go to the tuition, deposit it for admission."

Upon hearing these words, Jay's eyes lit up with unrestrained joy. Without a moment's delay, he hastened back to his room, propelled by the anticipation of discovering the much-anticipated draft. With bated breath, he opened the drawer, and there, amidst papers and documents, lay an 8 lakh rupee draft made out to Dream Coaching. The sheer magnitude of the opportunity before him ignited his heart with hope, a fire of ambition burning brightly within his chest.

But as he examined the contents of the drawer further, his elation gave way to distress. Nestled beside the draft was Srivastav's cheque book. Jay's inquisitive fingers seized it, flipping it open to reveal a meager balance of 8,000 rupees. A cloud of confusion and concern cast its shadow over his once-blissful countenance.

Compelled by a gnawing sense of unease, Jay swiftly called out to his mother, Pushpa, his voice carrying a note of urgency that cut through the stillness of the house. "Mom, come here for a moment."

From her station in the kitchen, Pushpa responded to her son's summons. Her steps echoed the gravity of the moment as she approached Jay, a mother's intuition sensing the impending storm of questions.

"Why, what happened?" Pushpa inquired, her voice laced with a mixture of curiosity and concern. "Didn't you find it?"

Jay, his eyes reflecting a myriad of emotions, from bewilderment to anxiety, directed his mother's attention to the cheque book. With a somber expression, he pointed at the account balance displayed within. The figures revealed a stark truth, and Jay's unspoken question hung heavily in the air, begging for answers. In the face of this unsettling discovery, Pushpa found herself momentarily speechless, her silence echoing the weight of a revelation that would reshape their understanding of their family's financial reality.

– 33 –

After a long, weary day, Jamal trudged back to Raqib's house to take Shahrukh home. As he approached the door, Raqib welcomed him with a smile that didn't quite reach his eyes, as if a weighty matter loomed on his mind. Jamal sank into the sofa, his gaze searching for Fatima, but she was conspicuously absent. He turned to Raqib with a furrowed brow.

"Where's Bhabhi? I can't seem to find her," Jamal inquired. Raqib met Jamal's gaze, his expression filled with mixed emotions. "She's taken Shahrukh to the shrine. They should be back soon. I'm glad you came now; I wanted to talk in private."

Jamal's serious countenance betrayed his curiosity. "What's troubling you, Bhai Jaan?". Raqib sighed, his hands nervously rubbing together. "Well, brother, it was bound to happen sooner or later - my transfer. And the most important news is that Fatima is pregnant. She's in her third month. We only found out last week... I need to leave as soon as possible, for her sake."

Jamal's initial seriousness melted into a warm smile. "Oh, these are both good news. Why the long face, then?". Raqib, instead of sugar-coating the situation, decided to lay it bare. He let out another sigh and continued, "Brother, do you realize the predicament we're facing? Once we leave, who will look after Shahrukh? Are you prepared to leave your job and raise the child at home?"

Jamal waved his hand dismissively. "Don't over think it, Bhaijan. You've done everything in your power. Let's see what the future holds. God will watch over us."

In the midst of their conversation, Fatima returned with Shahrukh. Jamal turned to see them, a wide grin spreading across his face. His eyes lit up with joy as he spoke, "Congratulations, Bhabhi... Many congratulations!" His gaze then shifted to Shahrukh, and he spoke with enthusiasm, "Son, you're going to be a big brother!"

Fatima blushed and attempted to divert the conversation, saying, "Please, have a seat; I'll prepare breakfast." Jamal, however, shook his head and insisted, "No, no, Bhabiji. You should rest for now." Fatima playfully waved him off. "Oh, hush, you're too kind. I'm perfectly fine." She smiled and disappeared into the kitchen.

Raqib turned back to Jamal, his voice now tinged with concern. "I have a friend who runs a primary boarding school for the poor and orphans. It's a bit far from Kolkata... I was thinking of sending Shahrukh there." Jamal, puzzled by the term 'orphans,' paused and hesitantly asked, "What do you mean by orphans?"

Raqib who was struggling to find the right words, mumbled "Orphans are children who don't have parents. Or..." Jamal's cheerful face immediately turned somber, and he interjected, "But he has a father, doesn't he? I'm still here!"

Realising his misstep, Raqib tried to clarify, "I didn't mean it that way." Jamal, resolute in his decision, shook his head. "No, Bhai Jaan. That won't happen. Come what may, my son will stay with me." He scooped up Shahrukh into his arms and declared, "I'm leaving."

Raqib stood there, guilt gnawing at his conscience, and implored, "At least have breakfast before you go." But Jamal had already made up his mind. He nodded once more and uttered, "Not today, Bhai Jaan. Some other day. Take care of Bhabhi. Goodbye." With those words, he turned and left.

– 34 –

Riya and Rahul found themselves parked on the outskirts of Kolkata in Riya's car, surrounded by the picturesque beauty of nature. Sunlight filtered gently through the leaves, casting a soft, dreamy glow. Riya gazed at Rahul and couldn't help but appreciate the serene setting.

"What a beautiful place, don't you think?" she remarked.

However, Rahul's mind was elsewhere. He absentmindedly replied, "Hmm..."

Sensing something amiss, Riya looked at him with concern. "What's wrong? You don't seem happy," she inquired.

Rahul quickly shook his head, denying any unhappiness. "No, it's not that."

Riya felt a pang of unease, so she tried to lighten the mood. She leaned in closer to him with a playful smile. "You're not happy? Should I make you happy?"

A blush crept across Rahul's cheeks, but he didn't move closer. He sat there, gazing at her with a mixture of love and guilt. Riya sensed that something was amiss but persisted in trying to cheer him up. She whispered, "What's bothering you? Come closer... Don't worry, my love, I won't bite. Look, this is for you."

Rahul glanced at the white iPhone box and then back at her. Riya moved even closer, her intent clear, and added, "My first gift to you... Oops, my apologies, the second one." She planted a tender kiss on his cheek and chuckled. "The first one was this."

After pulling back, Rahul looked at the expensive phone and remarked, "I assume this is the latest iPhone model?"

Riya nodded, her excitement evident. "Yes, indeed! Is there any other model worth gifting? I have the same one. Do you like this colour? It's as cool as you, don't you think?"

Rahul hesitated for a moment, then asked, "What's the price of this phone? It must be around a lakh, right?"

Riya looked at him, frustration creeping into her expression. "More than that... Why? What's the issue? Don't you like it? You know, I used to receive gifts from others all the time. This is the first time I've bought something for a guy."

Rahul tried to choose his words carefully. "It's really nice of you, Riya... but I can't accept it right now." Rolling her eyes, Riya questioned, "May I ask why? Is it about swag?"

Rahul shook his head, his hands gently cupping her face. "I may not know the exact meaning of 'swag,' but it's definitely not about that. Riya, you're the first girl in my life, and obviously, you're very special. That's why we should be clear with each other before moving forward."

Riya tenderly rubbed his hands and asked, "Rahul, why are you acting so strangely? What's bothering you?"

Rahul nodded and withdrew his hands. He looked at her earnestly. "I'm fine, Riya. I just need to tell you something." "Okay," Riya responded calmly. "I'm all ears."

Taking a deep breath, Rahul began, "A few days ago, I was telling someone that a person should live within their means. But today, I feel like I'm not following my own advice. Krish told me about your dad's shipping business, a third-generation enterprise that's one of the most renowned in the city. A luxurious house in the upscale part of town... If they were to find out that my father's annual income is roughly equivalent to the cost of your iPhone, or that we live in a small room in a Howrah colony, what would that mean to them? Riya, you can understand, right? You're a mature girl. This is my reality, Riya, and you have to accept it. Not every story has a 'happy' ending, like in movies."

Riya gazed at him with eyes filled with hurt. She wanted nothing more than for him to stay by her side, but deep down, she knew he was right. However, she desperately wished he could see himself the way she saw him. She took a deep breath and said, "But you're not ordinary, Rahul!"

Rahul was taken aback to hear his father's words mirrored by Riya. It made him question whether he was right. He looked at her with teary eyes and responded, "I need to prove that." Riya nodded, her own eyes moist. "I'll miss you."

Rahul replied, "Me too."

They exchanged a meaningful look and then embraced beneath the enchanting sunlight, amidst the poetic vibes of the serene location.

– 35 –

Rohan and Shaket found themselves in a meeting with the eminent business magnate and President of the Bengal Chamber of Commerce and Import-Export Association, Mr. Mehta. Their discussion revolved around matters of business when an unexpected guest, Hasmukh Parekh, joined them.

Shaket's surprise was evident as he gazed at his father. He turned to face Parekh and inquired, "Dad, how are you here?"

Before Hasmukh could respond, Mehta intervened, shedding light on the situation. "I had invited Mr. Parekh. I had some important business matters to discuss with him. When I called him, he mentioned there might be some ongoing interior work at the office, making it unsuitable for a meeting. At the same time, we had a meeting scheduled for your presentation. So, I thought, why not invite Mr. Parekh here? We can delve into our business affairs while enjoying some casual conversation. After all, you two are family, aren't you?"

However, Hasmukh addressed Mehta, expressing his concern, "But Mehta, you should have informed Shaket about your intentions. He's now handling everything."

Mehta acknowledged Hasmukh's point and continued, "If the office renovations had been completed, there would have been no need for the call. Parekh Saab, I have full confidence in

Shaket. His vision and intentions are clear to me. I understood his proposal as soon as I reviewed it. However, he could benefit from some experience, guidance, and support. Times have changed, and there are numerous protocols and heightened competition now. Shaket and his partner haven't engaged in any import or export transactions through their new company, and without a successful transaction record, the association won't register their new firm. I'm uncertain about the way forward. Back in your day, anyone facing such a critical situation would have turned to you for advice. I'm doing the same now. Please consider a solution. Weave your magic once more, Hasmukh Parekh."

As Shaket and Rohan stood there somewhat bewildered, Mehta shifted his focus. "Shaket, don't misunderstand me. You should discuss these matters with Mr. Parekh. He's the one who can comprehend and resolve your issue better than anyone else. Learning from someone who possesses knowledge is a fundamental principle of business. He has always been our business mentor, even today."

"Mehta, why delve into such discussions in front of youngsters?" Hasmukh intervened "I'm just a simple businessman, with no expertise beyond the realm of business. Anyways, tell me, what task do you have in mind for me?". Mr. Mehta, clearly pleased with Hasmukh's response, smiled and remarked, "That's the mark of a true businessman. I spoke in circles, but we eventually reached the point: 'What task do you have for me?' This is Mr. Hashmukh Parekh."

After a brief pause, Mr. Mehta continued, "Next month, the Chamber will hold its Annual General Meeting. You'll be responsible for handling all the printing collateral. Time is, as always, in short supply. Here's the file with all the item details.

Provide a quote and initiate the work. Now, I must leave for another meeting. Shaket, we'll catch up soon. Take some time to ponder what I've said, Parekh bhai, and commence the work."

Mr. Mehta shook hands with Hasmukh Parekh and took his leave. Shaket and Rohan, still somewhat perplexed, followed Hasmukh out of the meeting. They got into the car, with Shaket in the driver's seat and Rohan beside him. Silence filled the car until Hasmukh's phone rang, prompting Shaket's curiosity.

As Hasmukh answered the call, Shaket couldn't help but wonder about his next steps. Hasmukh greeted the caller, "Hello, Anwar Bhai... Waleikum Assalam... How are you? Is everything fine in Dhaka? Yes, yes, I'm fine too, Inshallah! Bhai, I need a favor... No, not for myself. I have everything I need from the Almighty, except for your prayers and friendship. Tell me, do you source cotton for your garment mill from Vietnam and India? My son and his friend have started a new import-export business. Could you give them a small consignment to see how these young people work? Your son has also joined your business, right?"

After a pause, Hasmukh continued, "That would be great. They'll reach out to you directly. Our time is running short, and it's these young individuals who need to take the reins. So, I'll provide your number to my son and instruct him to contact you. You can negotiate rates on your terms. Just offer them a smaller order for now, but finalize some consignments by next month for me."

Following another pause, Hasmukh resumed. "What? Should I take that as a yes? Thank you, Anwar bhai. Thank you very much. How's everything else over there? Are Hilsa fish back in the market? Yes, yes, we'll visit this year. Alright then, thank you very much once again. Take care. Allah Hafiz."

Shaket had been listening intently, and as soon as the call ended, he couldn't contain his curiosity. "What happened, Dad? Who was that?"

"Anwar Hossain, a prominent industrialist from Bangladesh," Hasmukh Parekh responded. "He is an old friend. I've shared his number with you on WhatsApp. You should talk to him."

Shaket nodded but had more questions. "Alright, but..."

"For the association's registration, we need overseas transactions," Hasmukh interjected, his tone firm. "Bangladesh may be nearby, but it still qualifies as overseas. Present your transaction records and adhere to the association's protocol to secure your membership. After that, you can engage in business with any country on your terms. For now, this contact will resolve your immediate issue. Talk to him."

Shaket agreed with a nod but refrained from saying more. The remainder of the car ride was marked by silence. Upon arriving home, Hasmukh Parekh was about to exit the car, but he couldn't resist imparting the wisdom he had been pondering throughout the journey. He paused for a moment and said, "And always remember, son, never judge anyone by their status, and never assess a businessman solely by his balance sheet. Business relationships are founded on something that doesn't appear on a financial statement."

Hasmukh stepped out of the car and made his way towards the gate. Shaket observed him entering the house before turning his attention to Rohan.

"What are you thinking?" Rohan asked.

Shaket glanced at him for a moment and then replied, "Nothing... Please ask the interior team to halt the renovations for a day or two. I need to make some changes."

– 36 –

Srivastav sat in his office cabin, engrossed in discussions with some long-standing agents when Jay made an unexpected appearance. Startled by his son's presence, Srivastav promptly ended his call and redirected his attention towards Jay.

"Jay Beta, why are you at the office? How did you get here? Didn't you go for the tutorial?" Srivastav inquired.

Jay nodded and replied, "I did, Dad."

Srivastav sensed that something was amiss, a brewing storm inside his son's mind. Concern etched his features as he spoke in hushed tones, "Is the admission done?"

Jay anticipated this question, yet he didn't immediately respond. Instead, he reached into his bag, retrieved a draft, and handed it to Srivastav. Srivastav continued to scrutinise Jay, waiting for an explanation. Jay finally broke the silence.

"Dad, it's not needed," he said calmly.

Srivastav accepted the draft but couldn't comprehend his son's change of heart. "What do you mean? You told me you wanted to secure admission there."

Jay sighed and explained, "I did say that... Then I pondered it further and realised that I could crack the IIT without this coaching."

Srivastav shook his head in disagreement, concern etched across his face. "No, son, I don't want to take any risks."

Jay countered, his hand gesturing in emphasis, "You're taking a risk, Dad. Putting everything on the line for my education—isn't that a big deal?"

"But, son..." Srivastav attempted to intervene, but Jay cut him off.

"Dad... Mum told me everything," Jay interjected. "You could have told us the truth. Do you think I'm so selfish that I won't understand your point? I know you want to shield me from every problem to ensure it doesn't affect my career. But for how long, Dad? How long will you and Mum keep solving my problems? How long will you keep me insulated from reality? One day, I will have to confront this world independently. So, let me face it my way. I am a good student at the end of the day. I can achieve excellent marks even without specialized coaching. What's the worst that can happen? At most, a 2-4% difference. That won't matter in real life. Keep this money with you; it will come in handy for all of us later."

Srivastav gazed at his son, love and admiration in his eyes, and then said, "Think about it once more. Are you absolutely sure?"

Jay nodded resolutely, stating, "100 percent sure, Dad. There's a common misconception about our generation among parents... We aspire to be self-made, not perpetually self-absorbed. And one more thing, Dad: I want to be an engineer, but I also want to learn about business starting now. That's why I've decided that after my tutorials each day, I'll dedicate 2 hours to learning from you, Sir. Who could teach me business and management better than you? As your only son, I'll eventually have to take over the family business! So, what do you think of the plan?"

Srivastav smiled, his eyes betraying a tinge of guilt, and said, "That's the spirit... In that case, I'll prepare you to teach Harvard professors about business management within a year. I'm sorry, son... my perception of you was not entirely accurate."

Jay, empathetic and considerate, chose to change the subject. "Now, let's put these discussions behind us and grab a quick meal. I'm famished."

Srivastav, back to his cheerful self, suggested, "Let's head to the Royal... We'll invite Ushman Bhai for some special biryani." Jay nodded and said, "Let's go." Srivastav swiftly organised his documents, placing them neatly in one pile and stowing the draft securely in his pocket. He affectionately patted Jay's shoulder, and together, they left the office.

– 37 –

Jamal was in the kitchen, busy cooking, when he suddenly realised that his gas cylinder had run empty. His attention shifted to Shahrukh, who was playing in the room with a tiny car. The gravity of the situation struck him - he couldn't take Shahrukh to Raqib's house due to his impending transfer. Jamal was gripped by fear, concerned that Shahrukh might wander off or hurt himself. After all, he was only two years old and couldn't speak properly yet. Jamal, feeling helpless, decided to tie Shahrukh with a rope on the balcony until he returned.

Initially, Shahrukh didn't react, but as soon as Jamal stepped outside the room, he panicked, and started crying and yelling. Jamal knew he had to act quickly, so he rushed to get his small gas cylinder refilled, paid for it, and hurried back home. Meanwhile, Shahrukh's cries echoed throughout the colony, but no one came to his aid.

Fortunately, it was Razia who emerged from her house, drawn by the sound of Shahrukh crying. She immediately rushed to Jamal's room, untied him, and cradled him in her arms, trying to soothe him. Within a few minutes, Shahrukh stopped crying and began to smile. She carried Shahrukh to her room and engaged him in play.

When Jamal returned, he couldn't find his son. He searched the room and then asked his neighbours if they had seen him, but no one had any information. Frustration mounting, Jamal rushed to Razia's house, and what he saw, warmed his heart. Razia was feeding Shahrukh with a smile, and Shahrukh looked content and happy in her presence. A smile crept onto Jamal's face.

Razia, upon seeing Jamal, turned to him and scolded, "What kind of behavior is this? How could you tie up a child and leave him alone like that?"

Jamal retorted, "I had to go and get gas; otherwise, how would I cook dinner tonight?"

Razia, still concerned, replied, "You could have informed someone. Imagine how scared he must have been!"

Jamal knew he was in the wrong and spoke in a hushed tone, "What could I do? I'm all alone and have to manage everything!"

Razia empathized with his predicament and said, "Listen, I have a suggestion. Either consider getting remarried or find his mother and bring her here. This child desperately needs his mother. Your stubbornness is making life difficult for both of you."

Jamal turned towards her, scoffing at the idea of remarriage. He looked at Razia and inquired, "Remarriage? If someone is willing to treat him like their own child, then I'll think about it. With my current situation - no stable job, no home, and dealing with this child's troubles on top of it - who would even consider marrying me? Besides, if his mother genuinely cared, she would have come back by now."

Razia paused for a moment and then acknowledged, "That's also true."

Curiosity got the better of Jamal, and he wondered why Razia was single. She was beautiful and seemed to have turned her life around. He seized the opportunity and asked, "But why do you live alone?"

Razia gave him a piercing look and said, "By choice. Sometimes, I can't decide whether you're incredibly foolish or just pretending to be one!" Jamal didn't argue; he knew what she was about to say. Razia continued, "The stories of women like me are not uncommon, Jamal. You must have heard plenty of neighborhood gossip."

Jamal waved his hand dismissively and said, "Why should I care about the neighborhood? They gossip about me too. Look at that guy; his wife ran away." Razia understood that they both had been victims of betrayal. She looked at him and said, "Yes, that's one thing we have in common. Your wife left you, and my lover sold me off here. Let's have a drink to that."

By this time, Shahrukh had fallen asleep on Razia's lap. Jamal declined the offer, as he had never been fond of alcohol. He glanced at her for a moment and then said, "Let's not drink anymore. Some wounds can't be healed with alcohol." Razia stared at him intently and inquired, "Then, how do you heal them?"

Jamal gazed into her eyes and replied, "By being with someone who understands and has experienced those wounds, you can heal them. Someone who knows how to handle their pain." Razia nodded in agreement and said, "Alright, so no more drinking."

Jamal smiled at her and gently picked up Shahrukh from Razia's lap. As he prepared to leave, Razia looked into his eyes and made a heartfelt offer, "Listen. If you don't mind, you can leave him with me every evening until sunset. This child needs me, and I need him."

A smile spread across Jamal's face, and he left, grateful for the support he had found in Razia.

− 38 −

Rahul sat alone in the canteen, consumed by his thoughts. Since that pivotal night, he had embarked on a journey of self-reflection, confronting his own flaws and the burgeoning sense of ingratitude that had taken root within him.

In the midst of this profound introspection and the weight of his overwhelming guilt, Ansh and Sanjay entered the canteen. Ansh immediately noticed Rahul's distant demeanor and inquired, "Hey, where have you been? No one seems to have spotted you, and everyone's been asking…"

Yet, Rahul was so deeply ensconced in his own sorrow that he scarcely registered their presence or the words they uttered. It was only when Sanjay placed a comforting hand on Rahul's shoulder and queried, "Hey, Devdas! Are you with us? Do you even recall that today happens to be Ansh's birthday?" that Rahul was jolted back to the present.

He gazed at his friends standing before him, catching the tail end of Sanjay's sentence, and replied, "Happy birthday, my friend… I'm sorry; it completely slipped my mind." Ansh responded with a tinge of exasperation, "Don't sweat over it. Listen, I don't have the means to throw a grand party for a crowd of 40-50 friends. At best, I can treat 4-5 close friends to some street food in Dalhousie after school."

Sanjay chuckled softly and chimed in, "You won't even find many people eating on the footpath, even if you tried. Alright... Let's meet after school then..."

Rahul simply nodded. "Goodbye!"

– 39 –

Ansh was treating his friends to a birthday feast at Dalhousie Street's bustling food corner. Amidst the delectable dishes and the joyous atmosphere, Rahul noticed an unexpected sight - Prashant, seated at a local tea shop, sipping a cup of tea. Puzzled by his father's presence in such a place, Rahul abruptly stood up, leaving his plate behind, and discreetly made his way towards Prashant.

"Where are you off to?" Ansh inquired.

Rahul glanced at him and replied, "I'll be back in two minutes." His friends exchanged curious glances but refrained from asking further questions. Rahul observed Prashant from a distance as he finished his tea, returned to his desk, and resumed typing on his typewriter.

Rahul couldn't believe his eyes. He was stunned to witness his father toiling under the scorching sun. He returned to his friends, his face a mixture of confusion and disbelief. Turning to Ansh, he asked, "Can I borrow your phone for a moment?"

Ansh nodded and handed him his phone. Rahul swiftly Googled "Hasmukh Parekh Diary & Calendar Company" and retrieved the address. Without waiting a moment longer, he decided to visit Prashant's former workplace.

Meanwhile, renovation work was underway at the office. Labors were busy, bringing in a new chair to one of the cabins. As Shaket observed the new addition, he couldn't help but smile, touching it with a sense of fondness. When Rahul reached the office and was met with the ongoing construction. With no nameplate to guide him, he approached a paanshop and inquired, "Is this the Parekh Diary and Calendar?"

The shopkeeper gestured towards the office and replied, "It's closed. A new office is opening up now."

"When did it close?" Rahul inquired further.

"It's been more than a month." the vendor responded.

Rahul was taken aback to learn that his father had been laboring under the scorching sun for over a month. Overwhelmed by emotions and guilt, he quickly retraced his steps to the Dalhousie Collectorate Area, where he concealed himself behind a tree. From his vantage point, he witnessed Prashant packing up his typewriter and handing it over to a shopkeeper. He then approached Jamal.

"Jamal, this is for you and Shahrukh," Prashant said, handing Jamal a polybag. "Also, for Raziaji, from me."

Jamal looked at Prashant, concern in his eyes., "Why, brother? You should keep your money. You need it," he replied.

Prashant smiled and reassured, "It's for my own happiness. You've done so much for me. Although the office has shut shop, I'm still earning a living, thanks to you. Isn't your son like my own? And what's this – all your bananas are sold out. Is there nothing left for me?"

"Brother, who could come between your son and your bananas when I'm here?" Jamal replied, waving his hand in a dismissive gesture.

Jamal retrieved the bananas he had saved for Prashant and handed them over. A warm exchange of smiles passed between them.

"Your name shouldn't be Jamal; it should be 'Kamaal'," Prashant chuckled and remarked.

Jamal laughed heartily and responded, "If that's your wish, we can arrange to have my name changed legally. A new name, a new life."

Prashant joined in the laughter and concluded, "Alright then, let's meet tomorrow. Goodbye!"

Jamal bid him farewell. "Goodbye!"

Rahul overheard the entire conversation, and when he saw Prashant departing, he followed him surreptitiously. Prashant boarded a crowded bus, and Rahul trailed behind him. He took a seat at a distance from Prashant, hoping to remain unnoticed. During the journey, the bus driver suddenly hit the brakes, causing Prashant's bag of bananas to tumble to the floor. He swiftly retrieved it, cradling it as if it were a precious infant. Rahul continued to observe from a distance.

– 40 –

Prashant and Durga were enjoying a quiet tea together when Rahul returned home. He approached them and joined their company. After a moment of silence, Prashant inquired, "How's your practice going?" Rahul remained wordless; his thoughts heavy.

Prashant presumed that Rahul might be longing for a branded phone, so he continued, "Just be patient. You'll have a branded phone soon."

Rahul looked at Prashant as these words reached his ears. He had been holding back his tears for an extended period, but now he teetered on the brink of an emotional breakdown. Without a word, he abruptly rose from his seat and made his way to the washroom. In the solitude of that space, Rahul finally let his emotions overwhelm him. Guilt washed over him, and he resolved to mend his ways.

– 41 –

After months of construction, the long-awaited inauguration day had finally arrived. The once-dilapidated Parekh Diary and Calendars office had transformed into an elegant and inviting workspace. A gathering of people had assembled to witness the grand opening.

In due time, a car pulled up, and Hasmukh, accompanied by his wife and Shaket, stepped out of the vehicle. Hasmukh admired the exterior of the office, where bright and pleasing colors adorned the façade. With anticipation building, he made his way towards the office entrance. Shaket, standing nearby, handed his father a pair of scissors. Applause erupted from the crowd as Hasmukh ceremoniously cut the ribbon.

Once inside, Hasmukh was equally impressed with the interior. The old, worn-out chairs had been replaced with high-quality ones. Hasmukh cast a grateful glance towards Shaket and then noticed a cabin with his nameplate designating him as Chairman. He was momentarily taken aback by the surprise.

Turning to Shaket for an explanation, Hasmukh found his son ready to reveal his intentions. Shaket wore a warm smile as he addressed his father, saying, "Dad, even though I studied business management in the US, there's something you possess that would take me years to acquire. And right now, I need it the most."

Hasmukh stood in bewildered silence, waiting for Shaket to elaborate.

Shaket continued, "Dad, I'm referring to your experience! Also, I think it's time to bring back those few employees who were with us until the end. They deserve it too. From this point forward, Parekh Printing and Parekh Export will be jointly managed by father and son. I have no desire to continue my partnership with Rohan. We're more than capable of independently managing our respective businesses."

Hasmukh's eyes welled up with tears of joy, and an immense smile graced his face. He embraced Shaket tightly, expressing his deep gratitude and pride.

– 42 –

Prashant emerged from his room, scanning the house for Rahul, but he was nowhere to be found. Concerned, he headed to the kitchen where Durga was busy preparing tea. She glanced up and said, "I was just about to wake you up. Have some lemon water, and then I'll make tea."

Prashant, checking the clock and Rahul's room, which was still closed, returned to the kitchen and inquired, "Is the bathroom still occupied? Where's the young master?"

Before Durga could answer, Rahul appeared in his school uniform, clutching his cricket kit. He looked at her and said, "Give me my lunch, Mum." His mother complied, handing him his packed meal.

Rahul asked, "Banana?"

Durga nodded and replied, "No, no bananas. I can't bear your daily complain over banana."

"Give it to me," Rahul insisted.

Durga was taken aback; it was the first time he had asked for them. She handed him four, and he put two in his lunchbox. He then turned to Prashant and said, "Oh, I almost forgot to tell you, Papa! Bananas are rich in vitamins, protein, and minerals. But did you know they're great for your heart too? They lower cholesterol and have high fiber content. So, starting today, two bananas for you too... every day! It's essential for your health. You've turned so weak. Check yourself in the mirror."

He gave Prashant the remaining two bananas and headed for the door. Durga and Prashant exchanged astonished glances as Rahul added, "And this time, I'll become the 'Man of the Series' in the tournament. Don't worry." As Rahul left, his parents were still in shock. Prashant's eyes glistened with tears as he hurried to Rampiyari and hugged her, his delight palpable.

Meanwhile, Durga served tea and turned to him, asking, "He's going to practice with so much enthusiasm after such a long time, and he spoke to you so affectionately. Why didn't you say anything?"

Prashant smiled but remained silent. Instead, he reflected, "I wanted to say so much to him, but I didn't feel the need to say anything. For a brief moment, it felt like we had both returned to each other. But the truth is, neither of us had ever gone anywhere. We've always been in each other's hearts. No one else knows us like we do."

Prashant took a sip of tea, a content smile crossing his face. Their lives were finally getting back on track. Prashant soon resumed work in the newly refurbished office alongside Hasmukh Parekh and Ghosh Babu. One fine day, Shaket gently warned him about a typing mistake and gifted him brand-new glasses. Later, when Prashant returned home and saw the "Man of the Tournament" trophy, he felt that he had been granted all the happiness in the world. He hugged Rahul tightly.

In the interim, Srivastav was engaged in a video call with his son, Jay, unable to suppress his grin. All his investments in Jay's education had paid off as he had successfully cracked the IIT.

Meanwhile, Shaket embarked on his business education under Hasmukh's guidance. He sat in the office with Hasmukh, Khanna, and some foreign clients, eager to learn the ropes of the trade.

Lastly, Razia found her happiness in playing with Shahrukh, while Jamal discovered comfort in the love and care that both Shahrukh and Razia provided. Their lives had been a rollercoaster ride, but in the end, they all found their true comfort and happiness at home!

Abbu Ki Naaz

– 01 –

It was another bustling day at Jupiter Incorporation, a renowned advertising agency in the heart of Delhi. The office buzzed with the controlled chaos typical of creative environments. At the entrance, Yogesh, the ever-smiling security guard, stood sentinel, greeting each person who walked in as if they were family.

As Naaz approached the office, her boundless energy and confidence were evident.

Yogesh's eyes lit up at the sight of her, and he respectfully nodded, his welcoming smile beaming. "Good morning, Didi," he greeted her.

Naaz returned his smile with her trademark warmth. "Very good morning, Yogesh."

Her presence exuded cheerfulness as she entered the office. The receptionist acknowledged her with a polite, "Good morning, ma'am."

Naaz turned to the receptionist, Sharon, and corrected her with a friendly tone. "Sharon, I've told you before, I'm not your 'ma'am.' Please, just call me 'Naaz.' Good morning, anyway."

Walking towards her cabin, Naaz contemplated, "Excessive respect or animosity, I fear both, as my life is already brimming with these emotions. There's no space left for anything extra. Right now, I'm in a happy place, or am I?"

Inside her cabin, the office peon had left a steaming cup of coffee on her desk, accompanied by a note. The note read, "Life's just like a cup of coffee. It's all about how well you make it."

Glancing at Aditya's workspace, located just across from her own, Naaz couldn't help but smile before turning her attention to the design layouts scattered across her desk. She summoned her team, which included Sana, Kabir, and Hardik.

"Guys, please, let's avoid writing captions that lack genuine belief. Instead of spending so much time scouring the internet for such captions, if we put in a bit more effort to think creatively, I'm sure we can come up with something better. We're not here to merely copy and paste. Where's the originality?" Naaz advised her team as they gathered around her desk.

With a marker in hand, she scribbled a message on a whiteboard: 'Ctrl + Alt + Del; control yourself from copying; alter your thoughts; delete the fear of failure.' Setting the marker aside, she continued, "Please, pay close attention, follow this advice, and give your minds a fresh start. I believe we can generate a far better idea than this. Come on, team, let's give it another shot."

Aayaan strolled past her cabin and gave her a thumbs-up, to which Naaz responded with a warm smile.

"Alright, let's give it another go," Sana chimed in enthusiastically.

The team nodded in agreement and exited her cabin. Along the way, Hardik complimented Naaz. "By the way, the Ctrl + Alt + Del analogy was clever," he remarked.

Kabir, on the other hand, couldn't hide his frustration. "Honestly, anyone can occupy a chair handed out by Aditya

Thakur and preach like this. Do you really think a Creative Director gets promoted solely on talent within a year? Especially with zero experience? Meanwhile, we've been slogging in this field for a decade."

Sana interjected, "Kabir, please, don't blame Naaz for this. The decision came from the management, and while she may lack experience, let's not doubt her talent. After all, the agency's most prestigious campaign, 'India... By Nature,' was Naaz's brainchild."

Kabir sneered, "That so-called inexperienced intern's idea? Is that what you're calling a campaign? Ridiculous!"

Hardik chimed in, "But Kabir, that campaign was the only entry submitted for 'Campaign of the Year!'"

Kabir waved off the comment with a dismissive shrug. "Come on, buddy, we got the nomination solely because of the agency's reputation. Don't read too much into it."

Here it must be noted that it woukd be hard to judge a person like Naaz based on her brief presence in this chapter. To know about her one has to be aware of her life before she, Naazneen Qureshi, became the Creative Director at Jupiter Incorporations

In the meant time she caught sight of Mr. Madhab Thakur, the CEO of Jupiter, waving her over from his cabin. With a curious anticipation, she stepped into Madhab's office and he informed her of an impending announcement.

– 02 –

With a warm smile, Naaz nodded and exited her cabin. As she descended the staircase, she was joined by Aditya Thakur, the Deputy Managing Director, and CEO Madhab Thakur.

Aditya and Naaz positioned themselves beside Madhab as he addressed the entire office. Madhab cleared his throat before making the exciting announcement, "Hey everyone, I've got some fantastic news for you all! Jupiter has once again clinched the Campaign of the Year Award! Our 'India by Nature' campaign did it. And that's not all; we've also secured the Indian Tourism account! I want to extend my special thanks to Naaz and her team. Outstanding job, Naaz. This achievement is the result of your relentless hard work and dedication. Keep it up, and stay tuned for a special bonus."

Smiles erupted across the faces of the staff, and they cheered in jubilation. Madhab acknowledged their enthusiasm with a nod and continued, "Addi and Naaz, please come to my office. Everyone else, enjoy the celebration."

The employees dispersed to their respective workstations, while Aditya and Naaz followed Madhab to his office.

Seated behind his desk, Madhab gestured for them to sit. "Please, have a seat, both of you. I wanted to personally congratulate you both. This was a prestigious campaign for Jupiter, and you delivered."

"Thank you, sir," Naaz replied with a smile. "But I must say, I had an exceptional team, a conducive work environment, and, most importantly, strong support from the management, especially from Addi. Without him, achieving this milestone in just a year and a half would have been nearly impossible."

Aditya blushed modestly when Naaz mentioned his name in front of his father. He glanced at her and humbly responded, "I didn't do much, really."

Madhab chimed in, expressing his pride in Aditya. "I'm proud of you, Beta, for discovering this exceptional talent for Jupiter. I'd like to throw a party in celebration of this accomplishment, and I want the two of you to arrange it for tonight. Invite everyone to join us."

Aditya and Naaz nodded in agreement before rising from their seats and leaving Madhab's office. They exchanged a glance and then proceeded to their respective offices to carry out the task at hand.

– 03 –

As the evening draped the city in twilight, the rooftop of the Jupiter Incorporation building became a canvas for celebration. Aayaan, bearing a radiant smile, approached Naaz to extend his heartfelt congratulations, effectively kick starting the festivities.

As the hours waned on, Naaz found herself encircled by friends and colleagues, the jovial spirit of the party becoming palpable. Though offered drinks, Naaz graciously declined, her attention soon captured by the arrival of Aditya and Madhab, who sauntered into the gathering. All eyes turned towards the pair, with Aditya's gaze magnetically drawn to Naaz.

While other guests gathered around Madhab, Aditya manoeuvred through the crowd to reach Naaz. A warm embrace was shared, and Aditya offered her a drink. Naaz accepted it with a smile, and the affection between them was apparent to all; Aditya was undoubtedly the love of her life. Their proximity didn't escape the notice of the staff and Madhab, yet it remained unspoken.

United by their shared desire to celebrate both their professional achievement and their year-long relationship, Aditya and Naaz decided to leave the party. They retreated to Aditya's cabin, where they cherished not only their career success but also the bond they shared. As the evening grew late, Naaz became aware of the hour, prompting Aditya to offer her a ride home.

Before parting, they shared a tender kiss, and Aditya, his eyes locked on Naaz, expressed his love, saying, "Good night, and once again, thank you for everything. Love you."

Naaz returned his gaze with equal affection. "Good night. Love you!" she replied.

– 04 –

Naaz's steps were measured as she unlocked the gate and entered quietly. She made her way to her room but was met by Irshad, who inquired about her dinner plans.

Naaz regarded Irshad with a contemplative gaze and replied, "I'll keep it in the fridge."

Irshad, his tone tinged with mockery, quipped, "Why bother? After working tirelessly, you must be exhausted. I'll handle it."

A trace of frustration crossed Naaz's expression as she retorted, "You should know by now that beating around the bush doesn't work with me. What's bothering you? Is it because I'm late? Because I dined out? Or..."

Naaz's gaze was fixed intently on Irshad, who offered an impatient response. "You're drunk!" he declared. "You work is just an excuse. What is that you really want?"

Naaz rolled her eyes and sighed. "You're getting to the point now, aren't you? But you've misunderstood me. Challenging you or undermining you isn't my life's mission. I have a mind of my own, and I live life on my terms. If that bothers you so much, I can leave this house. After all, it's yours. Everything belongs to you. And one more thing, I'm not a habitual drinker, nor do I have a particular inclination for it. It was merely a social occasion, and I can quit it whenever I wish. But can you change your habits?"

Irshad observed Naaz with curiosity and annoyance, retorting, "What habits? What are you talking about?"

Naaz waved her hand dismissively."The habit of imposing your opinions on others," she replied, her tone casual. "The habit of believing you're always right and everyone else is wrong. Can you give it up? Not in this lifetime. Reflect on that. Good night."

With that, Naaz turned on her heel and made her way to her room.

Irshad, who stood stunned, frozen in disbelief, watched her leave. "You don't know what you're saying. May God forgive you," he muttered under his breath.

– 05 –

Naaz reclined in her cozy living room was sharing a moment with her mother, Shahin. The tedium of the day had compelled her to seize her mother's diary. With a mischievous glint in her eye, she recited one of Shahin's poetic verses aloud.

"Woh jo dard ka sama hota hai... Har shakhs is main fanah hota hai. Kaise keh dete hain unhe haal-e-dil. Suna hai zamane me har koi bewafa hota hai."

"Wow, Mom, that's amazing!"

Shahin's cheeks tinted with embarrassment as she chided, "Naaz, give me back my diary. Reading other people's diaries without permission is hardly mannered."

In response, Naaz rolled her eyes playfully. "Manners, Mom, aren't really my strong suit. As for this diary, Ammi Jaan, I have no less right on them as you have. But tell me, why is it that your diary is always filled with melancholic verses? Why not something cheerful or light hearted?"

Shahin paused thoughtfully before responding, "I don't know, darling. I simply pen down what I feel, what I hear, what I learn. And if you fancy light-hearted poems, why not read jokes instead of poetry?"

Unsatisfied with her mother's reply, Naaz leaned closer, curiosity dancing in her eyes. "No, I don't want jokes. I want to hear something you've written, aside from themes of 'betrayal, loneliness, and unfaithfulness.' Quickly, share one before 'Hitler' makes an appearance."

Aware of Naaz's nickname for her father, Shahin pointed out, "Who talks about their dad like this?"

Naaz nodded nonchalantly. "Well, there's no harm in calling 'Hitler' a 'Hitler.'"

"You don't even know how much he loves you. How much he worries about you," Shahin replied in a desperate attempt to defend her husband

But Naaz remained unperturbed. "I've never seen it."

Shahin persevered, "Perhaps his way of expressing it doesn't align with yours. Everyone has a different way of showing love, but he truly loves you."

Not particularly interested in her father's affection, Naaz redirected the conversation. She turned to her mother and asked, "And what about you?"

With a warm smile, Shahin recited a touching shayari.

"Choti si hai Zindagi Khushi se jiyo, Gam main kya rakkha hai. Maze se sar utha ke jiyo, Udasi kya cheez hai, bas muskura ke jiyo. Apne liye na sahi, Apno ke liye jiyo."

Naaz's eyes widened as she heard the shayari. She smiled and exclaimed, "Whoa! Mom, that's amazing. But it's not in your diary."

Shahin smiled back. "Because I haven't written it in the diary yet."

Impressed, Naaz marvelled in disbelief. "So, you composed it just now? My goodness, Mom, you're incredibly talented."

Realizing that she had indulged in lengthy conversation, Shahin remembered her husband would soon return home. She promptly got up and headed to the kitchen. "Enough playful banter, my spirited daughter," she said. "Now, let me attend to the kitchen; your dad will be back soon, and there's still much to do."

Naaz chuckled lightly, watching her mother go about her business.

– 06 –

After a few minutes, Naaz heard a knock on the door. Initially, she assumed her mother would handle it, so she lazily stretched out on her bed. However, as the knocking grew insistent, Naaz realized it was Radha Masi at the door, arriving promptly at 9 a.m, and jolted out of her languor.

Greeting Radha Masi with an affectionate smile, she said, "Good morning, Radha Mausi."

Radha didn't bother with morning greetings; instead, she inquired, "Another argument between the daughter and father last night, I presume?"

Naaz looked at her quizzically. "How did you know?"

Radha placed the breakfast on the table and explained, "I've been part of this household for years. I'm acquainted with every nook and cranny. Both of you skipped dinner last night, and this morning, no sign of either of you. He must be sitting at Mr. Kohli's house for sure. I still can't fathom what the issue is between you two. And what's with this enmity with food, dear? If you don't want to eat, you should at least inform me in advance."

"Apologies, Radha Masi," Naaz replied with an air of innocence. "There was a sudden office party arranged yesterday, so I had to go. But I'm clueless about why Dad skipped dinner."

Radha waved her hand dismissively. "Let it be; you wouldn't understand. Today's Sunday. Do you plan to have breakfast at home or dine out? Let me know in advance. Otherwise..."

Naaz glanced at Radha and said, "Yes, boss, I'm staying home today. You can plan as you wish, but please allow me a bit of rest."

Rolling her eyes, Radha exited Naaz's room. She knew that discussing these matters with Naaz was akin to talking to a wall.

Naaz emerged from the washroom, her Smartphone beckoning her with an array of unread messages. Her fingers danced across the screen, responding to Aditya's message before guiding herself towards the study table. There, nestled among the carefully arranged items, was a photograph of her mother, Shahin. She reached for it tenderly, her eyes drawn to the image as a wave of affection and nostalgia washed over her.

In the soft illumination of her study, Naaz found herself whispering, as though sharing her innermost thoughts with her mother's image. "Life, it's an intricate puzzle, Mother. Difficult to fathom," she murmured, her voice barely more than a sigh. "It was your deepest desire for me to pursue a career in the creative realm, to achieve something of significance. Yet, now, at 27, having accomplished just that, there's no one to share this achievement with. You're no longer here, and Father shows no interest in my work, much like he never appreciated your poetry. Lately, even Aayaan has been distant, behaving strangely, barely speaking. He, too, seems to have withdrawn. But it was Aayaan who re-entered my life, right after your sudden departure when I was shattered. He was my pillar of support. In terms of my success, however, there's no comparing Addi's contribution. The way he, a seasoned professional, believed in and supported a newcomer like me is beyond imagination. Besides, there's an emotional connection between us. Yet, I cannot discount Aayaan's role. If not for him, I might never have dared to dream of working at Jupiter."

– 07 –

Naaz reminisced about the time she was browsing handicrafts in Janakpuri, Delhi, when she was teased from behind. She whirled around in annoyance, her retort on the tip of her tongue, but her irritation dissipated when she saw Aayaan's familiar face. She greeted him with genuine surprise, "Aayaan, it's you? What a pleasant surprise! Where have you been all this time?"

Aayaan, sporting a warm smile, replied, "Yes, it has been quite a while, hasn't it?"

As Naaz engaged Aayaan in conversation, her curiosity piqued. "Indeed, but what kept you away for so long?"

Aayaan's gaze met hers as he casually explained, "After college, I ventured into various pursuits. On the advice of a cousin pursuing a PhD at the University of Fine Arts in Helsinki, I decided to attempt the entrance exam there. Miraculously, I secured a scholarship, spending the next three years in Finland before returning to work at Jupiter for the last two years."

The mention of Jupiter intrigued Naaz. "The renowned Jupiter? India's premier advertising agency?"

Aayaan gestured dismissively and remarked, "This idea of being 'top' is rather peculiar here. Everyone seems to fancy themselves as such. What's even more amusing is the excessive emphasis placed on degrees from foreign universities."

Naaz rolled her eyes, jesting, "True, but it certainly worked out for you, didn't it?"

Aayaan agreed, "Yes, it did. And you? You've vanished from Facebook and Instagram. What's going on?"

Naaz's demeanour shifted, her expression turning pensive. "I don't know, Aayaan. I feel lost. Completely lost."

Concern etched into his features, Aayaan probed further. "What are you talking about? That doesn't make sense. Let's find somewhere to sit and talk."

But Naaz disagreed, her mind wandering to the heavy loss she had endured. "No, Aayaan, you can't understand. No one can. When my mother passed away, I didn't realise the depth of my despair until months later. After the condolences and departures, I was left with the stark reality—I couldn't bear to be without her. I'd feel her presence everywhere in our home, hear her voice. Still do, in fact. It's unfathomable how someone so vibrant and full of life could simply be gone."

Aayaan's voice softened, sympathy in his eyes. "I can't imagine what you went through."

But Naaz's frustration simmered. "No, you can't. Its not possible. Do you know why my mother really left us? It wasn't just heart failure. She didn't want to live."

Aayaan was taken aback by her revelation. "What? Did your mother tell you this?"

Naaz responded, her words heavy with meaning, "Some things don't need to be said. Those close to your heart can be understood without words."

Concern etched deeper into Aayaan's expression. "But why didn't she want to live?"

Naaz scoffed, bitterness in her voice. "It's because of my father. He killed her, you know, emotionally. Year after year, he stifled her talents, her creativity, her emotions, making her nothing more than a puppet. Did you know how skilled my mother was at writing poetry? How incredibly talented? But my father never encouraged her. Why? Because he thought it was all nonsense. He didn't appreciate her interests and my mother paid the price. My father always imposed his views on others, perhaps thinking that poetry wasn't suitable for women. Cunningly, he labelled my mother as the 'perfect housewife,' suppressing her talents and dreams. Poetry was her life, but over time, bowing to my father's wishes and fulfilling her responsibilities, she left her passion behind—then eventually she left us forever. The day she was laid to rest, I made a promise. I swore never to forgive my father, and never to abandon her dreams. Since that day, this battle has raged within me. I tried everything, from meditation to medication. Nothing worked. Despite my mental state, I cleared the NSD exam and completed a Diploma in Dramatic Arts last year. But I still feel like I'm drowning in that abyss of depression. I'm sinking, and I don't know how to stop it."

Aayaan tried to offer solace, his voice gentle. "I may not fully understand, Naaz, but I can help. Counselling, a good job—those can be the answers. In fact, I think I can arrange both for you. My uncle is a renowned sports counsellor, associated with the Indian Archery Team. He can assist you. And why not join Jupiter?"

Naaz's eyes widened in disbelief, "Jupiter? Are you serious? I have no work experience; they don't hire freshers."

Aayaan's smile held a glimmer of hope. "I know your capabilities, Naaz. You're immensely talented. I'll personally speak to Aditya Thakur; he won't refuse. So, relax, it's all sorted."

Naaz couldn't help but return his smile. "How do you stay so composed, Aayaan? Why can't I be more like you?"

A playful twinkle lit up Aayaan's eyes as he quipped, "To be cool, you need to drink 'Amul Cool.' I know, it's a lame joke, but let's run with it. My throat's parched."

Naaz rolled her eyes, a sense of comfort enveloping her. "It's good to hear your famous lame jokes after all this time. Alright, no more, okay?"

Both shared a hearty laugh before making their way to a nearby Amul stall for lassi, relishing the rekindling of old memories.

As Naaz snapped back to the present, she couldn't help but reflect on Aayaan's significant role in her life. He had been her best friend, the one who shattered the barriers she had erected around men due to her father's indifferent nature. Aayaan had shown her that there were trustworthy men, friends who selflessly supported her, friends like him.

She delved into the memories of her first days at Jupiter, marked by moments when Aayaan accompanied her to the counselling sessions, where she felt she was conversing with a mirror—unjudged and understood. It was Aayaan who brought her to Jupiter for her interview. Naaz had given her all, aware of the tremendous opportunity at stake. When she learned of her selection, she couldn't believe it. Turning to Aayaan, disbelief in her eyes, she had received his confident, knowing smile, solidifying her faith in herself.

– 09 –

In her initial days at Jupiter the relationship with her father, however, remained strained, marked by frequent arguments, but Naaz had grown resilient to his attempts to stifle the women in his family. Meanwhile, Aditya and Naaz had grown closer at work. While initially discreet, it became evident to their colleagues that their relationship was more than just professional. Naaz, unburdened by the speculations, believed in pursuing what she valued. Aditya, in his own way, had transformed her life, teaching her the essence of love at a time when she had shunned the idea of it.

She remembered the first day of her job, Naaz arose promptly, her eagerness palpable as she meticulously readied herself in front of the mirror. She couldn't wait for the office driver to arrive at her doorstep.

After a brief interlude, Goutam, the driver assigned to Naaz, pulled up to her residence. As she stepped into the car, he greeted her with a courteous "Good morning, mad..." But before he could utter 'madam,' Naaz interjected, asserting, "Naazween Qureshi... You can call me Naaz."

Goutam offered a warm smile and responded, "I am Goutam Tripathi, and you can address me however you prefer. Didn't William Shakespeare once say, 'What is in a name?'"

Naaz chuckled softly and acknowledged, "Interesting."

Goutam nodded with a knowing grin and commented, "Delhi is an intriguing city, allowing even its residents to be fascinating. And when you step into Jupiter, you'll encounter an even more captivating cast of characters, my dear."

Naaz concurred with a nod, her curiosity piqued as she spotted a shayari adorning Goutam's car dashboard. She couldn't resist and inquired, "The shayari on your car's dashboard; who penned it?"

Goutam turned to examine the shayari, which read, "Zindegi ka safar toh ek haseen safar hai. Har kisi ko kisi na kisi ki talash hai. Kisi ke paas manzil hai toh Raah nehi, aur kisike pass raah hai toh manzil nahi."

A smile played on Naaz's lips as she complimented, "Wow, you have a knack for poetry."

Goutam's heart swelled with delight, elated that someone had acknowledged his poetry for the first time. He beamed and inquired, "Do you have an interest in poetry?"

For a fleeting moment, Naaz's thoughts drifted to her mother, and she paused before responding, "My mother used to write. She had a profound passion for it." As curiosity piqued, Naaz probed further, "But you didn't tell me whose poetry it is."

Goutam paused thoughtfully, a nostalgic smile gracing his face, and replied, "Oh... I told you, dear, what's in a name? I composed it in some bygone era."

Naaz appreciated his artistry and complimented, "Wow! That's remarkable. You write exceptionally well."

Goutam's mind briefly wandered back to his days of composing poetry, but he swiftly brushed aside those thoughts, stating, "I used to write, but not anymore. Anyway, let's put that behind us. We've arrived at our destination."

As Naaz gazed out of the car window, her eyes fell upon her workplace, and she inhaled deeply, remarking, "And I didn't even notice. What a delightful journey. I hope everything here is as enchanting!"

Goutam turned to face her, offering a reassuring smile, and said, "I shall keep my fingers crossed for that. All the best!"

Naaz returned his cheerful smile and quipped, "Merely uttering 'All the best' won't be enough to rid yourself of me. I'm going to pester you quite a bit. Goodbye... See you in the evening."

Stepping into her workplace, Naaz felt a touch of nervousness, but the presence of Aayaan instantly comforted her. He greeted her with a warm smile as she entered the office, introducing her to the rest of the staff. It was her first encounter with Aditya, and she sensed a flutter in her heart. Yet, she remained resolute in her determination to fulfil her mother's aspirations. She snapped back to reality and dedicated herself to relentless work for the company. Her dedication and tireless efforts did not go unnoticed, both among her colleagues and the management. Aditya, in particular, found her qualities appealing and her capacity to manage substantial tasks impressive.

One day, Aditya appointed her as the head of a significant project, with Aayaan as her subordinate, further bolstering her confidence in her career. The workplace transformed her into a wholly different person, transcending from a despondent teenager into a vibrant and exuberant individual.

While her father continued to harbour disapproval for her job and certain aspects of her life, Naaz was unfazed by his criticisms. She had become well-versed in recognising his tendency to suppress the women in his family. Concurrently, her relationship with Aditya progressed in the office, albeit discreetly at first. Though rumours swirled that they were becoming romantically involved, Naaz remained unperturbed. She was steadfast in pursuing her passions, and Aditya had a profound impact on her life, teaching her the true meaning of love at a time when she had dismissed the notion entirely.

– 10 –

The vivid memories seemed to fade away when Radha Mausi turned towards her and asked, "Shall I set the table? It's already late."

Naaz met Radha's gaze and responded by asking, "Have you seen dad since this morning?"

Worry crept into Radha's eyes as she responded, "That's exactly what I was about to ask. Where did he go? When will he be back? He didn't even have breakfast. Now, I don't even know if he'll have lunch."

Naaz nodded in agreement and pondered aloud, "He must have gone to Mr. Kohli's house. Or maybe...". Before Naaz could finish her sentence, Radha interrupted, "Why don't you call and tell that he is a grown up person, but still he hasn't lost the habit of worrying everyone. He should've just made a phone call." Naaz rolled her eyes in mild irritation but reached for her phone to dial Irshad Qureshi's friend and neighbour, Dr. Kohli.

As Dr. Kohli answered the call, Naaz greeted him, saying, "Hello, Kohli uncle, how are you?"

Kohli replied warmly, "All good, beta. What about you? How are things at work?"

Naaz got straight to the point. "All good, uncle," she replied. "Sorry, uncle, I just wanted to confirm: Is Dad with you?"

"Qureshi? No, he didn't come for our morning walk either. I thought it was Sunday, so maybe he's taking a rest. I even tried calling him around noon, but his phone was switched off. In fact, I was about to call you in a little while," Dr. Kohli replied.

Naaz paused for a moment. "That's strange!" she noted.

Concern laced Dr. Kohli's voice as he inquired, "Why? Hasn't he said anything? Has something happened?"

Naaz chose not to share her suspicions with Dr. Kohli and simply replied, "Not as such. Okay, I'll check... I will keep you updated. Bye, uncle."

As soon as the call ended, Radha queried with a childlike curiosity, "What happened? Where did he go?"

However, Naaz kept her thoughts to herself, her mind racing with negative possibilities. All she said to Radha was, "Just a minute, let me check."

Radha nodded, her concern evident, while Naaz attempted to call Irshad's number, but it was switched-off. In frustration, she rolled her eyes and decided to call her uncle, Ishmile Qureshi, Irshad's elder brother.

When Ishmile Qureshi answered the call, Naaz greeted him with the traditional "Asalam Walekum, Bade Chachu!"

"Walekum Salam!" Ishmile replied.

"Did Abbu come to your house?" Naaz inquired.

Ishmile responded casually, "No, he didn't! Why? What's the matter?"

Disappointed by the lack of leads, Naaz replied, "No, it's nothing like that. He left in the morning and hasn't returned yet. His phone is also switched off. So, I thought maybe he went to your place. Anyway, I'll check; maybe he went to some other friend's house. Alright, Uncle? Is everyone doing well?"

"Allah ka shukr... Everything is fine," Ishmile cheerfully shared. "Muddashar has come on vacation from Canada. And by Allah's grace, Saba is going to become a mother again."

"That's great news, Uncle. I'll call you later with an update," Naaz responded.

Ishmile couldn't help but feel disappointed by Naaz's curt tone, expecting her to at least offer congratulations to Saba. He asked, "Has Nimmi Mausi been informed?"

"Nimmi Mausi is currently in Dubai. Anyway, I'll let you know. Goodbye," Naaz replied.

"Allah Hafiz!" Ishmile bid her farewell.

"Allah Hafiz!" Naaz echoed before ending the call.

Growing increasingly anxious, Naaz tried Aditya's phone number several times, but it remained 'out of reach. Frustration etched across her face, she decided to leave a voicemail. Her next call was to Aayaan.

As soon as Aayaan answered the call, Naaz plunged into the heart of the matter.

"Aayaan, listen. Dad left home this morning, and it's 5:30 now. He hasn't returned yet, and his phone is also switched off," Naaz said, her tone panicked.

"Did you talk to him this morning?" Aayaan inquired in his calm voice.

" I was sleeping at that time. There was a minor argument last night, but that's become a part of our daily lives. I don't think it's related."

"All right! Hang on; I will be there in half an hour. Let's go looking for him."

As Naaz bit her nails, consumed by worry, she asked, "But where? Dad doesn't go out much, and I've already checked all the usual places." Aayaan's calm tone remained unwavering as he suggested, "Then we need to inform the local police station."

As anxiety gnawed at Naaz, she felt responsible for her father's disappearance, her mind brimming with fear and uncertainty. She could only wait with bated breath for Aayaan's arrival.

– 11 –

Irshad emerged from his home in the early hours of the morning, his weariness mirrored in the depths of his eyes. But more striking than his fatigue was the pain etched across his face. He embarked on a journey devoid of purpose, his steps carrying him to a solitary destination—a graveyard. There, he lingered for an extended moment, seemingly lost in contemplation amidst the silence of the resting souls.

Resuming his aimless march, Irshad found himself navigating the bustling thoroughfare of Chandni Chowk. His searching gaze darted from one direction to another until it landed upon a sullen-looking man. In an unspoken exchange, their eyes met, and without hesitation, Irshad began trailing the enigmatic figure. Soon, they both entered a shedy printing press, where Irshad initiated a terse interaction with the press owner.

With an air of urgency, he handed over a plain white packet, receiving another in return. As they conversed, Irshad gleaned information that seemed to hold significance for him. Eventually, he exited the establishment and headed towards the grandeur of Jama Masjid. There, he discreetly stowed away his newly acquired possession and assumed a serene posture to engage in Namaz. Completing his prayers, he resumed his solitary expedition through the labyrinthine streets of the city.

– 12 –

Unbeknownst to Irshad, Naaz's anxiety had reached its zenith, compelling her to seek help from the local police station, accompanied by Aayaan. Her father's actions had set a chain of events in motion, of which he remained blissfully unaware.

The sub-inspector ushered Naaz into a weathered wooden chair, its creak echoed through the modest police station office. He observed her with a practised yet empathetic gaze, coaxing her to divulge the details of her distress. Retrieving a pen, he poised it over a well-worn notepad, prepared to document her account meticulously.

"What name should we associate with the missing individual, madam?" he inquired, his voice was measured. Without hesitation, Naaz responded, her tone imbued with urgency, "Irshad Qureshi." The sub-inspector maintained his composed demeanour as he proceeded with his inquiry, extracting essential particulars to aid in the search.

"His age, if you please?" he asked.

"66 years."

"And his occupation?"

"He's a retired IAS officer, Delhi Cadre."

"When did Mr. Qureshi disappear?"

"He's been missing since morning."

A moment of contemplative silence hung in the air as the sub-inspector digested the provided information. He exhaled audibly before addressing Naaz with a reassuring tone. "I understand your concern, ma'am. But it has not been even 12 hours since his absence was noted. Have you attempted to contact his friends or relatives in the vicinity?"

Naaz shook her head despondently, her voice tinged with frustration. "We've reached out to everyone we could think of. He seldom ventures out, which makes his sudden absence all the more perplexing. Furthermore, his mobile phone is switched off."

The sub-inspector nodded in understanding, sympathetically regarding Naaz. "Please share his mobile number with me. While I may not be able to file a missing person report immediately, I will expedite our efforts to locate him, considering his distinguished background. In the interim, I advise you and your companions stay at home. Let us exercise a bit more patience; we will explore all avenues to resolve this situation."

With those words, he turned his attention to his assistant, Panday, issuing a swift directive. "Panday, fetch the list of accidents for today."

Returning his focus to Naaz, the sub-inspector took a step further to ensure her peace of mind. "Now, madam, kindly take note of my personal mobile number. Send me a message on WhatsApp from your number, and I shall promptly respond."

Aayaan, who had been standing by Naaz's side, seized the opportunity to intervene. "I'll note it down?" he said. The sub-inspector turned his scrutiny towards Aayaan, briefly assessing the newcomer.

Aayaan, unfazed, introduced himself confidently. "I am Aayaan Malik, a colleague of hers from the office." Satisfied with Aayaan's explanation, the sub-inspector offered his contact details for further assistance. "Very well, Mr. Malik. Please record this number: 9910937813." Aayaan complied, typing the digits into his phone with a nod of gratitude. "Thank you, sir."

With their mission at the police station concluded, Naaz and Aayaan silently exited the premises, their unspoken concern for Irshad Qureshi hanging heavily in the air.

– 13 –

Naaz's impatience simmered as she pressed the doorbell, her gaze focused on Radha Mausi, who answered the door with an embarrassed expression. Stepping inside, Naaz's eyes quickly sought out Irshad, who was calmly engrossed in watching television. A mixture of relief and irritation washed over her upon seeing him.

Without hesitation, she marched towards him, her tone stern as she confronted him. "When did you return?" she asked.

Irshad turned his gaze towards Naaz, puzzled by her intensity."Just a little while ago. Why?"

Naaz's voice remained firm as she questioned him further. "Where were you?"

Irshad hesitated, his eyes avoiding hers as he replied nonchalantly. "I had some work."

Her temper flaring, Naaz blocked his view of the television, demanding an explanation. "Yes, that's exactly what I want to know. Was that work so important that you had to keep your phone off all day? Couldn't you have informed someone earlier?"

Irshad finally met Naaz's gaze, his expression blank as he explained, "Last night, I wasn't in a state to say anything. And as for the phone being off, I forgot to charge it last night. When I realized it, it had already run out of battery."

Frustration welled up within Naaz as she vented her exasperation. "Wow! Wonderful. Do you have any idea how much trouble your absent-mindedness can cause others? No, you don't, because you always think about yourself. Understanding someone else's feelings or troubles is beyond you. You are just so full of yourself."

With that, Naaz turned away from Irshad, addressing Radha and Aayaan. "Radha Mausi, please go home. It's getting late," she said. "And sorry, Aayaan, for all the trouble." Aayaan attempted to intervene, his eyes pleading with Naaz to calm down. "Come on, Naaz," he urged. Turning to Irshad, Aayaan inquired about his well-being. "Uncle, are you okay?"

Before Irshad could respond, Naaz interrupted, her frustration unabated, "Oh, he is perfectly fine. Can't you see how peacefully he's sitting and watching TV? Why would he be worried? Are we not here to worry?

Though her words were harsh, Aayaan discerned a trace of concern hidden beneath Naaz's anger. He rolled his eyes at Naaz, making a final attempt to soothe her. "Come on, Naaz. Everything is okay now. Please calm down. I'm leaving," he said.

Naaz glanced at him, her expression remaining unyielding as she made a request. "Please do me one last favour," she said, her tone soft. "When you leave, call the sub-inspector and tell him that everything is fine now. I feel very embarrassed."

"Don't worry, I will do that," Aayaan assured. "Please take care of yourself. Uncle, you also relax a bit. Radha Mausi, come with me. I'll drop you off."

"No, beta... I'll go on my own."

"Come on, Mausi. Come with me. Good night, Naaz. Good night, Uncle."

Irshad remained seated in silence, while Naaz replied with forced politeness, "Good night. See you."

As Aayaan and Radha left, Naaz stormed into her room, slamming the door behind her.

Frustration seeped into Naaz's voice as she muttered, "Disgusting. Simply disgusting." She tossed her belongings onto the bed, her irritation mounting. It was then that she noticed Aditya's call flashing on her phone screen.

Reluctantly, Naaz answered the call on the fourth ring, her silence speaking volumes. Aditya's voice, tinged with concern, immediately filled the line. "Hey Naaz, what happened?" he asked.

Naaz responded with a blank tone, her emotions a whirlwind, "Nothing."

Aditya hesitated for a moment before pressing further, "What 'nothing'? You texted me that your father is missing!"

"You were also missing for the whole day!" Naaz replied, her eyes rolling heavenward.

"I was just sleeping, so I switched off my phone," Aditya explained, his tone casual.

Naaz couldn't conceal her exasperation. "That's great. Some people go out without charging their phones; some go to sleep during the day with their phones turned off; and some are needlessly worrying about these people. Funny."

Aditya struggled to grasp the connection between her words and his own actions, his voice filled with puzzlement. "But what's the connection between my sleep and theirs? What are you talking about?"

Sighing, Naaz clarified, "Nothing... Papa hadn't been at home since this morning. His phone was also switched off when I tried calling, so I was worried, and that's why I called you. Anyway, after causing me a lot of worry, he has finally come back home and is probably sleeping in his room now. You should go back to sleep too, and let me get some rest as well. It's been quite hectic. I'm not in the mood right now. Sorry, I'll catch you later. Good night."

"Hey, bye... Good night. Take care!" Aditya replied, his tone caring.

– 14 –

Months passed and Naaz found herself immersed in a load of work. One such ordinary day as she was seated in her office chair, gazing around the familiar workspace. A sudden ring of her phone broke her meditative state. As she casually checked the inbox, she found an impending text. It was the result of her recent pregenancy test, and it was positive.

Naaz got engulfed in a peculiar sense of ennui. After the demise of her mother she had to face innumerable challenges to assert her existance. But once she joined Jupiter and could explore her true potentials that is when life has started being benevolent to her, showering success now and then. Infact even the news of her pregnancy felt dreamlike to her.

She couldn't feel at ease until she shared her excitement with Aditya. Little did she know by then that dreams are ephemeral. Not only was Aditya uncomfortable with the news but he immediately he seeked for his father's advice. This was followed by the expected turn of events, when Madhav Thakur expressed his views by stating that there was no other option but to abort. To Naaz's utter surprise Aditya agreed to his father's decision.

Though she felt humiliated and defeated, it didn't stop her to calmy write her rignation letter and pack her things from the office. She realized that the shelf life of this beautiful dream which constituted Aditya and Jupiter was destined to be short. By that time she had found in herself the strength to face harsh realities of the world without any hesitation

As Naaz began packing her belongings, Aayaan entered her cabin, concern etched on his face. "Are you resigning for official reasons or something personal?" he inquired.

Naaz responded with a weary sigh, "What difference does it make?"

"What do you mean, 'What difference does it make?' Is something serious going on?" Aayaan pressed further.

Naaz'a answer remained vague, "Maybe... maybe not... I don't know. I really don't know. But one thing is for sure: I don't want to stay here. They don't deserve me, but I deserve better. Emotional fools like me should end up like this, there is no doubt. I completely deserve it."

Worried by Naaz'a cryptic response, Aayaan fixed his gaze on her and implored, "Naaz, are you okay?"

Naaz offered no immediate reply, choosing instead to ask for a solemn favour, "Will you do me one last favour? Just one last... Can you help me find a girls' PG?"

Perplexed, Aayaan probed further, "A PG? But why?"

Without hesitation, Naaz responded, "I need a place to stay alone. I have to leave my home, and it has to be quick. Please..."

Concerned Aayaan questioned her, "Have you lost your mind? You're quitting your job, thinking of leaving your home... What's wrong?"

Naaz, in a tone laced with resignation, quipped, "Be thankful ... I'm not leaving this world."

Aayaan nodded solemnly and conceded, "Alright, you don't have to explain anything now. Take your time and try to calm down."

Naaz gazed at him with a mixture of innocence and gratitude, whispering, "Aayaan, I'm sorry. Please..."

Aayaan softened, assuring her, "It's okay. I'll catch you later. Take care of yourself. Goodbye."

As Aayaan exited the cabin. Naaz's emotions overwhelmed her, and she silently broke down. After a few minutes, she wiped away her tears, cast one final glance around the office, and left Jupiter Incorporation. Curious eyes within the office followed her as she carried her belongings in a box. Goutam, noticing her presence near the left corridor, hurried over to assist her, taking the box from her hands.

"Thank you, Goutam bhai," Naaz expressed her gratitude.

Goutam regarded her with a touch of sadness and inquired, "Are you really resigning?"

Naaz nodded solemnly, confirming, "Yes."

He further inquired, "So, from tomorrow?"

With a resigned sigh, Naaz answered, "I'll be on vacation."

Goutam hopped into his car and glanced at Naaz, "Shall we?"

In agreement, Naaz entered the vehicle, and as they drove towards her home, she couldn't help but ponder aloud, "Goutam bhai, do you believe in destiny or karma?"

Goutam let out a sigh, revealing his inner thoughts, "I used to believe in destiny initially. When I started writing lyrics, I thought destiny would favour me. I aspired to become a lyricist. In Mumbai, I had a friend in the music industry, a genuine guy with good connections. We arrived in Mumbai with a handful of poems. We met a few music directors, and some of them liked my lyrics. I thought my hard work would finally pay off."

With curiosity piqued, Naaz prodded, "And then?"

Goutam's voice held a hint of bitterness as he continued, "And then, I waited. I kept making trips to that music director's office, but one day, I saw a music video on TV with lyrics slightly modified from my poems. Within days, I came across a couple more songs with the same fate. I understood..."

Sympathetic, Naaz inquired further, "What about your friend?"

Goutam nodded, his eyes filled with disappointment, "I couldn't find him. He had probably vanished after making money from selling my work."

Curious, Naaz probed, "And the music director? Did you confront them?"

Goutam heaved a deep breath and explained, "They knew I couldn't do anything to them. But what they didn't know was that I had no intention of doing anything. If they had asked me for the lyrics before stealing them, I would have gladly shared. The poetry resides within me. I didn't desire to profit from someone else's theft; a little respect would have sufficed."

As Naaz absorbed the story, she exclaimed, "But that's deceitful! They betrayed your trust."

Goutam nodded in agreement. "Well, dear, I may not be highly educated, just a simple driver. But I believe it's better to deceive oneself than to cheat or betray someone else's trust. Because then, you don't bear the weight of guilt. I find contentment in knowing I've done no wrong. Whatever they did, that's their problem, not mine. After that incident, I decided not to solely rely on destiny.

The poetry still resides within me, but now I write only for myself and work for my family. So, for now, I believe in karma."

Their conversation continued as they reached Naaz's home. She offered a warm smile and thanked Goutam, "Thank you, Goutam bhai. You've shared something profound during our conversation. If I haven't done anything wrong, why should I be concerned about those who have wronged me? I shouldn't carry the burden of guilt. When someone else did wrong it is their problem. Thanks again, Goutam bhai. Take care of yourself and continue writing. Goodbye."

– 15 –

With a sense of finality, Naaz stepped out of the car and made her way into her home. She placed her belongings on her bed and, within moments, heard a knock on her door. She opened it to find Radha Mausi standing, a warm smile on her face.

Radha Mausi's surprise was evident as she found Naaz at home earlier than usual. "Beta, you came early today?" she asked. "Yes," Naaz replied, a gentle smile gracing her lips.

"I was preparing food. Should I make some for you too? I've just cooked some piping hot aloo parathas," Radha offered warmly.

"Yes, alright!" Naaz responded, though her thoughts seemed to be elsewhere.

Noticing her unusual behaviour, Radha furrowed her brow. "Alright, freshen up then. I'll set the table in the meantime."

"You can leave the food on the table and go," Naaz shrugged. "It'll take me a little while."

Accepting her request, Radha nodded. "Alright, but please eat while it's still warm."

A short while later, Naaz and Irshad found themselves seated at the dining table, about to eat their meal. Naaz hesitated for a moment before speaking, "I want to talk to you about something."

Irshad continued eating but acknowledged her with a soft, "Hmm..."

Taking a deep breath, Naaz bravely confessed, "I've been in a relationship with Aditya Thakur, a colleague from the office, for the past year."

Irshad paused mid-bite, his gaze shifting to Naaz as he inquired, "The son of the owner of your company?"

Naaz nodded and continued, "Yes, we were very close to each other."

Irshad's shock was palpable as he sought clarification, " 'We were' means?"

Taking a moment to compose herself, Naaz closed her eyes briefly and stated, "I am pregnant!"

Irshad's eating came to an abrupt halt. He sat there in silence for a moment, then slowly asked, "Do I have to talk to them?"

Naaz nodded resolutely and explained, "I've already spoken to them. Aditya and his father both suggested for an abortion. But I won't do it. So, I ended the relationship and left the organization."

The room fell into a heavy silence as Irshad continued to stare at her, his disbelief evident. Breaking the silence, Naaz pressed on, "I've decided to raise this baby as a single mother. Do you have any objections?"

Irshad, still wearing a look of dismay, set his plate aside, rose from the dining table, and retreated to his room. Naaz sat there in the quiet aftermath, her thoughts racing.

As the moments ticked by, it became apparent to Naaz that she was resolute in her decision to keep the baby. She felt the need to reach out to a friend for support. Picking up her phone, she dialed Sana's number.

"Hey, Sana. It's Naaz," she said when Sana answered, her concern evident due to the late hour of the call. "I apologise for reaching out so late."

Sana reassured her, "No apologies needed, Naaz. Just tell me, what's going on?"

After a brief pause, Naaz confided, "Can I stay at your apartment for a few days? Just for a little while."

Sana's voice was filled with immediate concern as she responded, "Of course, anytime you need. Do you want to come over now? Should I come to pick you up?"

A sigh of relief escaped Naaz's lips as she responded, "Not now. Tomorrow morning. I'll let you know. Thank you, Sana."

Before ending the call, Sana asked with heartfelt care, "Naaz, I won't pry, but are you alright?"

Naaz's response was unguarded and authentic, "No, I am not."

With that, Naaz concluded the call and lay on her bed, her mind consumed by the tumultuous events of the day.

As dawn's light gently seeped through the curtains, Naaz began the solemn task of packing her belongings into a large suitcase. Her heart weighed heavy with the gravity of the situation that lay before her. With each folded piece of clothing, she mentally steeled herself for the uncertain future that awaited her.

As she carefully folded a dress, the insistent ringing of her phone interrupted her thoughts. Aditya's name flashed on the screen. A surge of irritation coursed through her, but she reluctantly answered the call.

"Why are you calling? What's your problem?" Naaz's voice held a hint of annoyance. Aditya, on the other end, took a deep breath before speaking. "Naaz, please, try to understand. Dad is right. We're not ready for this responsibility. You've got a promising career ahead, and this decision could ruin everything."

Naaz's reply was sharp and unforgiving, "You should've thought about that before our night together."

She paused briefly, her words laced with bitterness, "When you lack the courage to stand by your choices, perhaps next time, discuss it with your father before sleeping with someone else."

Aditya's voice grew heated, "You're crossing the line now, Naaz."

Naaz interrupted him, her tone resolute, "No, I'm not. I have no intention of causing trouble for you or your family. I've already left your life and your father's organisation. My principles forbid me from committing sins, but they also give me the strength to make my own choices. And my choice is this: I'm keeping the baby. Don't call me again or offer your suggestions. You're nothing but an opportunist. Be happy and stay out of my life."

With that, Naaz ended the call and blocked Aditya's number. A solitary tear rolled down her cheek as she crumbled under the weight of her emotions.

– 16 –

The rhythmic knocking of Radha Mausi on her door pulled her out of her misery. Through her sobs, Naaz instructed, "Radha Mausi, please place breakfast on the dining table. I'll eat it later."

But the knock persisted, irritating Naaz further. "What is it?" she snapped.

Naaz hastily wiped her tears and turned to face the door, only to be greeted by a sight that left her in disbelief. Irshad stood before her, bearing breakfast.

Irshad looked at her tenderly and asked, "Have you thought of a name for the child?"

Naaz's heart swelled with a mix of emotions. She rushed into Irshad's arms, much like the first time they had met. With a joyous smile, she met his gaze. Irshad patted her shoulder and said, "I'll ask Kohli Uncle to come tomorrow. He'll conduct weekly check-ups from now on. Have you informed Ayaan?" Naaz shook her head.

You should let him know," Irshad gently suggested. "Give me Ayaan's phone number; I'll call him."

Tears of gratitude welled up in Naaz's eyes as she whispered, "Thank you, Abbu."

Irshad nodded, his smile conveying reassurance. "Have your breakfast and take some rest. I'll be back soon."

With Irshad's departure, Naaz let the tears she had held back for so long flow freely. Meanwhile, Irshad made a call to his friend Kohli, arranging a visit for the evening.

Kohli agreed readily but questioned, "What's happened, Irshad?"

Irshad shot a sharp exhale and replied, "I'll explain when you get here. We need a check-up for Naaz."

Kohli's voice took on a serious tone. "Why? What's wrong with Naaz?"

Irshad uttered the unexpected news. "She's pregnant."

Kohli was taken aback, his response swift, "What? Alright, I'll be there in the evening."

With that call done, Irshad dialled Aayaan's number. As he relayed the situation, Aayaan's voice held calm determination, "Uncle, don't worry. I'll be there in the evening."

Irshad heaved a sigh of relief, "Thank you, Beta. Naaz needs you."

The next evening, the soft amber hues of twilight cast a warm glow over Irshad's quaint home. Dr. Kohli had arrived for a visit, and his comforting presence filled the air with a sense of reassurance. A cool breeze rustled through the leaves of the nearby trees, carrying with it a hint of jasmine blossoms through the windows.

As Dr. Kohli concluded his check-up on Naaz, a gentle smile graced his face. "Everything looks perfectly fine. No need to worry. Please bring her to my clinic tomorrow for a formal ultrasound. By God's grace, she'll give birth to a healthy baby within the next six months."

Meanwhile, Aayaan had also made his way to the house. When Irshad spotted him, a warm smile broke across his face. He greeted Aayaan with a nod and said, "Alhamdulillah, Aayaan, you've arrived just in time. Naaz is in her room. Go ahead, have a chat with her. I'll join you after Dr. Kohli leaves."

Aayaan acknowledged with a gracious smile and proceeded to enter Naaz's room. As he stepped inside, he couldn't resist a playful tease, "Well, well, what do we have here? I always thought you were a bit slow in matters of love, but it seems you're quite quick on your feet, eh?"

Naaz responded with a faint smile, "You've found an opportunity to tease me, haven't you? If your intention is to annoy me, you might as well leave."

Aayaan chuckled and countered, "I won't abandon you, Naaz. Without you, I have no place to go. I'll live and die by your side."

Naaz, though attempting to stay stern, couldn't help but laugh, "Is that so? Literally, live and die?"

Aayaan nodded with a grin, "Absolutely."

With their playful banter, they decided to head out for a meal. "Come on, let's go grab some chaat," Aayaan suggested.

Naaz smiled, "You know me too well. Chaat it is. Your manipulation skills are unmatched."

Aayaan winked. "I try my best."

They left the room, and Aayaan informed Irshad of their plans, "Uncle, I'm taking Madam out for some chaat."

Irshad agreed with a warm smile, "Of course, take care."

As they made their way to the car, Naaz gazed out of the window and sighed with relief, "It feels good to get out. I've been feeling suffocated for the past two days. Now, I feel a bit better."

Aayaan reassured her, "Don't worry; everything will be fine."

Naaz reflected, "I don't know what the future holds, but whatever I may have lost, or will lose, it's worth it. I've never seen my father like this. To see him like this, I'd endure a thousand breakups."

Aayaan playfully teased, "A thousand, really?"

Naaz chuckled, "Alright, maybe not a thousand. Park the car here; I want some ice cream first."

Aayaan grinned, "Ice cream before chaat? Unusual, but alright."

As they savoured their ice creams, Naaz couldn't resist teasing Aayaan as his ice cream started to melt. Their playful banter continued as they headed to their next destination, a chaat vendor. Naaz found the chaat a bit too spicy this time, and Aayaan took the opportunity to pull her leg in this context.

After their outing, Aayaan drove Naaz back home. The evening had brought a sense of normalcy and relief in her.

– 17 –

Meanwhile, on the verandah, Irshad and Dr. Kohli enjoyed a quiet moment over cups of tea. Their conversation was accompanied by the soothing chirping of crickets. Irshad's attention was drawn to a newcomer – his brother, Ishmile Qureshi.

Rising from his seat, Irshad warmly welcomed him, "Come, Bhai Saab. You've arrived quite unexpectedly. If you had called, I would have come to pick you up."

Ishmile's expression was less than cordial as he replied with frustration, "When has your daughter ever given me the chance to call? If it were up to me, I would have come last night."

Dr. Kohli, sensing tension, made a move to leave. Irshad, however, urged him to stay, saying, "Oh, Doctor, please stay. You've just arrived."

Ishmile's anger simmered as he questioned Irshad, "Do you discuss family matters in front of outsiders?"

Irshad maintained his calm and responded, "Dr. Kohli is practically family. You can speak freely."

Dr. Kohli tried to interject, but Irshad held up a hand, insisting, "Doctor, please."

Turning towards the kitchen, Irshad instructed, "Radha, bring some tea."

Ishmile rolled his eyes and bitterly remarked, "Fine, if you have no shame discussing this in front of outsiders, why should I?"

Irshad was quick to retort, "Shame? For what?"

"You've certainly become quite modern, haven't you?" Ishmile scoffed.

Irshad waved his hand dismissively, "Is that why you came here?"

"Yes, I came to tell you that because of your daughter's actions and what she's about to do, our family and community will be shamed," Ishmile replied, his tone sharp as ice. "It's best you put an end to this sin and get an abortion done to spare us this disgrace."

Dr. Kohli couldn't remain silent any longer, "What are you saying?"

Ishmile turned a stern gaze upon him. "Please, let us handle our family matters," he shot back.

Irshad, unfazed by Ishmile's words, responded calmly, "Bhai Saab, which family are you referring to? The family that never inquired about Naaz's well-being after her mother passed away? The family that never attempted to bridge the gap between Naaz and me? I've followed your guidance all these years, but have you ever truly engaged with Naaz?"

As the conversation continued, Naaz, along with Radha, secretly eavesdropped on the exchange, listening to the family's long-held grievances and unspoken tensions.

The amber hues of twilight painted a tranquil scene outside Irshad's cozy home as tensions flared within. Dr. Kohli had just completed his examination of Naaz, and the calming rustle of leaves filled the air. Inside, Irshad found himself engaged in a heated dispute with his elder brother, Ishmile Qureshi. The two were locked in a battle of words, their voices echoing through the room.

In his mind he could picture the poignant memory, one that had long stayed with him. It was a day when Shahin, his beloved wife, lay on their bed, and he sat at her side. Her gaze held a sweet innocence as she inquired, "Did you speak to the doctor? What did he say? How much time do I have?"

Irshad's heart ached as he recalled the pain in her eyes. He replied, though with a stern façade, "What do you mean, how much time? The doctor didn't say anything like that. You'll be completely fine."

A faint smile graced Shahin's lips as she gently chided him, "You're not very good at telling lies, my love. Why even try? I'm not worried. I've led a good life. But I worry about Naaz and you. You two are so different from each other, good in your own ways, but different. My greatest task in life has been caring for both of you. And now, in the midst of..."

Irshad halted, struggling to find words. "Are you suggesting that because of us, you've sacrificed your greatest joy?" he questioned.

Shahin responded with a calm resolve, "What sacrifice, my dear? I cherished nothing more than cooking and nourishing you with my own hands. You loved to eat, and I loved to feed you. Naaz, like you, requires a variety of dishes daily. If I'm not here, both of you will struggle with your meals."

Irshad acknowledged her words with a nod, his eyes revealing his confusion. "But you know what I'm talking about—the poetry," he pressed.

Shahin's smile remained gentle as she replied, "Then why ask? You should already know."

Irshad was puzzled. "Me?" he questioned in disbelief.

Shahin sighed, her gaze unwavering. "Look, I have no complaints about my life or about you," she reassured him. "In our 25 years together, I've received immense respect and companionship."

Irshad, however, couldn't hold back his own insecurities. "Perhaps not love," he confessed, his eyes reflecting his pain.

Shahin took his hand gently, her touch reassuring. "That's not true," she said softly. "Everyone has their own way of expressing emotions. You may not express love in the same way, but it doesn't mean you don't love us. You love Naaz and me deeply in your own way. Love is understood even when it's not spoken. That's why fulfilling your requests didn't trouble me."

Irshad remained puzzled. "My request?" he asked.

Shahin clarified, "I knew that in our society, married women don't typically write the kind of poetry I do. People would talk, and you, being an IAS officer, respected in society and your work, earned so much regard. So, when Ishmile Bhaisaab hinted that you didn't approve of my poetry, I understood." Her voice held a note of resignation. "Perhaps he didn't like it either. But I didn't want to confront you about it. Maybe you..."

Irshad couldn't believe his ears. "Oh, Allah," he whispered, his grief palpable as he looked at Shahin.

She gazed at him, her eyes filled with unspoken understanding. "There's something I need to share," she continued. "Naaz will forge her path in life, and though I don't know what she'll choose, I can tell you that she's a very creative-minded girl. She'll excel in any creative field with your support. Times are changing, aren't they? So, take care of yourself and your thoughts."

Grievously Irshad nodded, a sense of guilt weighing on him. "I've made a grave mistake," he admitted. "I should have asked you about this long ago. Allah, what a misunderstanding! Shahin, nothing will happen to you. Please, if you leave us, we'll all fall apart. Naaz, everyone... if you go!"

Shahin, with a hint of sadness, recited a poem, "Na koi kisi se door hota hai. Na koi kisi ke karib hota hai. Woh khud hi chalke aa jaata hai, Jo jiska nasib hota hai."

Irshad's panic set in as he shouted, "Shahin!... Doctor, doctor..."

As Irshad snapped back to reality, he turned to Ishmile and exclaimed, "Do you understand the ramifications of your baseless beliefs and futile attempts to suppress Shahin's emotions? Along with Shahin, my daughter has distanced herself from me."

Irshad's breath came in heavy gasps, and he continued, "Shahin never allowed me to understand, and I became entangled in my work. I should have questioned this matter much earlier. I thought that nurturing Naaz had perhaps extinguished her desire for poetry. But I was wrong. In truth, you stifled her most beautiful dream because of her belief in you, in me, and in this family. A misunderstanding has shattered everything. I have often contemplated confronting you about this, but by then, my life had unravelled. The burden of your lie still weighs heavily upon me today. Your false accusation created such a chasm, that I have still not been able to bridge it, neither has my daughter."

Ishmile glared at Irshad, his frustration palpable as he demanded, "Why bring up old matters now? What does your daughter have to do with all this?"

Irshad nodded, his voice unwavering. "There's a connection, only one. If that day we hadn't blindly trusted our traditions and way of life, then both Shahin and her poetry would have thrived. But this mistake won't be repeated. Naaz has decided to bring this child into the world, and, Inshallah, the child will be born. And you spoke of sin, did you not? If you believe Naaz made a mistake, then tell me what her mistake was. She trusted someone, didn't she? Someone took advantage of her trust. Go to any mosque, shrine, religious school, holy man, sage, or fakir, and inquire about who committed the sin. If you find evidence, return; if not, goodbye."

Ishmile regarded Irshad with dismay, questioning, "Are you throwing me out of your house?"

Irshad nodded firmly, resolute in his decision. "You are my elder brother, and I am giving you a chance to cleanse your conscience. Only then should you attempt to establish a relationship with Naaz and her child. Otherwise, these days, people even wish Eid Mubarak over the phone."

Dr. Kohli, sensing that Irshad's emotions was reaching their peak, tried to intervene. "Qureshi, calm down. Please, have a seat."

Irshad, however, gestured towards Ishmile and asserted, "No, Doctor, today I want to share this not only with him but also with myself and everyone else. I have unwavering faith in my daughter and her choices. I am proud of my daughter Naaz. You know the meaning of Naaz, don't you, Bhaijaan? 'Proud.' I am proud of my daughter."

Ishmile didn't linger for a moment after Irshad poured out his emotions. As he exited the house, Radha emerged with a glass of water, offering it to Irshad. Meanwhile, Naaz, who had overheard the entire conversation, stood in stunned silence. Tears welled up, but she concealed her emotions from the others.

− 18 −

Months drifted by, and the impending moment of Naaz's delivery drew near. Radha, wearing a loving smile, meticulously prepared nutritious meals for Naaz. She knew the paramount importance of Naaz's well-being during this period. Yet, Naaz frequently pushed her plate aside, her face a portrait of stubbornness, consistently resisting Radha's offerings of wholesome food. Undaunted, Radha Mausi persisted, coaxing and gently encouraging Naaz to take each bite. Slowly but surely, Naaz began to notice subtle changes in her body.

Whenever waves of nausea struck, Irshad was quick to rush to her side, his face etched with concern. Meanwhile, Aayaan adopted the role of the family's resident jester. He spun tales, cracked jokes, and shared humorous anecdotes, all in an effort to bring a fleeting smile to Naaz's face, if only for a moment. Dr. Kohli continued to showcase the baby's movements during ultrasound scans, each time revealing the tiny life stirring within Naaz, her eyes would fill with wonder and love at the sight.

On the other hand, Aditya's attempts to contact Naaz remained futile, a source of constant disappointment. Madhab noticed Aditya's growing desperation and urged him to endure the emotional turmoil.

In contrast, Irshad, with gentle care, accompanied Naaz to the dining table. There, they shared quiet dinners that spoke volumes about their deepening connection. Radha and Aayaan watched with a sense of relief, reassured by the family's growing unity. Naaz, in the meantime, felt nothing but loved.

One morning, as Naaz approached Irshad, she inquired, "Why did you give Radha Mausi the day off today?"

Irshad glanced at her, a twinkle of mischief in his eyes. "Who told you? Radha?"

Naaz nodded, her voice tinged with curiosity. "Of course, I spoke to her this morning."

Irshad paused for a moment before explaining, "Well, I was thinking..."

However, their conversation was interrupted by Aayaan's sudden arrival. Naaz casts a quizzical glance at him, remarking, "Oh, you? This early?"

Irshad interjected, "I called him."

Naaz's confusion deepened as she questioned, "What's going on here? I can't make any sense of it. Are you okay?"

Irshad nodded and reassured her, "No, no. I was thinking that you've been cooped up indoors for a while, and the delivery date is approaching. I don't know much about these things, so I asked Aayaan to take you shopping for the bacchi. Baby products, feeding bottles, toys, and, what's it called? A cot, I think. There must be more. Aayaan might have some ideas."

Naaz shifted her gaze to Aayaan, inquiring, "Aayaan?"

Irshad nodded and continued, "Yes, Aayaan might have some idea about what else is needed. Right, Aayaan?"

Aayaan stood there, slightly embarrassed, and mumbled, "Yes, of course."

Naaz fixed her gaze on Irshad, probing further, "And why did you refer to it as 'bacchi'? How do you know if it's a boy or a girl?"

Irshad beamed and replied confidently, "I'm 100% sure about that."

Naaz snapped, "But how can you be so sure? Did Kohli uncle say something?"

Irshad shook his head, disagreeing, and chuckled, "Do you think I have the guts to ask him about this?"

"Then?" Naaz inquired.

"Experience. Years of experience. You won't understand," Irshad responded, taking a moment to smile.

Naaz rolled her eyes and retorted, "Experience? As far as I know, you became a father only once, so how are you talking about years of experience?"

Irshad gazed at her lovingly and said, "It will be a daughter, and I've already chosen a name. Combining your mother's and your name, Shahnaaz."

Naaz paused, her eyes softening, and cautioned, "The name is lovely, but don't set your hopes too high. Anything can happen. Don't over think it."

Irshad nodded and replied, "I'm saying the same thing – that you shouldn't over think either. Go out for a while, shop, watch a movie, and then come back in the evening. It'll be good. You'll see."

Naaz looked at Aayaan, casting him a questioning glance. "Why are you getting involved with him and wasting your day?" she asked, her tone pointed. "Don't you have to go to the office?"

Aayaan sighed and explained, "How long can one stay cooped up in a cage? I'm a free bird now!"

Naaz's curiosity was piqued as she probed further, asking, "What do you mean?"

Aayaan replied vaguely, "I'm doing freelance work now. It's simple. I've got a lot of offers coming in. Let's see."

Naaz stared at him, her eyes searching, and pressed on, "And Jupiter?"

"I left that a long time ago," Aayaan revealed with a sigh.

Silence hung in the air for a moment before Naaz broke it, demanding, "When? After I resigned?"

Aayaan attempted to divert the conversation, suggesting, "Let's sit down and talk about this when we are back?"

"You're avoiding my question, aren't you?" Naaz persisted.

Aayaan met her gaze squarely and proposed, "Shall we go then? Or..."

Naaz rolled her eyes and conceded, "I'm coming... in 5 minutes. God knows what you two are up to."

"Don't worry, uncle. I'll take good care of her," Aayaan chuckled and reassured Irshad.

Irshad smiled, acknowledging Aayaan's words. "I know."

On their way, in the car, Naaz got consumed by her thoughts. She was awestruck to find out that her father has given Radha Mausi a leave while insisting Aayaa to take her out for shopping. She had never seen her Abbu like this before, to her he seemed to have gotten twentyfive years younger. None of his actions align with his nature, atleast the one known to Naaz since her childhood.

As Aayaan and Naaz entered the mall, their eyes landed on a shop named "Mother Care," brimming with an array of baby products. Aayaan's eyes sparkled with excitement as he began selecting various baby items. Naaz, however, shook her head and declined his enthusiastic suggestions. Aayaan responded with a playful eye roll, determined to have his way. Eventually, Naaz relented and picked out a few baby toys and clothing items. She knew Aayaan wouldn't easily yield to her stubbornness. After making their selections, they settled into a restaurant for lunch.

Aayaan excused himself briefly, returning with two movie tickets and a mischievous glint in his eye. Naaz, slightly irritated by his impromptu decision, sighed but reluctantly agreed to go along with the plan.

Throughout the movie, Aayaan made a valiant effort to lift her spirits. However, traces of annoyance still flickered in her eyes. As soon as the movie concluded, Naaz turned to Aayaan and expressed her desire to return home, unaware that another surprise awaited her.

Meanwhile, Irshad received a substantial package from a delivery person and placed it in his room. His curiosity piqued, he uncovered an old trunk and discovered a dusty notebook hidden within. Irshad regarded it with a fond smile, gently brushing off the dust. He lovingly traced the words inscribed on the notebook before carefully reading them. He then collected fresh vegetables from the refrigerator and proceeded to the kitchen. Yet he couldn't resist the allure of the package, so he momentarily left the kitchen to investigate further. Inside the box, he found another packet. Realising he was running out of time to prepare dinner, Irshad left the package in his room and returned to the kitchen. Following the instructions contained within the aged notebook, he prepared the meal with great care.

– 19 –

Some time later, Naaz and Aayaan returned home. As Naaz stepped inside, she felt a peculiar sensation wash over her. It was challenging to articulate, but it was something familiar, something lost—like a distant memory. The surroundings seemed subtly altered, as though they had been redecorated. A distinct fragrance permeated a dimly lit room, evoking a sense of nostalgia.

Moments later, Irshad emerged from the room, reciting, "Intezaar to bahut tha humein; Lekin aaye na woh kabhi. Ham toh bin bulaaye hi aa jaate, Agar hota unhe bhi Intezaar kabhi."

Naaz stood there, stunned to hear her mother's shayari. Her eyes glistened with lost memories as she said, "Abbu, this is Ammi's... But this book?"

Irshad smiled warmly and explained, "It's your mother's. It just took a while for it to get published. She had aspired to publish her book one day. But for now, freshen up, you two. I'll set the table."

Naaz looked at him curiously, asking, "Dinner... But, You..."

Irshad interjected, urging them to freshen up, "Come quickly!"

Naaz nodded and cradled the book in her hands. She read the title, "Ankahi," before making her way to her room.

As Naaz and Aayaan entered the dining room, they were greeted by a table laden with a sumptuous feast. Naaz looked at the spread in amazement and commented, "So many dishes, Abbu? Why didn't you order from outside?"

Irshad nodded and replied, "First, let's eat."

Naaz took a bite and exclaimed, "Oh, this is Ammi's recipe! The same taste, Abbu, you..."

Irshad nodded, acknowledging her delight, and confessed, "I borrowed the recipe from Ammi's book. If she were here, the Godh Bharai wouldn't have been so simple?"

"My God Bharai couldn't have been better than this," Naaz admitted, a tear glistening in her eye.

"Uncle, if this is just the first copy of the recipe, we can only imagine how the original would have tasted!" Aayaan looked at Irshad and quipped. "By the way, your Godh Bharai gift is still pending..." he added, turning his attention to Naaz

"You can still give it to me," Naaz interjected.

After savouring a mouthful, Aayaan inquired, "Now... how?"

Naaz offered a playful smile and proposed, "By reciting a cheesy, budget sher."

Irshad interjected, "Aayaan, my boy, I don't know if I can give this book away, but for now, you can keep one."

Aayaan waved his hand dismissively, stating, "Oh, forget about that, uncle. Just let me post it on my page once. I guarantee 1,000 copies from my side."

Irshad was taken aback. He looked at Aayaan in astonishment and asked, "A thousand copies... from a page? What page would that be?"

Aayaan grinned and brushed off the question, saying, "Don't worry about it, uncle. It's no big deal. But could you share another shayari by Aunty? Naaz never told me how skilled you are at reciting poetry."

Naaz turned to Irshad with a hopeful expression, urging, "Please, Abbu."

Irshad opened the book and recited, "Udaas hoon par tujhse naraaz nahi, tere dil main hi hoon par tere pass nahi. Jhoot kahu toh sab kuch hai mere pass. Sach kahu toh ek tere siwa kuch bhi khass nahi."

Naaz and Aayaan sat there, their hearts touched and their souls enchanted as they listened to Irshad's heartfelt recitation of Shahin's shayari.

In the days that ensued, they stumbled upon the cover of another book, bearing the title "Tanhai."

– 20 –

Within two months, the long-awaited day arrived when Naaz's life was poised for a transformation. Whether it was Irshad Qureshi's prediction or destiny Naaz gave birth to a beautiful baby girl. She embraced the infant and welcomed Shahnaaz into the world. Dr. Kohli took care of all the hospital formalities and escorted them home, shielding the old man from the anxiety of hospital stay. It was a momentous occasion. Aayaan and the new mother returned home with her precious daughter. When the grandfather laid eyes on his granddaughter for the first time, he cradled her gently in his arms, and in that embrace, a torrent of emotions swept over him, drowning out the cries of everyone else in the house. The years of distance and estrangement evaporated in an instant.

This was the instance when Naaz realized the profound truth about the fact that her most coveted Advertising Award seem to have fallen pale in comparison to this immaculate sensation of being a mother. All of a sudden, she is overwhelmed with gratitude, to have friend like Aayaan by her side is like a blessing. But above all when she witnessed her Abbu embracing the role of her Ammi as soon as he laid eyes on his granddaughter. She felt that her heart's desire was fulfilled.

It all started with Naaz's labour pains intensifying, as she clung to Aayaan's hand for support. The pain was excruciating, but

Aayaan's unwavering presence provided her with the strength to endure.

Irshad, upon hearing Naaz's cries of pain, was filled with panic. Aayaan rushed Naaz to the hospital, leaving the old man behind to shield him from the mounting anxiety. In the meantime, Irshad contacted Dr. Kohli, relaying Naaz's condition. Dr. Kohli's reassuring words served as a balm to Irshad's frayed nerves, assuring him that they were well-prepared to handle the situation.

Time passed, and Naaz eventually gave birth to a beautiful baby girl, and a profound sense of relief washed over her. The cries of the newborn resonated in the room, announcing her arrival. The nurse gently placed the baby in Naaz's arms, and tears of joy streamed down her face. Aayaan, too, was overwhelmed with emotions as he gazed at the two most important people in his life.

Dr. Kohli wasted no time in sharing the delightful news with Irshad. Irshad's heart was racing with anticipation when he answered the phone, and an immense smile graced his face as he absorbed the doctor's words.

Radha, who had been waiting anxiously for news, couldn't contain her curiosity any longer. "What's happened?" she inquired.

Irshad beamed with joy as he shared the wonderful news with Radha. A wave of relief swept over her, prompting her to pray and offer her heartfelt blessings. Irshad, on the other hand, headed to the prayer room to express his gratitude through namaz.

Meanwhile, Aayaan took charge of all the necessary discharge formalities at the hospital, ensuring that Naaz and their precious newborn daughter were ready to return home. He drove them back home, his heart brimming with happiness.

As they crossed the threshold of their home, Radha rushed to Naaz and showered her with blessings and affection. Naaz, with a serene smile, moved towards Irshad, who finally held his granddaughter in his arms, a flood of emotions washing over him. Irshad couldn't help but be transported back in time, reliving the same overwhelming emotions he had experienced nearly 28 years ago when he first held Naaz in his arms. His eyes welled up with tears of joy as he cradled Naaz again, and they wept together, their tears a testament to the immense love and enduring strength of their family.

The Kahete Papa

– 01 –

As the sun dipped below the horizon, casting an amber glow over Merlion Park in Singapore, the city burst into life, ablaze with the dazzling spectacle of neon lights. The towering skyscrapers, their glass exteriors creates a canvas for the vibrant evening hues, stood as majestic sentinels against the darkening sky.

Meanwhile, nestled within the opulent confines of the Presidential Suite at the Shangri-La Hotel, Singapore, Rajvir Mehta, a distinguished man of fifty, exuded an aura of self-assuredness. He stood before a gathering of Japanese investors, his local ally and friend, Patel, at his side. With each meticulously articulated point in his presentation, Patel offered a nod of assurance, enhancing Rajvir's conviction.

Finally, Rajvir paused, drawing a measured breath, and declared, "Ladies and gentlemen, this is my master plan, and I can assure you, as investors, that within a year, your investment will be repaid, with AUTO TECH INC. offering you a 30% share of our profits as a sweetener."

The investors exchanged contemplative glances, their thoughts conveyed in their silent interactions. It was the lady translator who eventually spoke. "Mr. Mehta, we appreciate your effort and the merits of your presentation. However, as you may be aware, the automotive sector is currently grappling with inflation."

Rajvir nodded gravely, his gaze unwavering. He replied, "Ma'am, I firmly believe this plan will succeed. All I request is your trust and support."

The translator relayed the response, "Very well, Mr. Mehta. Give us a few days to deliberate."

Rajvir accepted their decision with a nod, his anticipation palpable. As the investors rose to their feet, they adhered to customary Japanese etiquette, bowing respectfully before filing out one by one. Rajvir, though inwardly disappointed, maintained his composure. He extended his hand to the translator and offered a gracious, "I appreciate your consideration, ma'am. Thank you."

The translator, Akio, returned a final bow and offered a warm smile before departing.

With the room now empty, Patel approached Rajvir, his hand resting comfortingly on Rajvir's shoulder. "Don't lose heart, Raj! I'm confident they'll come around. And remember, we still have one more meeting. Hope can work wonders."

Rajvir sighed, his distress apparent. "Patel bhai, we've already had four meetings, and these were our most significant potential investors. This was the meeting I'd held the most hope for. I can't fathom why they need more time to decide. The last investor on our list isn't in good financial health either. I've checked his status; it's unlikely to work out. We need to explore other avenues. Nevertheless, thank you for your support. You've made a valiant effort when even close ones have deserted."

Patel nodded with understanding. "Raj, we're not just friends; we're family. Family doesn't require thanks. By the way, how is your father? I heard he's unwell."

Rajvir's expression grew somber. "Lung cancer. Likely in the third or fourth stage, he's undergoing chemotherapy." Concern etched on his face, Patel inquired, "In Kochi?"

Rajvir confirmed with a weary nod, "Yes."

"Why don't you get him over to UK? It has excellent facilities," Patel suggested.

Rajvir's gaze turned distant for a moment, and then he replied, "I wish that was possible. But let it be. I think you're getting late. Thank you again for your concern and support." Patel waved off the gratitude with a dismissive gesture. "Anything for you, brother. And no formality—dinner at my place tomorrow. It's settled."

Rajvir offered a warm smile. "Why be so formal?". Patel's tone brooked no argument. "No, you're being formal. I'm not asking; I'm telling. Tomorrow, sharp at 6:30 in the evening. Goodbye."

After Patel's departure, Rajvir found solace in the hotel's balcony. The cool breeze caressed his face as he closed his eyes, releasing a deep sigh. Retrieving a cigarette from his pocket, he lit it and took a long drag.

– 02 –

As he exhaled a plume of smoke, his mind was awash with worries. He tried to push them aside but found himself ruminating about him being Rajvir Mehta, the proprietor of Auto Tech Incorporation in the UK. Once who used to be a renowned player in the automobile parts trading industry in the UK and European markets. Unfortunately, Auto Tech has, over the past years faced substantial challenges. So his company is grappling with a severe liquidity crisis, exacerbated by fierce competition from Chinese companies offering lower prices. If this persists for a few more months, the bank may seize his villa in Manchester, and his family, consisting his wife and two children, could find themselves on the streets. For the first time in over two decades he is finding himself to have to rely on others so that he can salvage his company and safeguard the family's future.

Lost in his anxious thoughts, Rajvir's phone suddenly rang. He took a deep breath and answered, "Disha."

On the other end of the line, Disha stood outside the ICU of Kochi City Hospital, her grip on the phone betraying her anxiety. "Hi! I'm sorry to disturb you, but I think you should come here immediately."

Rajvir's voice trailed off as he inquired, "Did Dr. Parera...?". Disha's response was direct, her tone laden with gravity. "He asked me to call you."

Rajvir, though well aware of the implications, couldn't help but hope. "Can we seek a second opinion from another doctor?". Disha's reply was tinged with resignation. "Raj, he's on his deathbed now. It's your decision."

Rajvir turned his gaze to the sky, his eyes closed. He asked, "Alright. How much time does he have?"

Disha's response was terse. "I don't know. Goodbye." She hung up.

Left alone with his thoughts, Rajvir pondered for a few moments before reaching out to Patel. "I need to go to Kochi. Please arrange a ticket and initiate the e-visa process immediately. Also, cancel my Manchester flight. My father's condition has deteriorated."

Patel responded with genuine sympathy, "I'm sorry to hear that."

"While I'm away, can you manage things here?" Rajvir inquired.

"Don't worry. They haven't declined yet. We'll receive an update in 1-2 days," Patel reassured.

"I'll return as soon as I assess the situation at home," Rajvir declared.

"Agreed. I'll arrange your ticket," Patel confirmed before ending the call.

Taking a deep breath, Rajvir called his wife, Shalini, only to have their daughter, Bhavana, answer the phone. "Hey, sweetheart! Are you at home? Where's Aavesh?" Rajvir inquired.

Bhavana's response was light hearted. "Aavesh is in his gaming room with his friends. Mom and I went shopping today. When are you coming back?". Rajvir's tone grew somber. "Very soon, sweetheart. Where's Mom?"

Shalini took over the conversation. "Hi. Are you done for the day?"

Rajvir wasted no time in conveying the gravity of the situation. "Listen, Dad's condition has suddenly worsened. I need to go to India."

Shalini's concern was evident in her voice. "Oh God! How is he doing right now?". "I don't know exactly," Rajvir admitted, his uncertainty palpable. "But it must be serious. Apparently, Dr. Parera has given up."

Shalini offered words of comfort. "It's okay, Raj. He'll recover soon. Dad is mentally very strong. Don't worry." Rajvir nodded, hope mingling with his anxiety. "I hope so. I'll call you once I get there. Alright, I'm leaving for the airport."

"Take care. Keep me posted. Love you!" Shalini's voice conveyed her love and concern. "I love you too. Bye," Rajvir replied before ending the call.

As he prepared to depart for Kochi, Rajvir found himself consumed by a whirlwind of emotions, knowing that the next few days would be critical for both his family and his business.

Rajvir reclined on the plush lobby sofa, his fingers dancing across the screen of his phone. With a tap, he composed a message to Disha, "Arriving tomorrow morning," and gently closed his eyes. His intention was to find solace in the quietude of the moment, to clear his cluttered thoughts. However, tranquillity remained elusive as his mind was abruptly inundated by a tide of memories from his early days in Manchester—a moment etched vividly in his heart.

In his head, Rajvir found himself standing within a quaint phone booth, the scent of nostalgia clinging to its walls. The booth was dimly lit, and its wooden frame bore the marks of countless conversations. His fingers fumbled for change as he inserted coins into the coin slot.

"Hello," Gayatri, his mother, answered the call on the other end, her voice a warm embrace over the miles.

A smile played on Rajvir's lips, his tone imbued with a playful air. "Mom, are you cooking a pamphlet today? I swear, I can smell it even in Manchester!". A soft chuckle escaped Gayatri's lips. "You always had that nose, beta. You know it's Friday, and I've been preparing it for you and your father for years now. How much longer do you expect me to wait? You promised to come this month."

Rajvir's heart swelled with affection. "Maa, I called to share some wonderful news. I've landed a job at Ford." There was a pause on the other end, and Gayatri's voice held a tinge of concern. "You can work here as well, can't you?"

Meanwhile, Shalini stood by the door, her eyes conveying a sense of urgency as she silently urged Rajvir to wrap up the call.

Rajvir gently raised a finger, a silent request to Shalini for an additional minute to finish his conversation. He turned his focus back to the call, his voice reassuring. "Maa, trust me. Just let Dad know about the job at Ford. He'll understand everything. Okay, I really have to go now. I promise I'll call you again soon. Love you, Maa. Bye!"

"But..." Gayatri's plea was left hanging, her words fading away as Rajvir decisively ended the call. Stepping out of the phone booth, he embraced Shalini, a tender moment of shared understanding between them.

The night had fallen like a soft velvet curtain when Rajvir stepped to aboard the plane. Weariness washed over him as he found his seat, and he surrendered to the comforting embrace of slumber as the plane ascended into the dark expanse of the night sky. Hours passed in tranquil repose, and as dawn broke, casting a gentle glow, the aircraft descended gracefully onto the runway at Kochi Airport.

In the quiet of the morning light, Rajvir stirred from his deep sleep. His eyelids fluttered open, momentarily struggling to adjust to the newfound brightness. Rubbing the sleep from his eyes, he gathered his belongings and embarked on the journey through the airport's corridors.

– 03 –

Stepping out into the open, his gaze alighted upon a young man of twenty-three, Junior, who held a placard bearing Rajvir's name. With unwavering patience, Junior awaited his arrival.

Still groggy from his nap, Rajvir called out to him, "Hey, Junior?". A warm smile gracing his face, Junior rushed forward to relieve Rajvir of his backpack. "Ji, Bhaiya!". A smile played upon Rajvir's lips, his weariness momentarily forgotten. "How's Dad doing?" he inquired.

Junior nodded as he assisted Rajvir with his luggage. "Bhaiya, would you prefer to go home or straight to the hospital?"

"Hospital," Rajvir replied, his gaze meandering out of the car window. The lush landscapes of Kochi unfolded before him; their beauty heightened by the morning sunlight that streamed through the glass.

As they drove further, Junior ventured, "It's been twenty years since you last visited Kochi. How does it feel to be back?" A fond smile graced Rajvir's lips, and he leaned back in his seat. "Not twenty, Junior, but twenty-one. Let's do something—turn off the AC and roll down the window."

Junior obliged, and the cool breeze of Kochi enveloped them, carrying with it a rush of memories from Rajvir's youth. With a sense of nostalgia, he began to revisit the days of his youth.

In those days it was his father who owned 'Mehta Auto Service Centre', it was Kochi's oldest automobile workshop. Mr. Mehta was quite a competent automobile engeneer. Though he was not holder of a full fleged degree but did his diploma. Nevertheless he possessed an innate understanding of the cars. And this fact earned him the nickname of 'Doctor Saab' among the locals. It was a testament to his skills as the Car Doctor.

Infact Rajvir himself grew up surrounded by cars, both imported as well as exported. Each having its own unique story. His father could effortlessly diagnose and mend the most stubborn engines. There were times when he wouldnt even charge his customers. Though his approach of running the business was admiral, garnering him praise, but according to his son he was never interested in the path of prosperity. Whereas Rajvir craved for prosperity and wanted to climb up the ladder of automobile business. So instead of returning to India after completing his Master's Degree, he decided to work for 'Ford'. After working there for five years he started his own Company.

Minutes passed, and the car came to a halt, its blaring horn jolting Rajvir from his reverie. Junior informed him, "Bhaiya, we've arrived at the hospital."

Rajvir nodded, alighting from the vehicle and heading toward the hospital entrance. There, he found Disha, her demeanour heavy with concern. "Any updates?" Rajvir inquired.

Disha shook her head somberly. "No change. He's asleep right now."

Peering through the glass wall of the ICU, Rajvir caught sight of his eighty-year-old father, Avinash Mehta, lying still on the bed. With a deep sigh, he turned to Disha. "The visiting hours are from four to six, right? I'll come back in the evening. You should go home; I'm sure Aunty is waiting for you. Thank you for being here."

Disha nodded and offered a supportive smile. "You're welcome. Take some rest; you must be exhausted." Rajvir agreed with a nod. "I'll do that. See you in the evening. Bye."

On the journey home, Rajvir couldn't help but stare out of the car window, eagerly anticipating their arrival. The car eventually came to a stop, and Junior stepped out to retrieve Rajvir's luggage. The prodigal son stood there for a moment; his gaze fixed upon his childhood home. Ringing the doorbell, he was met by Kamla, and just beyond her, he could see Gayatri.

In a reflexive motion, Gayatri embraced him tightly, her eyes moist with tears. "Raaj, Beta, you've come! Disha told me you had gone to the hospital. Have you spoken to your dad?"

"He was asleep," Rajvir replied, his voice tinged with emotion. "I'll visit him again in the evening."

Gayatri's eyes were filled with concern as she scrutinized her son. "You've arrived at the right time. Who knows if anyone would have cared if you would have come any later. But enough of that for now, let me prepare some food. You go freshen up."

Rajvir's gaze shifted to Kamla, and Gayatri, following his glance, introduced her. "This is Kamla; she's new here." She turned to Kamla and asked her to start preparing for the meal.

Rajvir continued to survey his surroundings as he basked in the familiarity of home. Quietly, he admired the walls adorned with photographs, each frame holding cherished memories. He ventured into Avinash's room, drawn to a box containing miniature cars on the table.

Reaching for one of the cars, Rajvir's lips curved into a gentle smile as he revisited a time when he was just a ten-year-old boy. Memories flooded his mind as he placed the miniature car back into the box, each moment etched with love and nostalgia.

– 04 –

Returning to the present, Rajvir gently replaced the car and picked up a photo frame from the table. He gazed at it with a myriad of emotions coursing through him. The space seemed to echo with the laughter and joy of yesteryears.

Gayatri entered the room, her eyes reflecting a mixture of sadness and understanding. She gazed at the photograph in Rajvir's hands and remarked, "Your father used to look at these pictures with the same eyes. Perhaps through these pictures, he conveyed his love. But a picture is just a picture; it remains in a corner somewhere. I don't know what has come between you two. These pictures seem to speak more than you do with each other."

Rajvir stood silently, meeting his mother's gaze. She looked at him tenderly and urged, "Go take a quick shower. I'm preparing breakfast."

Rajvir nodded, and Gayatri left the room, leaving behind a sense of warmth and nostalgia.

In the soft, warm glow of the evening, Rajvir entered the hospital once again, this time accompanied by Disha. Together, they made their way to Dr. Parera's cabin, where he awaited them, reviewing Avinash's reports.

Dr. Parera, a seasoned physician with a hint of exhaustion in his eyes, greeted them. "Raj, let's get straight to the point," he began sombrely. "The reports aren't promising. I'm sure you're aware it's lung cancer, and it has advanced to the final stage. In this situation, you do have the option to continue with treatment, but realistically, it won't make a significant difference. It might be better to take him home, where he can spend quality time with his family before..."

Rajvir nodded gravely, his voice heavy with concern. "But, Doctor, are you absolutely sure? I mean...". Dr. Parera's gaze bore into him, the weight of years of medical experience in his words. "Consider his age, Raj. Chemotherapy at this stage would only prolong his suffering. As a doctor myself, I would advise you to bring him home and let him spend his remaining days with his loved ones, rather than in the sterile confines of the hospital. Your presence here means the world to him now."

Rajvir lowered his head, deep in thought. Finally, he nodded and asked, "May I see him?". The doctor nodded, offering a reassuring smile. "Of course, but keep the conversation light."

As Rajvir entered the ICU, his gaze fell upon Avinash, reclined on the bed, eyes dimmed by the ordeal but brightening as he spotted his son's familiar face. A smile played on his lips as he spoke in a soft, raspy voice, "Ah, Engineer Sahab! You finally made it, didn't you?"

Rajvir returned the smile with affection. "Yes, Doctor Sahab, I had to come. How are you feeling?"

Avinash playfully rolled his eyes and quipped, "Can't you see? They've tied me to this bed against my will."

Rajvir chuckled softly. "Dad, you'll get better." Avinash's smile remained, though his eyes held a hint of melancholy. "Well, sometimes in life, one needs a change of scenery too."

Rajvir, his voice tender, asked, "Would you like to go home, Dad? The doctor mentioned..."

"That fool Parera—what does he know?" Avinash interrupted, his eyes locking onto Rajvir's. "He cheated his way through medical school. He knows nothing about proper treatment, yet here I am, stuck. It's all a charade. And is it even a question? Of course, I want to go home. Thank God you have more sense than he does."

Rajvir nodded, his commitment unwavering. "Dad, I'll make the arrangements tomorrow morning. But for now, you need to rest."

Avinash's smile broadened. "Talk to Disha, son. She might understand better. She's looking out for us now."

Rajvir nodded in agreement. "I'll speak with her. Please rest, Dad."

With a nod of affirmation, Avinash settled back onto the hospital bed, his eyes heavy with fatigue. "Alright, Engineer Sahab. And how's Shalini? And the kids?". Rajvir assured him, "They're all well, Dad. Tomorrow, I'll arrange a video call so you can talk to them."

Avinash's eyes softened with gratitude. "That sounds wonderful."

"Now, get some rest, Dad," Rajvir gently urged.

In the dimly lit dining room, Kamla, their new addition to the household, diligently served the evening meal to Rajvir, Gayatri, and Disha. The clinking of cutlery against plates was the only sound as they began their meal, a heavy silence permeating the room.

Breaking through the awkwardness, Gayatri cleared her throat and asked, her voice tinged with concern, "What are your plans for the future?"

Rajvir, his brow furrowing in confusion, replied, "Plans? About what?"

Gayatri locked her gaze on him and said, "I was asking about your father."

Understanding her concern, Rajvir nodded, his expression softening. "Oh, I see. I was thinking of checking on him tomorrow. If everything looks stable, we'll bring him home." Gayatri lowered her eyes to her plate, her voice tinged with unease. "I don't know what's going to happen. I have a bad feeling about all of this."

Trying to offer reassurance, Rajvir responded, "Don't worry, Mom. Everything will work out." Turning to Disha, he expressed his gratitude, saying, "Disha, thank you for everything. You've been a pillar of strength." Gayatri interjected with a firm tone, "How many times will you thank her, Beta? She's the one who has managed everything for so many years."

Rajvir glanced at his mother, acknowledging the truth in her words. He fell silent, the weight of responsibility and gratitude settling heavily upon him.

The room descended into silence once more. After a few contemplative minutes, Gayatri finally spoke, her voice softened. "Raj, why don't you drop Disha off at her home? It's getting quite late."

Disha offered a warm smile and declined, "No, Aunty, I'll leave as I usually do."

Rajvir looked at his mother, then around the room, and finally asked, "Where are the car keys?"

After dinner, Rajvir retrieved the car keys, a subtle gleam of moonlight glinting off the polished metal. It was time to drop

Disha off at her home. He took the driver's seat, the car's engine purring to life, and Disha settled into the passenger seat. Her gaze wandered out of the window, embracing the serenity of the night.

With a sidelong glance at Disha, Rajvir gently inquired, "How have you been?"

Disha, her eyes fixed on some distant point beyond the glass, replied in a casual tone, "I'm good."

Minutes drifted by in silence, the world outside the car window bathed in the soft glow of streetlights. Finally, Disha turned her gaze towards Rajvir and reciprocated the question. "And you? How is Shalini? And the kids?" Rajvir nodded, a hint of warmth touching his voice. "They are doing well. Shalini and the kids are fine."

Disha continued the conversation, her curiosity evident. "Uncle mentioned your sugar levels have gone up."

Rajvir acknowledged her concern with a nod. "Yes, that's true. But I'm managing it well now."

Disha, her tone inquisitive, asked, "I thought you were in Manchester."

Rajvir explained, "I had a meeting with some investors, so I came to Singapore for a formal business visit. It was unexpected." He paused for some seconds, searching for the right words, before continuing. "Do you think it's a good idea to bring Dad home in his condition?"

Disha nodded, absorbing the information. "You should do what he wants. Why are you asking me?". To this Rajvir's response was thoughtful, tinged with a hint of vulnerability. "Because its you who understands him better."

Disha, in a matter-of-fact way stated, "Understanding comes from living together. You've never really tried to understand him."

Silence fell between them, a weighty pause that begged introspection. Eventually, Rajvir probed further, his voice gentle. "What motivates you?". Disha responded with a smile, her eyes reflecting a reservoir of emotions. "What do you mean?"

"It's very unusual. Putting your family's needs aside and choosing to shoulder the responsibility of another family. It's not easy. There must be a driving force behind it," Rajvir remarked, his tone laced with curiosity and respect.

Disha's smile persisted as she shared her perspective. "Raj, you're mistaken. Firstly, I've never forgotten my own family; they're always in my heart. Secondly, my uncle and aunt are like my mom and dad. Every ordinary Indian girl is expected to manage two families in her lifetime. It's not something new."

Rajvir paused to absorb her words, then ventured further. "I agree, but still..."

Disha nodded, her eyes focused on the road ahead. "I understand what you're trying to say. It's quite simple, really. In the absence of my parents, they've been like my mom and dad. Maintaining this relationship doesn't require legal or social recognition. And if you truly want to know what motivates me..." She directed Rajvir to take a right turn, her instructions guiding him along the familiar routes of their shared past. "You seem to have forgotten the old routes," she teased gently.

Rajvir chuckled softly. "It's been twenty years, so they've become a bit hazy. But here we are, we've reached your home." With an unwavering smile, Disha stepped out of the car. She turned to Rajvir and regretfully said, "It's quite late tonight, or I would've invited you in for coffee. Let's meet at the hospital tomorrow morning. Goodnight."

Returning her smile, Rajvir bid her farewell. "Goodnight."

– 05 –

The following morning, Rajvir and Disha found themselves in Dr. Parera's office. The doctor welcomed them with a warm smile and delivered the news that seemed almost miraculous. "Raj," he began, "there's some good news. Your father's vitals have surprisingly normalized overnight. It's like a miracle! I can't explain what caused this sudden change. Also, I've sent the biopsy report to Chennai for a re-examination. We should have the results in 3 to 4 days. Until then, I recommend you take him home and continue his medications as prescribed."

A sense of relief washed over Rajvir as he heard the doctor's words. He exchanged a glance with Disha, and they both left Dr. Parera's office to share the news with Avinash.

In Avinash's room, Rajvir looked at his father and asked, "Papa, would you like to go home?"

Avinash, with a playful twinkle in his eyes, replied, "Why ask, my boy? Let's go!"

With his father seated in a wheelchair, Rajvir and Junior carefully transported him home. As they crossed the threshold into their house, Avinash let out a sigh of relief, declaring, "Home, sweet home!"

Gayatri, holding a bunch of red chilies, approached her husband with concern in her eyes. She performed a ritualistic gesture, waving the chillies around his head to ward off any malevolent forces.

Avinash, bewildered by his wife's actions, inquired, "What on earth are you doing?"

Unperturbed, Gayatri replied, "Just sit quietly."

Avinash, amused, obeyed her without further comment. Meanwhile, Disha and Rajvir exchanged smiles at the sight of this endearing interaction. Guided by Rajvir, Avinash was wheeled into his room, where Disha helped him settle onto the bed.

Lying comfortably, Avinash humorously attributed his survival to Gayatri's "esoteric tricks." He remarked, "Here I am, in the fourth stage of cancer, still kicking, all thanks to her." Rajvir, with a reassuring smile, chimed in, "Dad, you're doing more than fine!"

The rejuvenated patient grinned and quipped, "Of course, son. It's been an 80-year journey for me. Cancer won't be the one to take me down. I'll go just like your grandfather."

Turning to Gayatri, he asked, "Isn't that right, Darling?"

Rajvir playfully assured his father, saying, "Dad, you're not going anywhere without hitting a century first. For now, just rest."

Avinash, satisfied, agreed, "Rest it is. But before that, catch me up on everything. How are you? How's the family? And how's the business faring?"

Pausing for a moment, Rajvir replied, "Dad, everything is going smoothly. I'm here for a few days, and we'll have plenty of time to catch up. For now, close your eyes and get some rest."

Avinash turned to Disha and humorously added, "By the way, Disha, remind Aunty to prepare some coriander chutney. Cancer might not get me, but the hospital food was on the right track."

Disha nodded, placing the required medications on the bedside table. With a playful smile, she reminded him, "Uncle, be a good boy and take your medicines. We wouldn't want Aunty complaining, would we?"

Avinash chuckled and agreed, "Yes, teacher ji."

Junior was meticulously tending to the verdant plants in the garden when Rajvir ambled in, capturing his attention. A momentary pause in his gardening activities signalled his curiosity as he observed Rajvir's focus on an aged signboard situated opposite the garden. The signboard, weather-worn and faded, bore the inscription, 'Mehta Auto Service.' Evidently, this workshop had shuttered its doors decades ago.

Junior regarded Rajvir, and with an air of intrigue, inquired, "Bhaiya, is there something you wish to say?". Rajvir, entranced by the relic of the past before him, turned to Junior and nodded thoughtfully, inviting him to speak.

With a light-hearted grin, Junior remarked, "Living abroad has certainly given you a fairer complexion, bhaiya. You almost look like a foreigner now."

Rajvir chuckled, his amusement evident. "You might be onto something, Junior. Let Maa know I'll return home after a short stroll around."

Junior concurred, saying, "Certainly, bhaiya. If you find yourself lost, just give me a call."

– 06 –

Rajvir acknowledged Junior's concern with a nod and proceeded to exit the house. He embarked on an aimless journey through the familiar streets, each corner holding a piece of his childhood memories. As he ventured further, fragments of his past emerged from the recesses of his mind.

After a few minutes, the mellifluous chime of the church bell reached his ears. His gaze fell upon the nearby church, awakening memories of Father John. With an irresistible pull, he made his way inside the church, where the sight of Father John ignited a spark of recognition.

Approaching the priest, Rajvir eagerly greeted him, "Father John!"

However, the pastor, initially baffled, struggled to identify the visitor. He gazed at Rajvir quizzically and responded, "Yes, my son?"

Rajvir beamed, asking, "Do you recognize me, Father?"

Father John, after a moment's contemplation, seemed to recollect, his confusion giving way to a radiant smile. "My goodness, Raaj! Weren't you away somewhere... abroad?"

Rajvir nodded affirmatively, explaining, "Yes, Father, I was in Manchester. I just returned yesterday. It's related to my father's health." With genuine concern, Father John inquired, "I know, I know! We've been praying for him. Such a fine gentleman! How is he faring now?"

Rajvir shared the latest news, saying, "He's back home from the hospital and in better spirits than before." The Father heaved a sigh of relief and expressed, "God has been merciful. Do you recall when you were a child? Your father used to bring you here every Sunday, and you'd sit eagerly in the front row."

Rajvir's smile was nostalgic as he replied, "I remember, Father. My visit here today rekindled those memories. Seeing the church reminded me of you." Father John nodded in understanding and noted, "You've done the right thing. How long will you be staying?"

Rajvir, uncertain about his plans, admitted, "I'm not sure Father. But before I leave, I promise to visit you again. I went on a walk to reacquaint myself with this city after 21 years. Goodbye for now, Father!"

Father John blessed him warmly, saying, "God bless you, my son!"

As Rajvir made his way out of the church, the pastor called his name once more. Their eyes met, and Father John imparted a heartfelt revelation, "I believe you should know that after you left, your father would come here every Sunday and pray for your return."

Rajvir stood in profound silence, deeply moved by this revelation. He had no words to convey his emotions, so he turned and left the church.

Stepping out into the daylight, Rajvir resumed his explorations of the streets he had once traversed daily. His wandering path led him to a familiar face, that of 63-year-old Liza Aunty, a flower vendor. Rajvir couldn't help but offer her a warm smile before approaching her humble stall by the street.

Coming to a stop, Rajvir greeted her, "Hello, Liza Aunty, may I have some daffodils, please?"

Liza, who had been tending to her colourful array of blooms, handed him a bunch of daffodils. As she studied his face for a moment, she remarked, "I've never seen you around here."

Rajvir nodded understandingly, remarked, "How could you, Aunty? I've returned after 21 years." Recognition slowly dawned on Liza's face, and her eyes sparkled with delight. She embraced him warmly, and Rajvir couldn't help but reminisce, "Your dimpled smile remains as charming as ever."

Liza chuckled lightly, her eyes dancing with mirth. "You haven't lost your knack for flirting, have you? You're still the same naughty boy! How have you been?". Rajvir assured her with a smile, "I'm perfectly fine, Aunty. How much for these daffodils?"

With a casual wave of her hand, Liza dismissed the notion of payment. "Silly! Put your money away. Take these to your father and tell him to get well soon. These are his favourite flowers, you know. And do you realize how much he's missed you?"

Rajvir nodded, promising to return later. "Thank you, Aunty. I'll be on my way now. Goodbye, and see you soon!"

Liza returned his farewell with a warm smile, "Goodbye, beta, come back soon!"

As Rajvir re-entered the house, daffodils in hand, he discovered his father engaged in lively conversation with his friends. Upon seeing Rajvir, Avinash paused and eagerly inquired, "Ah, Raj is back! Beta, quickly, tell me, is the sea fish better in Manchester or in Kochi?"

Rajvir fixed his gaze on his father, and with a loving smile, he responded, "Dad, there's no sea in Manchester, so where would we get sea fish from?"

Avinash, chuckling like a child, exchanged a playful glance with his 72-year-old friend, Sridhar, saying, "Come on, Sridhar, give me my 100 rupees!", Sridhar, feigning protest, handed a 100-rupee note to Avinash, retorting, "Mr. Mehta, this is cheating!"

The laughter of the group echoed through the room. Rajvir was greeted warmly by 70-year-old Peter, who addressed him with a grin, "Raj, now that you're here, take good care of him. He refuses to acknowledge that he's an old man now."

Avinash interjected playfully, "Why, you guys are here to take care of me, aren't you? Disha Beti is here too. What more could I ask for? Should he shut down his business and stay home? Sooner or later, he'll have to return."Rajvir gazed fondly at his father, who seemed as youthful and spirited as ever. Amidst the camaraderie of friends, conversations flowed effortlessly, and Rajvir savoured the joyous atmosphere.

– 07 –

In the afternoon, as everyone else took their much-needed rest, Rajvir peeked into Avinash's room and found him peacefully snoring, resembling a child. He couldn't help but smile before quietly closing the door. Proceeding to Gayatri's room, where she was engrossed in reading the verses of the Bhagavad Gita, he took a seat beside her.

Setting aside her book, Gayatri turned to her son who inquired, "You still read this?". Rajvir observed his mother saying "Maa, do you really need to read it? You probably know every word by heart."

The mother's smile radiated warmth as he continued, "Dad is taking an afternoon nap today."

Gayatri nodded knowingly, remarking, "He was tired, dear. So many well-wishers came by today, you wouldn't believe it, he seemed genuinely happy." Rajvir responded, his voice filled with affection, "Dad is always happy."

Gayatri concurred, sharing a revealing anecdote, "After you left, he tried his best to appear cheerful. It was Disha who filled the void you left. She cared for us as if we were her own family."

Curious, Rajvir inquired about Disha's marital status, "Maa, has Disha still not married?". Gayatri nodded, expressing her uncertainty, "Why she hasn't, only she knows. She never answers when asked. At one point, your father even wished for both of you to get married."

Rajvir, taken aback, sought clarification, "Me? With Disha?"

"Why not?" Gayatri reasoned, her voice softening. "I wished for it too. You two grew up together, studying side by side. You understand each other so well. If only..." She trailed off, her thoughts left unspoken. "By the way, Shalini is also a wonderful girl."

Rajvir fell into contemplative silence, then rested his head on his mother's lap, seeking solace. His thoughts returned to his father's workshop, and he gently asked, "Maa, why did Dad close down his workshop?"

With a melancholic tone, Gayatri recounted, "He continued to run it for a decade or so after you left. People came from afar for his expertise. But as time passed by and it became apparent you wouldn't return, his enthusiasm waned. One day, he handed Junior the keys and ceased to visit himself."

She continued, her gaze distant, "Your clothes must have dried by now. I'll ask Junior to fetch them."

Rajvir, not ready to part ways just yet, held onto her hand and implored, "Not now, Maa. Let's sit like this for a little longer, please."

In the tranquil evening, the soft chime of Rajvir's laptop signalled Shalini's incoming video call. As Rajvir answered the call, Shalini's radiant visage graced the laptop screen. Her warm smile radiated across the digital distance as she greeted him, "How are you?"

Rajvir mirrored her smile and replied, "I am good. What about all of you?"

"Everything is fine here too. How is Dad doing?"

"Better. He's back home now," Rajvir responded with a hint of relief in his voice.

"It's good to hear that. By the way, did anything happen in Singapore? Did you find any investors?" Shalini's concern was palpable.

Rajvir momentarily looked distant, pondering the outcome of his Singapore venture. After a brief pause, he replied, "They've asked for 2-3 days to decide. So, fingers crossed! Otherwise, we might have to sell the company."

Meanwhile, unbeknownst to Rajvir, his father had strolled through the veranda and inadvertently overheard Shalini's last question. He halted in his tracks, intrigued by the discussion. Shalini's voice broke the silence, "Don't worry. We will save the company. Once Dad gets better, you should come back immediately. I've talked to my brother; he has some clients in Australia. Maybe something will work out. Oh, and please let me speak with Mom and Dad."

"Mom should be in the kitchen. Just a moment," Rajvir said, and he stepped out to find Gayatri.

In the veranda, he found Avinash quietly seated, his expression a mixture of curiosity and concern. "Dad," Rajvir uttered, attempting to draw his attention. However, Avinash, perhaps not wanting to eavesdrop further, feigned ignorance and only responded when Rajvir raised his voice, saying, "Dad."

Avinash turned to look at his son and said, "Yes?"

Rajvir gestured towards his laptop, and Shalini's image promptly filled the screen. She greeted her father-in-law with enthusiasm,

"Hello, Dad! How are you now?". Avinash couldn't help but smile in response, "As healthy as a horse!"

Shalini chuckled, "You will be absolutely fine. Please come here once with Mom. The kids also want to meet you."

In the background, Rajvir was caking for for Gayatri, and she soon entered the room. Shalini's eyes shifted to her, and she cordially greeted, "Namaste, Mama!". Gayatri, wearing a warm smile, replied, "Be happy, Beta; where are the kids?"

Shalini's eyes sparkled, and she answered, "They are in their rooms. I'll call them."

With the laptop in hand, Shalini proceeded to find her children. First, she approached Aavesh, who was seemingly in a hurry to leave. She asked, "Where are you going?"

The kid hastily replied, "Mama, I am going out. My friends are waiting outside!"

Shalini called his name "Aavesh," but he rushed past her without paying much heed to her reprimand. Shalini looked at him sternly but said nothing as she moved on to Bhavana's room. She was engrossed in some task on her laptop when Shalini entered. She uttered a joyful "Surprise!" and revealed the laptop screen to Bhavana. "Look who we have! Say hi to Grandpa and Granny!"

Bhavana looked at the screen, her attention momentarily diverted from her task. She greeted her grandparents with a cheerful "Hello, Daddu! How are you feeling now?". Avinash's eyes twinkled with affection as he replied, "I'm absolutely fine, dear. How about you?"

Bhavana responded with assurance, "All good, Daddu. Can we talk later? I'm in the middle of something important. I hope you don't mind."

Avinash's smile remained unwavering as he replied, "Of course not, dear." Bhavana quickly added, "Thanks, Daddu. Please take care! Love you!". Avinash nodded, his love evident in his eyes as he said, "I love you too, dear."

Shalini, though, shot a stern glance at Bhavana for her apparent lack of enthusiasm during the conversation. Without vocalizing her disappointment, she maintained her composure. Rajvir, on the other hand, felt slightly embarrassed by his daughter's behaviour.

Brushing off the momentary discomfort, he commented, "Kids these days can't live without their laptops." Attempting to change the topic, Shalini said, "By the way, Mama, the Gujhiya you used to make, please teach me too. Raj misses it a lot."

Gayatri's smile widened as she replied, "Gujhiya? It's very easy. I'll send you some." They continued chatting, but Rajvir was quietly vexed by the interaction between Bhavana and her grandparents. Not wanting to dwell on it, he decided to conclude the call. "Okay, Shalu, I'll call you later."

Shalini, with a warm smile responded, "Sure. Take care, Papa." Avinash echoed her sentiments with a smile and a thumbs-up. Rajvir disconnected the call, leaving behind a somewhat subdued atmosphere.

As the video call concluded, Avinash fixed his gaze on Rajvir. A question weighed heavily on his mind, and he finally decided to voice it. "Will you tell me one thing, honestly, Beta?"

Rajvir nodded attentively, ready to listen to his father's query. "Yes, Dad, please go ahead."

Avinash locked eyes with his son and inquired, "How is your business going?"

Rajvir hesitated for a moment, choosing his words carefully before responding, "It's going okay, Dad. Business always has its ups and downs."

Avinash continued to hold Rajvir's gaze and implored, "Tell me honestly; look into my eyes."

Rather than maintaining eye contact, Rajvir casually let his gaze drift to the floor. Despite this, his old father offered words of encouragement, "Raj, business success comes after hard work, and experience is the biggest teacher. Experience always comes from failure, not successe. It's the small failures that lead to the big victories in life. You just need to have confidence in yourself. Do you believe in yourself?"

Rajvir, now making direct eye contact, nodded earnestly. Avinash continued, "And I believe in you. Don't worry. You're hardworking, and your hair has also turned a bit grey. Everything will be like it used to be. Just keep your mind's carburettor clean."

A faint smile played on Rajvir's lips as he listened to his father's words of wisdom. The exchange between them was heartfelt, an unspoken reassurance passed between father and son.

In the background, Gayatri's voice called out from the kitchen, "Dinner is ready; come."

Rajvir glanced at his father and said, "Let's go, Dad. The fish curry cooked today looks heavenly."

"You carry on. I'll join you soon," Avinash replied, his thoughts flooded by the memory of the day Rajvir had called to tell him about his new business.

– 08 –

Avinash Mehta could clearly recollect that particular day. The clinking of pots and pans filled the kitchen as Gayatri bustled about, tending to the evening's meal. The sudden trill of the telephone bell had disrupted her culinary rhythm, prompting her to hurriedly wipe her hands on her apron. With a hopeful heart, she dashed towards the ringing phone, her intuition whispering that it might be Rajvir on the other end.

As she answered the call, a familiar voice greeted her with a warmth that resonated across the miles. It was indeed Rajvir, and he asked, "How are you, Maa?". However, Gayatri chose to remain reserved, her longing mixed with a tinge of disappointment. She curtly replied, "Hang up the phone. There's no need to talk to you. You don't care about us."

Rajvir, accustomed to his mother's mixed emotions, gently retorted, "Come on, Mom. What do you keep saying that?". Gayatri's words took on a stern tone as she expressed her pent-up feelings, "What else should I do? Ask yourself. So many years have passed. Not even once have you shown your face." Rajvir, unwilling to engage in an argument, quickly redirected the conversation to Avinash, the reason behind his call. "I will come, Mom. Where is Dad?"

Gayatri, perhaps hoping against hope, looked at Avinash and said, "He's right here." She then handed the phone to her husband. Rajvir didn't waste time and immediately shared his news, "Dad, I'm starting my company in automobile spares. I've found investors. Now, I'll work for myself, not others."

Avinash's eyes lit up with anticipation. He entertained a fleeting thought that Rajvir might be considering a return. Encouragingly, he responded, "That's great, son. We have plenty of space in our house for an office."

However, Rajvir swiftly countered, "Actually, Dad, everything is finalized here. I've already taken an office. I have a plan for it. I was thinking of renovating our garage and turning it into a franchise office for my company. I believe it will do well in Kochi. How does that sound?"

Avinash's smile faded, and he hesitated before firmly responding, "All the best to your company, Beta. But this garage will remain as it is."

Rajvir felt a pang of disappointment but chose not to push the matter further. He sighed, "Dad, I think it will work. So, please think about it. I will call you again. Bye." With that, Rajvir ended the call. Gayatri, still harboring hopes of Rajvir's return, inquired anxiously, "Did he say he was coming?"

Avinash's gaze, however, was fixed on the stark reality. Resignedly, he replied, "Please make a cup of tea." The weight of the unspoken truth hung in the air, and they both silently carried their respective burdens of hope and reality.

Back in the present, amidst the vibrant ambiance of the park, Disha's athletic figure cut through the air as she jogged with her customary determination. Her regular presence during the morning hours was something Rajvir had come to anticipate. On this particular day, he decided to surprise her by joining her in the joggers' paradise.

Disha's brows furrowed in puzzlement as she noticed Rajvir approaching. She slowed her pace to match his and inquired, "Hey, how come you are here?"

Matching her stride, Rajvir offered a gentle smile and replied, "I've come to meet you."

Curiosity flickered in Disha's eyes as she questioned, "But, how did you know that I would be here?"

Rajvir, now breathing heavily due to the unexpected exertion, paused momentarily and explained, "Instinct, I suppose. Actually, Mom told me. So, is this the secret to your fitness?"

Disha, with a hint of playful exasperation, rolled her eyes and quipped, "I am fit. It's you who's put on weight." As they strolled together, Rajvir candidly confessed, "I never really had the time, to be honest. I've hardly done anything in life apart from work."

Inquisitive, Disha turned her gaze towards him and questioned, "But wasn't this what you wanted? Why the sudden complaint?"

Rajvir's admission came with a hint of introspection. "I'm not complaining," he clarified, "just reflecting. You see, not much has changed here. The city's rhythm remains unaltered, the people are still the same. They find happiness in the simplicity of life, whether it's the thrill of catching a fish or riding a roller coaster. After all these years, it feels as though in my pursuit of progress, I've distanced myself from who I truly am."

Disha gave him a searching look and remarked, "Only from yourself?"

Rajvir's silence spoke volumes, and Disha continued, "Remember our school days? Every Sunday, Uncle and Aunty used to bring us here for picnics. We were so content back then. The park seemed vast and boundless in our eyes."

Rajvir's smile hinted at nostalgia as he recalled, "I remember. It's changed a lot." Disha concurred, "The perspective may have shifted, Raj, but not the essence. If you look closely, everything remains largely the same. In my view, this park hasn't changed."

Seated side by side on a bench, Rajvir found himself captivated by some distant thought, his gaze distant and contemplative. Observing his introspection, Disha turned her attention to him and inquired, "What's on your mind?"

Rajvir heaved a sigh and admitted, "I'm thinking about how life can alter its course in an instant."

Disha held his gaze, her own eyes reflecting wisdom as she philosophically responded, "That's life's enigma, Raj. Sometimes, our destination is right before our eyes, but we veer off onto a different path. It's life's puzzle."

Rajvir acknowledged her insight with a smile, "You've turned into quite the philosopher." The conversation took a lighter turn as Disha shifted gears, "Uncle's birthday is in two days, remember?"

Rajvir nodded, recalling the upcoming occasion, and said, "Disha, I want to share something with you."

Disha met his gaze, encouraging him to proceed.

Rajvir let out a sigh before confessing, "You were right that day when you said I was full of myself. I've spent my entire life focused solely on my ambitions and desires. I wanted this and that, to build a business, earn money, and make a name for myself. It never crossed my mind that my father, just like me, might have his dreams and hopes. I thought sending him money each month was fulfilling my duties. I believed my father continually misunderstood me."

With a hint of frustration, Disha corrected him, "Raj, your father always spoke highly of you. He praised you incessantly. Whenever he mentioned you, his eyes would light up. He was always proud of you. His only regret was that you never visited him after your marriage."

Rajvir, overwhelmed with a mixture of emotions, expressed his helplessness, "Disha, I don't know where we went wrong, but I can't bear to see my father's life slipping away like this. I want to do something for him, but I feel so powerless." Following this she nodded empathetically and assured him, "Raj, we may not be able to change the past, but we can certainly create meaningful moments now. Let's celebrate his birthday like never before."

Rajvir, his eyes brimming with gratitude, turned to her and earnestly asked, "Yes, we will. Will you help me?"

With a playful roll of her eyes, Disha replied, "Do you even need to ask? Let's plan it when we meet tomorrow. I've got to head to the office now." As Disha prepared to leave, Rajvir called her name. She turned back to face him, curious about his parting words. Gazing at her, he simply said, "Thanks."

A small smile played on Disha's lips before she continued on her way.

– 09 –

The morning sun cast a warm, golden glow over Rajvir's family home as he decided to embark on an unusual mission - washing his father's cherished car. He beckoned Junior to join him and, armed with a hose, began to wash the vintage Ford Mustang Fastback with a heavy spray of water. The old car, a relic of another time, gleamed under their attention.

Junior, meanwhile, set about diligently scrubbing the car's window glass. Unexpectedly, Avinash appeared on the scene, drawing their attention. They were taken aback, not by his presence, but by the fact that he was walking without his customary wheelchair.

Rajvir, still in mild disbelief, asked, "Papa, where's your wheelchair?"

With a wink and a light hearted tone, he replied, "Wait a few more days, and I'll be trying out for Manchester United." His smile was a mixture of amazement and happiness as he responded, "What prompted this sudden morning stroll?"

Casually, Rajvir explained, "Just felt like it. And now since it's a vintage car, I thought I'd give it a little attention."

Avinash's eyes filled with affection and pride as he looked at his cherished Ford Mustang Fastback. Turning to Rajvir, he noted,

"This is no ordinary car, son. It's a Ford Mustang Fastback, a rare gem."

Junior chimed in, reminiscing, "It's been 8-10 years since it was last driven. Dad even used to buy groceries in this car."

Rajvir agreed, "Even after all this time, it's not in such a bad condition." Avinash nodded with pride, remarking, "Why would it be? I've always taken good care of it."

Rajvir, eager to bring the car back to life, turned to Junior and requested, "Pass me the keys; let me try starting it."

Junior complied, handing over the car keys. Rajvir settled into the driver's seat, a spark of anticipation in his eyes. He made several attempts to start the engine, but it remained stubbornly silent. Frustration began to creep in.

From distance the owner of the car was observing the scene with a patient smile, at last he approached and offered a piece of advice, "Mr. Engineer, try listening carefully." Perplexed, Rajvir queried, "Listen? Listen to what?"

With an enigmatic smile, Avinash continued, "Listen to what this car is trying to tell you." The utterly baffled son quipped, "Since when did the car start talking, Dad?"

Avinash chuckled and added, "It speaks, and when it's happy, it hums." Rajvir, now thoroughly intrigued, pressed, "What is it saying?"

With a fatherly grin, Avinash enlightened him, "Right now, it's telling you there's a problem with the differential bearing. Change that, and it'll be ready to race again." Rajvir raised an eyebrow and emerged from the car, playfully exclaiming, "Genius, Doctor Saab!"

Avinash, with a twinkle in his eye, shared his wisdom, "Son, there's a difference between you and me, just as there is between a doctor and a pharmaceutical company. You know how to sell, and I know how to save."

His words carried a deeper meaning as he continued, "You always used to ask me why I had such a passion for cars. Well, son, to me, cars and lives are analogous. Both need to keep moving. In a way, we're all on a long journey. Sometimes, the brakes fail us, and the journey comes to an unexpected halt. If you want to understand life, look at your past, and if you want to truly live, then look ahead."

Rajvir nodded in contemplation, acknowledging his father's wisdom, "You're right, Dad."

In the background, Junior set to work, changing the car's bearings with diligence. Soon, the engine roared to life. The overjoyed son, with a beaming smile, exchanged a proud glance with his father.

Avinash patted Rajvir's shoulder, and together, they headed back into the house. As the day transitioned into night and moonlight bathed the Mehta residence, a record of Shahnai music played softly in Avinash's room, where he slumbered like a contented child.

– 10 –

In the dining room, Gayatri, Rajvir, and Disha gathered, while Kamla, the housekeeper, arranged their dishes on the table. The air buzzed with anticipation as they gathered to plan a special celebration for Avinash's birthday.

Rajvir, ever the planner, turned to his companions and inquired, "Where should we get the cake from?". Disha, quick to respond, suggested, "Braganza! It's the best cake shop in Kochi. Papa loves their chocolate cake."

Rajvir nodded in agreement, envisioning the perfect cake, "The cake should be shaped like our Ford car, and let's put 80 candles on it. It should be a jumbo-sized cake."

Gayatri, brimming with warmth, reminisced, "Do you remember how, on every birthday of yours, your dad used to take you on a long drive? He insisted that celebrating without a long drive was incomplete. After you left, he never again went on a long drive."

Rajvir's heart warmed with memories, and he promised, "Well, we'll go on one this time."

Turning to Junior, he issued a directive, "Change the car's bearings today. Invite everyone. But make sure Papa has no inkling of the surprise we have in store."

Junior, energized by the mission, nodded vigorously and declared, "Bhaiya, this time, we'll make this party unforgettable. The entire neighbourhood will remember Bare Papa's birthday."

In the golden morning light, Junior threw himself into the task of restoring the vintage Ford car with unwavering dedication. Each turn of the wrench, each tightened bolt, and every ounce of effort he poured into the project was a testament to his commitment. The car, once dormant, now resonated with the promise of revival.

Meanwhile, Rajvir and Disha embarked on a mission of their own – to find the perfect birthday gift for his father. They set foot in the bustling marketplace, where myriad shops displayed an array of vividly coloured garments. Their first stop was a quaint boutique, where they selected a finely crafted kurta for Avinash and a resplendent sari for Gayatri. Rajvir, ever the considerate friend, contemplated buying a sari for Disha, but her polite refusal quelled his intentions.

With thoughtful presents in hand, they ventured into a retro bakery, where the rich aroma of freshly baked pastries filled the air. Amidst the inviting scent, they carefully deliberated on the design of Avinash's upcoming birthday cake – a task that required nothing short of perfection.

Their next stop, after the bakery, was an ice cream parlour. There, surrounded by colourful tubs of frozen delights, they indulged in creamy scoops of ice cream, savouring the sweet moments of companionship.

As the sun began its descent, painting the sky in warm hues, they entered a store adorned with an assortment of vibrant balloons and jovial clown birthday caps. Rajvir, seized by a moment of playfulness, couldn't resist donning a clown nose, which drew infectious laughter from Disha.

With their shopping complete, they returned to the vintage car, each taking their designated seats. Rajvir, now behind the wheel, radiated excitement. A casual smile graced his face as he confessed, "I can't express how happy I am today."

Disha, mirroring his elation, smiled warmly and replied, "I can feel it radiating from you. If you're not in a hurry, would you like to grab a coffee?"

Rajvir nodded appreciatively and asked, "Sure, where do you suggest?"

Disha, with a twinkle in her eye, proposed, "How about at my place?". Rajvir enthusiastically altered his course towards Disha's home, remarking, "Alright then!"

Within moments, they arrived at Disha's cozy abode. Stepping inside, Disha gestured for Rajvir to meet her mother, Devaki, who was seated in front of the television. Devaki, however, struggled to recognize the visitor due to her battle with dementia.

With a loving smile, Disha introduced Rajvir, saying, "Maa, look who has come to meet you."

But Devaki's vacant gaze remained fixed on Rajvir, devoid of recognition. Undeterred, Rajvir greeted her with a warm "Namaste, Aunty." Still receiving no response, Disha made another attempt, explaining, "Maa, this is Raj, Mehta uncle's son." However, Devaki continued to stare blankly, her memory faltering. Recognizing the futility,

Disha sighed and suggested, "Maa, why don't you watch some TV for a while? I'll set the table for dinner shortly." With the matter settled for the moment, Disha retreated to the kitchen to prepare coffee for Rajvir.

Later, after the aromatic coffee had been poured and the cups arranged on the table, a mellifluous piano piece played in the background. As they savoured their coffee, Rajvir complimented, "This coffee is excellent." With a gracious smile, Disha responded, "Thank you."

Curiosity then led Rajvir to inquire, "Do you still play the piano?"

Disha's eyes sparkled with a hint of nostalgia as she shared, "More than ever. Remember how you used to love country music? In college, you were always singing 'Country Roads.'"

Rajvir chuckled, reminiscing, "I sang it as I left the country."A pause followed, and Rajvir sought to understand, "Did you ever contemplate a different life abroad? You had so much talent; you could have thrived anywhere."

Disha, with sincerity in her eyes, confessed, "Raj, as content as I am here, I couldn't imagine being happier anywhere else."

Rajvir, intrigued by her perspective, pressed further, "How can you be so sure?"

With unwavering resolve, Disha met his gaze and posed a profound question, "Are you happy, Raj? If you are, does that mean everything you said in the garden that day was a lie?". Rajvir nodded, acknowledging her astute observation, "No, Disha. I meant every word I said that day. It was true. But sometimes, I feel a void inside."

Disha, struck by a memory, rushed to her room and returned with a photo album. As she flipped through the pages, the album became a window to their school days, where their youthful faces smiled in freeze-frame moments.

Nostalgia washed over Rajvir as he marvelled at the snapshots of their shared past. Taking the album from Disha, he exclaimed, "Hey! You've preserved these photos so well. I don't have a single one from that time. Look at us!"

Disha teased him gently, "Look at how skinny you were back then."

A wave of precious memories washed over Rajvir as he continued to peruse the photographs. He looked at Disha, a fond smile on his face, and remarked, "We were best friends then, and we still are." Disha, a glimmer of mischief in her eyes, raised an eyebrow and stated, "Friends? Yes, you're right. We are best friends."

Before Rajvir could respond, his phone rang, interrupting the moment. He answered the call, and upon hearing his mother's voice, assured her, "Yes, Maa, I'm with Disha. I'll return in a little while, and we'll have dinner together. Okay, Maa."

Rajvir turned to Disha, explaining, "I think I should get going now. After dinner, I need to give Dad his medication." Disha nodded understandingly, offering, "It was lovely having you here."

Rajvir rose from his seat, and as they headed toward the exit, he paused and said, "Disha, may I have some of those photographs?". Disha, conflicted, sighed and replied, "I wish I could, Raj. Those photographs are my life. But if you truly want them..."

Understanding the sentiment behind her reluctance, Rajvir quickly nodded, conceding, "It's alright, Disha. I understand."

Disha, however, countered, "No, you don't."

With an affirmative nod, Rajvir agreed, "You're right."

As Rajvir prepared to leave, Disha wished him well, urging him, "Tell Auntie I'll look forward to her next visit." With a warm farewell, Rajvir departed, while Disha watched him until he was out of sight. She then gazed at the photograph album, a gentle smile gracing her lips.

– 11 –

Just as Rajvir was about to step into his car, his phone rang again. This time, it was Patel Bhai on the line. The conversation quickly turned to their recent business dealings, and it was evident that their latest meeting had yielded disappointing results.

Disheartened, Rajvir inquired about the Japanese counterparts, to which Patel relayed the discouraging news of their lack of response, likely indicating a negative outcome. Rajvir, his face etched with concern, sighed and acknowledged, "Alright. I'll explore other avenues."

Concern for his father's health then took precedence, and Patel casually inquired about Avinash's condition. Rajvir shared the positive update that his father was improving, despite their business setbacks. Being a pillar of support, Patel, reassured Rajvir, "You did the right thing by being with your family during these times. If you ever need me, I'm just a call away."

Rajvir expressed his gratitude, and with a parting "Goodbye" and heartfelt "Take care," the call concluded. Rajvir closed his eyes briefly, grappling with a mixture of emotions, before finally driving away.

The next morning, the sun's gentle rays bathed the Mehta residence in a warm, inviting glow. As Avinash woke, he called out for Junior, his voice tinged with anticipation, "Junior?". There was no immediate response, causing a hint of concern to creep into the old man's voice as he tried again, "Junior! Raaj!"

The silence hung in the air, prompting Avinash to call for his wife, "Gayatri! Arey, where has everyone gone?"

Determined to seek answers, Avinash reached for his walking stick and slowly made his way out of his room. As he pushed open the door, a heartwarming sight awaited him. Gayatri, Rajvir, Disha, and Junior stood in a huddle just outside his room, their faces illuminated by radiant smiles.

Their joyful exclamation filled the hallway as they chorused in unison, "Happy Birthday!"

Avinash stood there, momentarily taken aback by the surprise. Rajvir approached him, a sense of reverence in his every step, and touched his feet, conveying his heartfelt wishes, "Happy Birthday, Papa!" A warm smile of gratitude graced the father's face as he blessed Rajvir, "Stay blessed, Beta."

Disha, too, followed suit, respectfully touching Avinash's feet, "Uncle, you've turned 80 today." Acknowledging the milestone, Avinash nodded with a gentle wisdom, "Beta, after a certain time, a human stops counting his age." Rajvir, who is always quick to add a touch of humour, playfully remarked, "Just 20 more, and your century will be complete."

Gayatri, radiating maternal affection, chimed in, "Please go and freshen up. Many guests and your friends will be coming." With heartfelt wishes and a thoughtful gift, Rajvir and Disha presented Avinash with a kurta, Rajvir noting, "Your favourite colour, green!"

Avinash's eyes shimmered with contentment as he acknowledged the choice, "If I wear this, I'll look just like Balraj Sahni."

With their mission to surprise him a success, they encouraged Avinash to retire to his room and prepare for the day's festivities. Gayatri watched with adoration as he went inside, humming a tune and sneaking a laddu, a subtle act of mischief that painted her cheeks a rosy hue.

In the afternoon, the parents made their way to the church, a place of solace and reflection. Father John, their longtime friend, greeted Avinash with warmth and familiarity. Within the serene ambiance of the church, he offered his prayers to Jesus Christ. However, he held a private contemplation, a secret that he chose not to divulge to Gayatri just yet.

As evening descended, Junior took the wheel, with Avinash and Gayatri settling comfortably in the backseat. The car journeyed onward, carrying its precious cargo through familiar streets.

Avinash, with a hint of wonder in his voice, mused, "It feels like I'm dreaming."

Gayatri, puzzled, inquired, "Why do you say that?"

Avinash, reflecting on the unexpected joy of the day, replied, "I don't know. Raj's sudden arrival and all of this feels like a dream." With a reassuring smile his wife noted, "Let it be a dream then. You're happy, and so are we. What more could one wish for?". The wishful husband, finding solace in her words, nodded in agreement, acknowledging the simplicity of happiness.

Their journey continued, the cool breeze seeping through open windows as the car glided through the streets. Avinash, lost in thought, ventured into a realm of introspection, sharing his concerns with his son, Rajvir.

"Sometimes, I feel like I couldn't become a good father," Avinash admitted, the weight of his doubts bearing down on him.

Gayatri, offering her perspective, consoled him, "It's all in your mind. You've done more than you could. Whether the kids understand it or not, parents always do. Don't overthink it."

Enjoying the cool breeze on his face Avinash gets lost in his thoughts. Recollecting the hurtful past suffered by them when they couldn't get to see their only son who refused to comply with the wishes of his father.

By the time they reached the house they found the garden decorated with colourful balloons and ribbons. Silver and golden strings tussled around making everything look delightful. Avinash was overwhelmed to be greeted by his old friends and relatives who were all waiting for his arrival. It was Disha and Rajvir who escorted the old man to the sumptuous looking birthday cake which had a shape of the Ford, that stood on the porch. The cake was covered in candles.

Avinash felt a rush of happiness surrounded by his loved ones. After the ceremony with the cake someone started the music which cheered the place with mirth and joy. The guests were happy to dance along the catchy tunes enjoying the party to its fullest. Disha swirled with the music as Junior and Avinash join her eventually.

Amongst the merrymaking Avinash gets to talk to his grandchildren over the video call which brought tear to his eyes. After the call Rajvir takes a selfie with his father to make the moment memorable. The air was filled with bliss and happiness. With time the party came to an end when Rajvir asked his parents to get ready for a long drive. But Gayatri refused as she felt exhausted. It was Disha who promised to stay with Gayatri till they came back from the drive.

Junior and the old man were unpacking the gifts like two children when Rajvir interrupted them asking his dad to join him for a long drive. The phrase made Avinash stop everything and look up at his son. He enquired about the destination, to which Rajvir reminded him of the place where his father used to take him on a long drive on his birthdays, Alleppey.

– 12 –

Rajvir took the driver's seat and his father sat beside him with an anticipated spirit to spend the next few hours alone with his child, on the highway which he always loved for such tranquil rides. Rajvir turned the radio on to enjoy the drive. Initially Avinash taunted his son enquiring whether he remembers the way or does he need a GPS like everyone else. This made him smile as he drove on listening to the old hindi song playing over the radio.

Reaching the destination both of them gets out of the car and sits by the river Alleppey, watching the setting sun in its golden glow. Mesmerised by the beauty Avinash states even if he had come to this spot after quite a considerable time but still everything seems the same, as if it was only yesterday that they witnessed the exact same sunset with all its hue and grandeur. But he is also aware of the universal truth that even nature, changes according to its convenience.

Rajvir, interjected, "Dad, can a person's needs remain the same throughout life? Everyone has different needs. When you were 30, your needs were different, and now they are something else. When I was 30, my needs were different, now they are something else. I don't think there's anything wrong in changing with time. It was you who used to say, 'Change is the only constant.'"

Avinash, in profound agreement, nodded in acknowledgment, "You did what was right for you, Beta. I have no complaints whether you think you shouldn't have come back or couldn't come back, I'm not upset about it. I'm happy that you achieved what you wanted. Sometimes, I do wonder where I went wrong that we didn't meet for 20 years!"

Rajvir, with a warm smile, reassured his father, "Dad, whether I came back or not, that was my problem. You never made any mistakes. Everything I am today is because of your guidance. You've always thought with your heart, and I've used my head. I wanted to start a business. I knew that a business starts with the heart, but to run it, you need to use your head. You were right according to you, and I was according to mine. Honestly, I was afraid to come back at one point. Do you know why? Because I thought if I came back once, I would never be able to leave again. At that time, I felt that all the big dreams I had nurtured would get buried in this small town. But I still tried. Do you remember when I told you I wanted to open my company's franchise here? But you didn't seem to like the idea. Your company could have become our company."

Avinash, sharing in the moment of levity, responded with a hearty laugh, "Yes, it could have. But what could I do, Beta? I've learned a lot in life, but I never learned how to do business. If I had, maybe people would be calling me Mehta Carwala instead of Dr. Car."

Both father and son laughed, the echoes of their shared laughter filled the air with a strange familiarity. Avinash, while reminiscing, couldn't help but muse, "Sometimes, keeping quiet can make the distance between people grow too long. And I don't want you to have the same distance with your children like we do. Parents need to step into their child's world and become a part of it. Maybe I couldn't become a part of your world, but, Beta, try your best to ensure your children don't drift away with time."

Rajvir, wholeheartedly accepting the advice, nodded resolutely, "I will try my best, Papa."

As they started their drive back home, Avinash's gaze was drawn to the serene riverside scenery. It was a place of cherished memories, and he fondly remembered the times they had spent here.

"We used to catch fish by this riverbank, remember?" Avinash asked, his voice laced with nostalgia.

Rajvir chuckled, recalling those times, and replied, "You were the one who used to catch them, Dad. I couldn't catch a single one." With a dismissive wave, Avinash urged them to leave the past behind, "Never mind! Let's not dwell on the past. There isn't much time left to look back."

"Dad, please!" Rajvir protested, a genuine plea in his eyes.

Avinash, gazing at the moonlit river, whispered to himself, "Ujale apni yaadon ke hamare saath rahne do. Jane kis gali men zindagi ki shaam ho jaye." He then looked at Rajvir and said, "Let's go home. I will get a good sleep today."

As the car drove on, an unspoken bond of love and understanding connected them.

Back at home, the family eagerly awaited their return, and as the doorbell rang, Junior was the first to answer. The moment father and son entered the house, they were greeted by a concerned Gayatri.

"How long did you both take? I was getting worried. I'm going to set food on the table. It's time for your medicine," Gayatri fretted, her voice tinged with exhaustion.

Avinash, however, seemed resolute, waving away her concerns, "Bhai, I'm already full from talking. I'm going to bed now. I don't need any medicine today." As he walked toward his room, Rajvir offered his goodnight wishes. Disha, too, bid her farewell, "Good night, Uncle."

Avinash turned to face them, his eyes holding a profound warmth, "Good night, Beta."

Disha sought Rajvir's opinion on how the day had transpired with a questioning look. Rajvir responded with a reassuring thumbs-up and a smile.

– 13 –

The following morning, Rajvir embarked on his routine jog beneath the expansive, clear sky. His path led him to Liza Aunty's quaint shop, where he paused to purchase daffodils, a thoughtful gift for Avinash. Further along his route, he took a moment to savour a cup of tea at the Basant Tea Stall, cherishing the simplicity of the moment.

However, the tranquility of the morning was soon to be shattered, as Rajvir returned home to find Gayatri standing before Avinash's room, her eyes brimming with tears. Beside her, Junior too was visibly distraught, and Rajvir's heart sank with a sense of foreboding.

Moving closer to Avinash's room, Rajvir was met with a heart-wrenching sight. His father lay lifeless on the bed, surrounded by an atmosphere of profound grief. Tenderly, Rajvir placed the daffodils by his bedside, paying his final respects to the man who had been both, a father and a friend.

In the end, Rajvir led the sombre final rituals, a poignant tribute to his father's enduring legacy.

One week had passed, and the inevitable moment for Rajvir to depart had arrived. In the dimly lit room, he carefully packed his belongings, his eyes locking onto a framed photograph of his father, Avinash. Tenderly, he slipped the photograph into his travel bag. The soft click of the bag's zipper resonated in the room as he sealed it shut.

Just as he was about to finish, Gayatri entered, her weariness evident in her eyes. She approached Rajvir, a mix of resolve and vulnerability in her voice, "Beta, I wanted to talk to you about something. When you go back, talk to a property dealer and sell this house. Your father also wanted this. I won't be able to manage all of this alone now."

Rajvir, taking a moment to contemplate, nodded thoughtfully, "Maa, give me some time to think." With a final, resigned nod, Rajvir closed his luggage, and then a sudden realisation struck him. Urgently, he called out, "Junior!"

Junior, swift to respond, entered the room, his question evident in his eyes, "Yes?".

Rajvir, his thoughts racing, instructed, "Bring the box from my room, the one with the car."

Gayatri, her eyes filled with fond memories, interjected with a touch of nostalgia, "Even after you left, your father used to make a new car for you every birthday. He used to say that one day when Raj visits, he would be very happy to see it."

Junior, attentive to Rajvir's request, returned with the box, and Rajvir instructed him, "Put it in the car as well."

He turned to look at Gayatri, a mix of emotions in his gaze, "Maa, I have to leave now. I will call once I reach."

Gayatri, her heart heavy with a sense of finality, nodded in acceptance, "Take care, Beta!"

With a last glance at his mother, Rajvir left the room, and in the hallway, he found Disha waiting for him. Their eyes met, and a shared understanding passed between them, reflected in their smiles. Disha gestured with her hands, conveying her intention, "I thought I should leave the office early to see you off. Who knows if you will come back again or not?"

As they prepared to leave the house, Gayatri approached them, carrying a plate with sugar and curd. She offered a spoonful to Rajvir, a symbol of her love and blessings.

Meanwhile, Junior efficiently loaded the car with Rajvir's luggage and the box containing the miniature car. Rajvir, displaying a sense of tradition and respect, turned to touch his mother's feet before departing. As Disha and Rajvir entered the car, Gayatri approached Rajvir once more, her eyes revealing a hint of longing, "If possible, bring your wife and children here someday." Rajvir, with genuine intent, nodded in agreement, "Sure, Maa. Bye!"

Junior started the car's engine, and they left for the airport. However, Gayatri remained rooted to her spot, her gaze locked on the receding car, tears escaping her eyes, an expression of inner turmoil etched on her face.

Upon their arrival at the airport, everyone disembarked from the car. Disha exchanged a glance with Rajvir, and they both smiled, the unspoken bond between them palpable.

Disha gestured with her hands, offering him an envelope. "Papa had kept this envelope in the locker. He told me to give it to you when you come. And this box as well," she said, pointing towards the box hiding the toy car.

Rajvir, curious about the envelope's contents, accepted it, his question evident, "What's in it?"

Disha, with a nonchalant nod, encouraged him, "I don't know. Open it later." She retrieved a photograph from her bag, presenting it to him, "This is a photograph from when you graduated. I took it. Show it to Shalini and the kids. They'll be very happy. And give them my love. Come on, you must be getting late. Check-in quickly."

Rajvir nodded and expressed his gratitude, "Take care. I'll call you once I reach."

Junior, too, offered his parting words, "Bye, Bhaiya. Come back soon!"

As Rajvir made his way towards the airport entrance, Disha called out to him, her voice tinged with sincerity, "Raj!"

Rajvir turned back, and Disha continued, her tone earnest, "Remember the day you said we were best friends? You know what? It is the best relationship we can ever have! Initially, we stayed together but were still very different from each other. It's good that we remained friends. We are still connected because we are friends; otherwise, some other relationship might have broken up a long time ago."

Rajvir, his gaze locked onto Disha, contemplated her words and opened up about his own experiences, "I met Shalini 22 years ago. We started as friends. Then slowly, love happened. When love happened, friendship ended. When we got married, love ended. But honestly, I have nothing to blame Shalini for. She has always been supportive of me. But with time, I didn't even realise when that friendship, that love, became a habit. Maybe relationships are like that—like sand! The more tightly we try to hold it, the faster it slips away. And before you know it, life takes on a certain shade. In reality, it's all a façade meant to show the world that everything is fine. We are fine! Maybe this is the truth of life, or maybe that's just how life is! Today, when you said that if we had any other relationship, it would have shattered long ago, you were right!"

Disha, touched by his words, smiled with a hint of sadness, "Take care!"

Rajvir nodded and waved a farewell gesture as he continued on his journey. Disha tried to offer a handshake, but Rajvir, driven by emotion, pulled her into a heartfelt embrace. They stood there for a moment, a silent connection between them. Disha's eyes glistened with unshed tears, but she regained her composure when Rajvir released her from the embrace.

Rajvir, looking deep into her eyes, uttered a final farewell, "Stay well"

Disha reciprocated his farewell with a heartfelt, "Bye!"

– 14 –

As Rajvir turned to proceed in the aisle of the plane, he was on the verge of succumbing to fatigue and emotions. An air hostess approached him, offering beverages, and he accepted a drink absentmindedly. Then, in a sudden rush of memory, he remembered the envelope Disha had given him.

With trembling hands, Rajvir retrieved the envelope, and as he tore it open, he discovered a letter within. It began with words penned by his father, a poignant message of love and reflection. Rajvir's eyes welled up as he continued to read.

"Raj, Beta,

By the time you read this letter, perhaps there won't be much left to say or hear between us. You will go about your life in your world, and I will be in a different world. I've never had any complaints against you. Just one small grievance, though. That is, during the difficult phases of your life, at least once, you should have remembered me. After all, I am your father. There is a draft of 6 crores in with your company's name on it in the envelope."

Rajvir's eyes widened as he gazed into the envelope, revealing the draft enclosed within. His tears flowed freely now as he continued reading, absorbing every word with reverence.

"This money belongs to you. For the past 20 years, I saved the money you used to send me every month. And yes, I have a surprise for you. I've had a miniature model of your favourite car, a Lamborghini, made for you. Your birthday is in two months, isn't it? Happy birthday, Beta! Give my love to the children and Shalini.

Your Father!"

With a trembling hand, Rajvir also opened the accompanying box and found the intricately detailed miniature of a Lamborghini car. Overwhelmed by the depth of his father's love and the unexpected gift, Rajvir could no longer contain his emotions. He burst into tears, and despite the attention of fellow passengers, he wept openly, clutching the heartfelt letter and the miniature car close to his chest. The anguish, love, and gratitude swirled within him, and he found solace in the profound connection with his father, although it was beyond the boundaries of life itself.

– 15 –

Two years later, Rajvir found himself standing centre stage at the prestigious Mehta Automobile Engineering College. Eager students filled the auditorium, their faces reflecting a mixture of anticipation and hope. Beyond them, a diverse crowd of spectators had gathered to bear witness to this momentous occasion.

Rajvir, exuding confidence and a sense of purpose, cleared his throat, his voice resonating through the hushed room, "This college is exclusively dedicated to those exceptional young minds who, due to financial constraints, may otherwise be deprived of the opportunity to pursue their dreams of becoming engineers." As he continued, his words carried conviction, "In my role as the founder and principal of this institution, I solemnly pledge to each and every aspiring student in Kochi that we will nurture your dreams and shape you into engineers—without burdening you with any tuition fees."

The promise hung in the air, echoing with hope and potential. Rajvir, acutely aware of the weight of his words, allowed a brief pause to let them sink in. Then, he moved on, his tone infused with both pride and sadness, "Today marks a moment of profound significance in my life. However, it is not without a touch of regret, for the person whose unwavering vision has brought us here today is no longer with us. My father!" Rajvir's voice wavered with emotion as he spoke of his father, his gaze momentarily distant, remembering the man whose legacy he now carried forward.

Seeking to honour his father's memory and continue his legacy, Rajvir took a deliberate step forward. He turned towards the audience and extended an invitation, "I would like to invite my mother to join me on this stage and inaugurate this college." With a warm and appreciative smile, he beckoned Gayatri, "Maa!"

Gayatri, the embodiment of grace and strength, made her way to the stage, her presence commanding respect and admiration. She approached the lectern where candles stood ready to be lit. As she ignited the flames, a collective wave of cheer and applause rippled through the room, the sound filling the space with hope and optimism. The flickering candles symbolised not only the beginning of a new journey but also the enduring spirit of a family united by a shared vision.

In this moment, the promise of the Mehta Automobile Engineering College hung in the air like a beacon, a testament to the power of dreams, determination, and the legacy of a father cherished by his son and carried forward with unwavering resolve.

Following the grand inauguration ceremony, the atmosphere was alive with jubilation as everyone gathered together to celebrate Rajvir's remarkable achievement and, in essence, the fulfillment of Avinash's cherished dream. Laughter and camaraderie filled the air, blending harmoniously with the shared sense of accomplishment.

Amidst the joyous revelry, Junior, with enthusiasm dancing in his eyes, approached Rajvir. He eagerly proposed, "Bhaiya, this calls for a celebration, doesn't it?". Rajvir nodded thoughtfully, acknowledging the sentiment. He responded, "Indeed, we should celebrate today. But you know what, Junior..."

Before he could finish his sentence, Junior chimed in, completing Rajvir's thought, "Every celebration..."

"...is incomplete without a long drive," they declared in unison, sharing a hearty laugh that reverberated through the gathering.

In the spirit of their shared tradition, Rajvir's family assembled around a vintage Ford car, ready to embark on a scenic journey—a long drive to Alleppey Riverside. The anticipation and excitement were palpable, with Shalini and Disha eagerly making their way to a badminton court, Gayatri tenderly tending to Bhavana's hair, and the rest of the family preparing for the drive.

Rajvir and Avesh found themselves beside a serene fishing spot, their lines cast into the tranquil waters. As they patiently waited for a catch, Rajvir turned to Avesh, his gaze steady on the horizon, and struck up a conversation. "Avesh, have you ever thought about the fundamental difference between nature and humanity?"

Avesh met Rajvir's gaze, intrigued by the question. He responded, "Tell me, what's that difference?"

Rajvir turned his attention to the breathtaking surroundings, the natural world unfolding around them. With a nostalgic smile, he began to explain, "You see, Avesh, nature operates according to its own immutable laws. It changes and adapts within the framework of those laws. But humanity, on the other hand..."

Avesh leaned in, captivated by Rajvir's words, and prompted him, "What about humanity?"

Rajvir's eyes reflecting the fading hues of the setting sun, he continued, "Humanity adapts and changes itself not according to laws but to fulfil its needs, desires, and ambitions."

Intrigued by the wisdom of these words, Avesh inquired further, "Who imparted this insight to you?"

Rajvir's gaze lingered on the sun as it dipped below the horizon, casting a warm, golden glow over the landscape. He fondly remembered his father and, with a heartfelt smile, revealed, "Papa kehte theh!"

www.ingramcontent.com/pod-product-compliance
Lightning Source LLC
LaVergne TN
LVHW061607070526
838199LV00078B/7201